ELIZABETH

Chisholm Manor

~~ Book Two ~~

~~ ~~

ANN M PRATLEY

BY ANN M PRATLEY

Chisholm Manor
Alessandra ~ Elizabeth

Power Moore Investigation Tales
Resolution of Happiness
Home by the Sea
Tiger in our House
Catch a Catfish Killer
DJ of Incapacity

Forbidden Conflicts Series
Amethyst of Youth ~ Ruby of Law
Diamond of War ~ Sapphire of Prejudice
Emerald of Wisdom

Copyright © 2025 Ann M Pratley
ISBN: 978-1-0670454-2-5

1

As Elizabeth Chisholm sat near the fire in the drawing room of her vast home, Chisholm Manor, she felt discontent. At eighteen years of age, every time she looked at her mother and father - Alessandra and Edward - she felt her unhappiness grow.

Throughout her whole life, she'd watched the love that her mother and father shared. When she'd been younger, it had been something she'd taken for granted and not given any thought to. As she'd grown and matured, the kind of love they shared had become something she deeply desired for herself. *How* she could ever find such a thing, she couldn't fathom.

For most of her life, she'd been resident in the great estate, leaving only for short durations when her family travelled to visit other members of family. Even though she had never experienced intense sadness or loss in her life, she did often feel like there must be a different path for her to embark upon. She was sure it must be time for her to be married and on her way to becoming a mother herself, but broaching that subject with either of her parents seemed far too daunting.

Resolved yet again that it must be wrong to think such unhappy thoughts, she silently told herself to stop thinking so much at all, and instead refocus on what was happening around her.

Also in the room were her parents and her sisters, Isabella - now seventeen - and Florence - still considered the baby of the family even though she was already fifteen. Elizabeth's only brother, Charles, was staying with school friends in London for the weekend. That was usually the way. With him studying away from the estate for much of the time, his life seemed infinitely more interesting to Elizabeth than her own did, even though he was two years younger than she was. He got to make and spend time with friends. He got to learn about wonders of the world, and see a great many new things. She accepted his life was so different from hers primarily only because of the genders they each were, and the order they'd been born. Unfortunately, accepting it didn't make it any easier for her to be happier about.

"Why do you sigh so, Elizabeth?" she heard her mother, Alessandra, ask.

"Forgive me, Mother," Elizabeth said, delivering as much of a smile as she could. "I have nothing to sigh about. I am fortunate, as we all are."

Determined to not let her parents see how unhappy she felt at times, she moved closer to Isabella and began a conversation with her. One year apart in age, they were as close as she was to any of her siblings, but they were also very different. Every time Elizabeth looked at her sisters, she knew they were both content in their lives, in their home, on their family estate. There was always much to do, but they were the same things every day. That was what Elizabeth felt was the worst thing of all. Nothing ever changed, and everyone else in her family appeared quite happy with that.

Listening to Isabella talk about whatever she'd learned or done that day that she found particularly interesting or funny, Elizabeth maintained eye contact with her sister. She smiled when she was expected to. She laughed softly when she could see Isabella would have wanted her to. There was nothing for Elizabeth to dislike about her life. She just wished something different would happen.

2

"Our daughter seems out of sorts," Edward said when he and Alessandra retired for the night. Throughout their marriage, their time alone in their bed chamber had remained his favourite time of day. To begin with, it had been due to the passion they'd shared. While he was glad that continued, sometimes he found himself simply yearning to just have any alone time with his wife, even if only to sit and say nothing.

Alessandra had also sensed the obvious loneliness of her oldest daughter. Earlier, in the drawing room, she'd seen Edward deep in thought as he'd studied the face of their firstborn. It was never difficult for her to see his thoughtfulness, or consider what might have been on his mind in those moments.

As their children had begun to grow, there had been many discussions between Alessandra and Edward, centred around anything they should do to ensure each of their children were secure and happy in their futures. Alessandra knew their discussions would continue long before they found any resolution. Perhaps it would have been different if their firstborn had been a son. In that situation, Alessandra suspected Edward wouldn't have found it so hard to consider the possibility of his oldest child marrying. A son, he would have gladly inspired to find a wife and settle down. With Elizabeth being their oldest, Alessandra knew Edward found the prospect much more difficult.

"Elizabeth, I believe you may be referring to?" Alessandra asked as she smiled at him. She knew when Edward had something stuck on his mind, quietly ruminating over it again and again. Sometimes he took much time getting to whatever he truly wanted to say, but he always got there in the end. All she had to do was nudge him a little, and then be patient.

Edward chuckled and nodded as he began undressing his wife. It was a small task that he embarked upon each evening, and always took great pleasure in.

"Yes," he said. "I cannot fathom what could possibly drive her discontent when she is like this. Do you have any idea?"

Alessandra turned around to face him, stopping him in his efforts to remove her gown. Every time she looked at him, she still saw the same man she'd known from the moment she'd met him - not handsome in a traditional way but certainly the most handsome man to her. The little quirks of his personality had amused her at the start of their marriage. Since then, they'd started to merge with her own, leaving Alessandra in a calm peace whenever she thought of her husband of two decades.

"She is eighteen, Edward," she said. "She is the same age I was when my parents brought me here to meet you."

As always when the particular topic of Elizabeth marrying was approached, even indirectly, Alessandra saw her husband sigh.

"She is younger than you were," Edward said, quite determined to not acknowledge the truth that his oldest daughter had actually grown into a young woman.

Alessandra laughed with affection as she moved forward and pulled him into her arms, then kissed him before she turned her back to him once more.

"And I say again, she is the same age as I was, and you know it," she said, teasing him. "Edward, she is of age to be wed. Why do you continue to make excuses for her not to?"

"She … she is our child," Edward said as he completed the undoing of Alessandra's gown and helped her to step out of it. "She is not ready."

"I believe it may be you who is not ready, my love," Alessandra said. "But we must think about her future."

"Her future is here," Edward replied. "She is our heir. She will be the rightful owner of the estate when ... when our time comes."

"Yes, but she will need help, Edward," said Alessandra. "And if she does not wed, there will be no-one to inherit Chisholm Manor estate from her."

As they followed their familiar nightly routine of undressing and climbing into their marital bed, neither said anything more. Once Alessandra was nestled into his arms, Edward finally spoke again.

"I do know you are right, Alessandra," he said. "However, it feels very difficult for me to contemplate letting her go."

"Yes, but this is how things must happen, and consider this - when Elizabeth weds, there is a strong possibility she will still remain here to continue taking over management of the estate, but she will have a husband to stand beside her and help her," said

Alessandra. "Our parents brought you and I together, and we have had a wonderful life together, have we not?"

"More than wonderful!" Edward exclaimed, making Alessandra laugh softly.

"Yes!" she said. "Would you deny your daughter the same level of happiness as you and I have shared through all of these years?"

"No," Edward replied. He knew he didn't truly have any valid argument against his oldest daughter marrying. "Let us talk more of this tomorrow. Perhaps if the weather is fine, you and I could ride up to the summit. I am certain we could better discuss this up there."

Alessandra grinned at him before leaning toward him and kissing his waiting lips. After all of their years together, they still had their little areas of the estate that Edward had wanted them to keep just as their own.

"Gladly," Alessandra said.

No more words were spoken.

3

The following morning, as Alessandra and Edward sat with their children, enjoying the morning meal, it was noticed by all as a messenger on horseback swiftly approached the house. After hearing the loud knock on the manor house door, Edward rose and walked out to see what the urgency was all about.

"Message for Mrs Chisholm, Sir," the messenger said when he saw Edward.

"Thank you," Edward said before inviting the young man in to rest a short while with food and ale from the manor kitchen.

Glancing at the letter, he turned it over and immediately identified the red wax seal.

"My love," he said when he returned to the dining room. "This has come for you. It appears to be from your aunt."

"Our great aunt?" Elizabeth asked,

excited.

She'd only been five years of age when her parents had taken her to Venice to meet what relatives were there. Despite the many years that had passed since then, that short but happy time had remained etched in Elizabeth's memory. She could remember the wonder she felt about the waterways and the way she and her family had moved around the strange city, plus snippets of conversations with her mother's aunt. At first, it had all seemed foreign. By the time they'd left Venice to return to England, Elizabeth had adapted to the strange language and accent, and the oddness of the location.

"Yes," Alessandra replied as she accepted the envelope from Edward, then proceeded to open and read it. "Oh dear," she finally said before glancing at her husband. "My dear Aunt Caterina is unwell. She speaks ... she speaks as if she is not expected to live much longer, Edward! She wishes for us to go there to see her."

"To Venice?" Edward asked. He had many fond memories of his two previous visits to the strange but beautiful place, but he'd not considered he might be going back a third time. "Do you wish to go alone, Alessandra? The children and I can remain…"

"Oh, no, Edward," Alessandra said. "My aunt has given strict instruction. She wishes for all of her relatives to go to Venice. I gather from this letter that it will not be just us who visit, but many people from different lands."

"Many people who are all related to her?" Edward asked.

"Yes," said Alessandra. "That is what she implies."

She took some time to watch Edward's face and see the look that suggested his mind was busy completing calculations. Although he was easy mannered and not bothered by most things that happened, she'd grown to learn that he was a man who loved the comforts of home. They'd previously gone to Venice twice together - once without children, and once with Elizabeth, Isabella and Charles - but she knew he might not wish to leave the estate to travel such a distance a third time.

As Edward processed the information, he felt some conflict. There was no reason not to take his family to Venice again. In truth, he'd loved each of the times he'd gone, and when he thought about how eager he'd been to do and see new things when he'd first married Alessandra, he couldn't help but feel a renewed eagerness to travel. In contrast, he did love the busyness of being on the large estate he'd grown up on.

"Father..." Elizabeth started to ask before remembering her manners. She desperately wanted to provide her thoughts on the prospect but knew better than to do that. As soon as she'd started to speak, she closed her mouth and looked down, her face red from the embarrassment of having even thought it worth trying express her opinion.

"I fear our daughter is about to plead a case," Edward said, smiling at Elizabeth and then Alessandra. "However she need not put in the effort, as I believe this is a good idea … as long as you think so, my love."

Alessandra didn't try and hide her happiness or excitement, instead simply reaching out her hand and happily grasping Edward's in it. Once again she would be visiting the homeland of her late mother. There was nothing to be sad about in that.

"When shall we go, Father?" Isabella asked. Still not yet interested in marriage or becoming a mother, she was excited simply at the prospect of seeing her great aunt one more time - a woman who'd seemed to understand Isabella perfectly even though Isabella had only been four years of age when she'd met her.

"That shall be the decision of your mother," Edward said before placing his napkin on the table. "In the present moment, however, I must go and see Mr and Mrs Jones, who have been having some problems with their new hedging."

"I'll walk you out," Alessandra said. It wasn't a usual thing for her to do, but she was excited.

Although surprised by her words, Edward said his farewell to his children and followed his wife out into the foyer. Once the door was closed behind them, he was further surprised by Alessandra placing her arms around him, pulling herself close against his chest, and reaching up to kiss him passionately.

When she pulled away, Edward couldn't help but grin. There were many things he knew he'd never grow tired of when it came to intimacy with his wife, but kissing was the greatest of all.

"That was very bold of you, my beautiful wife," he teased her before leaning down and returning a kiss with the same passion. "Best we put that out of our minds until this evening, however."

Alessandra smiled but nodded. She agreed wholeheartedly.

4

On returning to the dining room, Alessandra looked around the faces of her three daughters. One of her children was missing, but she knew where he was, she knew he was safe, and she knew he was happy. She hoped Charles would also be enthusiastic about going to Venice, but with how much he loved school and being around the friends he'd made, she could already see he might not wish to join them on whatever adventure they might embark upon.

"Are you happy to be going back, Mother?" Isabella asked.

"I shall like very much to see Venice again, Isabella," Alessandra replied as she grabbed a sugared bun that had been tempting her for quite some time. "But I shall be sad if my aunt is very unwell."

"I liked our great aunt," said Elizabeth. "I found her to be very kind and pleasant toward us."

"And I!" Isabella added. "She is a great spirit."

Alessandra smiled at her second daughter's terminology but didn't ask what she'd meant. When last in Venice, she'd viewed the odd friendship that had grown between Caterina and Isabella, often putting their heads together as if they shared a code that nobody else knew about. At first she'd wondered what they could possibly be talking about, before she considered how little she actually knew about her aunt.

"Shall I go too, Mother?" Florence asked, breaking Alessandra out of her thoughts. "I have not yet had the pleasure of visiting Venice. I should not like to miss out again!"

"Of course you shall come this time, Florence," Alessandra replied. "We shall all go, as was the request of my aunt. Unless any of you do not wish to…" she added, teasing her daughters.

"No!" all three exclaimed, making her

laugh softly. Alessandra was pleased. She'd always felt sadness when considering that her mother had never taken her or her brother, Nicholas, to her homeland before she'd passed.

Because Alessandra had never had the opportunity to experience Venice through her mother's eyes, she was grateful for the two times her Aunt Caterina had welcomed her into her home. On those occasions, her aunt had told many stories about the childhood she and Alessandra's mother had experienced. The stories had caused mixed emotions in Alessandra - sadness that she'd never heard them directly from her mother, but also joy in the stories themselves. It had felt like she was getting to know who her mother had been before Alessandra and Nicholas had entered her world.

Now the opportunity to visit Venice yet again had presented itself. Once more Alessandra would see the few relatives she'd met on previous visits.

Once more she would visit the wonders of the small but quaint place that had touched her heart. With each holiday in Venice, she'd enjoyed each moment, but then ended up looking forward to getting back to Chisholm Manor. It was good to be away, but she knew it was equally good to get home.

5

In the middle of the day, Elizabeth took some time to be alone. It was something her mother had always encouraged her to do from a very young age. Initially, Elizabeth hadn't understood why her mother would be trying to inspire her to do such a thing. Surely it couldn't be preferred that people didn't interact with others, given how important people seemed to regard society as being.

Over the years as she'd grown and matured, Elizabeth had discovered a strong appreciation for enjoying solitude. She sometimes wondered if it was healthy, especially when she found her mind wandering to places she wasn't sure it should. Then she'd find herself in a world where there was no room for anything negative or naughty in her head, and she'd start enjoying her alone time once again.

As she set up her easel, pencils and

paints where the midday sun met shade, her mind wandered back to the prospect of returning to the homeland of the grandmother she couldn't remember. Even though she'd been so young when she'd previously visited Venice, in her mind she could still visualize the strangeness of the waterways, and the beauty of the bridges and buildings that were so different from what she'd always known in England. The idea of returning to visit the place again now that she was of marrying age also excited her.

Without thought, she picked up a pencil and began to draw. As soon as the first piece of an image appeared in front of her, her conscious mind closed down. It was often the same when she indulged in her love of drawing or painting. Sometimes she liked to recreate what was before her, taking her time to present an almost perfect likeness to whatever it was that had captured her attention. At other times, the pencil or paintbrush seemed to take over like it had a mind of its own, creating images on paper purely from an unknown source of imagination in her mind. She wasn't sure where her skill in it came from, or even her enthusiasm for it. Neither of her parents spent any time drawing or painting, and her siblings, Isabella, Charles and Florence, had all expressed their extreme dislike for the activity, not understanding at all how Elizabeth could love it.

After a lengthy period of time, she felt herself come out of what had felt like a daze. It was sometimes like that - when she painted, she was pulled into a dreamlike state, as if her body was creating something quite without her input at all.

Standing back, inhaling deeply and then consciously looking over what she'd created, she recognized the scene. On the paper was a bridge, perched prettily over a waterway. Even though it was she who'd drawn and then painted it, Elizabeth was surprised. She hadn't consciously decided to create an image based on her childhood memory of Venice, but she knew she had. It was surprising, but pleasantly so.

She would soon be going back to the unique but highly likable place. What would be waiting for her there? Would she meet many new people? Might she meet someone who would deem her worthy of being a wife and a mother? Those questions passed fleetingly through her mind before she forced herself to focus only on the present moment.

Looking closer at what she'd created, she smiled to herself. There weren't many things she regarded were good about herself, but she knew she did have skills in creating imagery on paper. What was before her, facing her, was a good painting. The buildings looked as old as she knew they were. The water glistened in all the right places, creating almost a shimmer that made it look real. Yes, there were many things that she'd never learned to master in the classroom or in life, but art wasn't one of them.

Satisfied with her creation, she sat it facing toward the sun to ensure it was sealed with the unique dryness and colour setting that she'd learned direct sunlight provided. As she allowed it to bake before her, she moved her seat to the angle she loved to admire at the end of each painting session.

From where she sat, she could see the rolling green of the estate, and the large trees in the distance. She suspected it was a view that was no different than anywhere else in her country provided, and yet when she sat alone, in peace, and just watched, she always felt a particular kind of calm flow over her.

When she heard the familiar sound of her sisters' voices, she opened her eyes. It was usual for Florence and Isabella to spend time together, running around the garden and laughing. It was an activity that Elizabeth could certainly remember doing herself, however she could no longer summon the same childish enthusiasm for it. That discovery saddened her. She was eighteen. It seemed too old to be unwed, so it made her feel as if she was too old to have childish fun. Was that right? Was she now 'old'?

Not liking that thought, she finally stood and forced herself to start to run toward her sisters. It was a small thing to do but it worked. Finally, after far too many serious thoughts about what wasn't in her life, she remembered what it felt like simply to laugh and be the child she'd once been.

6

"I am not sure I can forgive you, Alessandra," Edward said that evening, using a stern voice as he spoke. All of the children had retired for the night, making Alessandra wonder what was coming next.

Suspecting he was teasing her, she held back from expressing humour or surprise, just in case he was serious. Over their twenty years of marriage, she'd grown to know him well, but he still managed to surprise her rather often.

"Oh?" she asked as she closed their bed chamber door behind them, then followed him toward the warmth of the fire.

"All day, I have been thinking … about that kiss," Edward said, finally grinning at her. "Now, how did it go again?"

Alessandra laughed out loud before

moving right up to him, then gladly indulged in kissing him with the full degree of passion she'd felt all day long.

"I have been thinking about it also," she said when she pulled away. It was the truth. While their passion for one another had never lessened over the years, they had both succumbed to real life encroaching on their private time together, and the reality of exhaustion at the end of many a day. "Touch me, Edward."

Without any further hesitation, Edward did as he was asked. They had their long nights of lovemaking when it was possible - when they were both awake enough to have the energy - but when she spoke those words, he knew it was something far less eventful that she was asking for.

Gently guiding her to sit on the chaise lounge near the fire, Edward knelt, assisted her to be free of any barriers, then leaned forward to give her the kind of kiss that he knew she loved.

"Oh, yes, Edward," Alessandra said as she felt his tongue touch her at the core of where she'd needed it. It seemed such a small and simple thing to do, and yet produced so many pleasurable feelings in her. It was a short time before she began building on her path to climax, and then toppling right over into orgasm.

As he felt and heard his wife reach her desired level of pleasure, Edward smiled to himself. He loved that she was so responsive to his efforts. It was something that had never ceased to amaze him throughout their marriage.

"Yes, thank you, Husband. That was certainly required," Alessandra said in a whisper before hearing Edward laugh in response.

Hearing his happiness, she smiled at him. She hadn't lied. Often, there was too much on her mind to even contemplate such pleasures. When it was on her mind, however, it seemed to build in her a desperation to be pushed over the ledge of pleasure.

"And now, my wonderful husband," she said as she lowered her gown and then stood up, holding out her hands to invite him to stand with her. "You appear to be far too warm in these layers. Please allow me to assist you..." she said as she started to undress him.

When Edward was fully naked, Alessandra instructed him to lie down on their bed. Once he was where she wanted him to be, she took a moment to glance over his body from head to toe. Although they'd both aged over the duration of their marriage, she appreciated how toned he remained. All of his body was muscular, and even though he generally looked relaxed as he lay still, watching her remove her own clothing, Alessandra could also appreciate how his hardness stood tall, as if waiting for her to claim it.

"You are so very beautiful," Edward whispered when she was fully naked. Every night they lay together, and often they still indulged in intimacy. Even so, every time he saw his wife without any clothing, it was as if he was seeing her beauty for the first time, all over again. "Come here."

Alessandra gladly moved onto the bed and positioned herself on top of him, aligning her body with his as she leaned down and indulged in kissing him with all the love that she felt. Things had been slow between them when they'd first met. Once things had heated up, she'd never ceased to look at him and know he was the one man in the world that had always been intended for her.

"Oh, my darling," Edward said as he felt her move down onto him ever so slowly and softly, not in any rush to take him fully into her.

As she watched his face, Alessandra enjoyed seeing and hearing how much she affected him in their private moments. Having known each other for so long, she could still appreciate how different things might have been between them if either of them had known pleasures of the body before they'd met. They'd discovered that path together, and she maintained the belief that their bond was all the more powerful because of it.

She knew his levels of arousal. When she saw his eyes close completely, she knew it was time to move a little bit faster. It was something she did for herself, as much as for him. The feeling of him inside of her had always felt like a magical state to be in.

Thankful that her body appeared to have decided, all by itself, to stop making children after the birth of Florence, she was glad that she and Edward no longer had to be aware of monitoring when he was close to climax. It had seemed a lengthy period when they'd had to monitor his state of arousal to ensure a child wasn't created, when they weren't sure they were ready for another. After Florence, they'd tried one more time. Her body, however, seemed to have decided that four children was quite enough, and the new generation of the Chisholm family was complete.

Feeling Edward begin to thrust upwards from his position beneath her, Alessandra moved with more power, driving him on. When she saw his eyes open again and focus on her, she knew he was very close. Leaning forward and presenting her breast close to his mouth, she enjoyed the pleasure of his lips caressing her nipple before that sent him over the edge.

"Oh, Alessandra!" Edward said out loud while attempting to maintain quiet. It was something he always strived for. It was also something that always made Alessandra giggle at his attempt, since he still hadn't learned to be very quiet at all in the moments his pleasure peaked.

"Shh, Husband!" she pretended to scold him. "You'll wake the household!"

Edward grinned at her before pulling her head down and kissing her. He, too, was appreciative that the years of child making appeared to be over with for the two of them. He loved being a father, and he loved all of his children, but to be able to fulfil his passion with his wife without worrying about her being with child again was something else indeed.

"I cannot deny that you lead me to not think clearly in these moments, Alessandra," he said. "One day I shall conquer my weakness."

"Shall?" Alessandra teased him as she pulled off him and lay down in his arms.

"May," Edward replied as they moved to face one another. "One day I *may* conquer my weakness."

"But I very much love the sounds you make," said Alessandra.

"Yes, I do believe you do," Edward said, chuckling. "And I understand fully, since I also love the sounds that you make," he added as he lowered his hand and began to caress her with his finger. When he heard a small gasp, he grinned further. "Yes. That one."

7

Two weeks later, Alessandra, Edward and their three daughters were rushing around in their home, preparing for their latest journey to Venice.

Correspondence had been entered into with Alessandra's aunt, confirming their dates of arrival and departure, and all travel had been arranged. All that had to be done was actually complete the long and arduous journey.

"Elizabeth, are you as excited as I am?" Elizabeth heard Isabella ask while they continued to organize themselves. The two of them were still attempting to adequately fill their travel cases, even though their departure time was so close.

"Yes, of course, Isabella," Elizabeth said as she felt frustration at not being able to fit her last gown into her case. "May I put this in your one?"

When she looked at Isabella, she

saw her grin.

"If you did not prioritize all of those paints, pencils and papers in your case, Elizabeth, you might be able to fit that gown in!"

Elizabeth knew it was Isabella's form of teasing - not answering the actual question that had been asked until she'd made Elizabeth wait for long enough to be worried.

"Yes, of course you may put your gown in my case," Isabella finally replied. "I care not what gowns I take with me. None of what we have will match up to the fashions of Venice, I am sure. I say, do you think Father shall let us buy some new gowns while we are there? I believe even he will see that we do not own anything so grand as what the people there will wear, I am sure."

Elizabeth had been wondering the same thing. Day to day, each of their family purchased clothes as they were truly needed, but she knew neither of her parents could be considered extravagant people. What her sister had said was right - even the nicest gowns they owned might never be considered good enough for being in society.

"I know not," she said as she carefully folded her last gown into Isabella's case and then closed it. "I suppose we shall have to wait and see."

"That might be your way, Sister, but I shan't be just waiting to see," Isabella said. "If you do not ask for something, how can you ever know what the answer will be? No, once we are settled in our great aunt's home, I shall ask Mother and Father if we may get a new gown each. I am sure they will not deny us."

Elizabeth nodded and smiled at her sister. How they were so very different in nature, she didn't know. She couldn't remember ever asking her parents for anything, or even considering daring to. Isabella was very different to her, and Florence was different again to both of them.

"Shall I call for some assistance in getting these down to the carriage?" she heard Isabella ask, the subject of new gowns quite forgotten for the moment.

"Yes," Elizabeth replied. "I believe I have packed all that I shall need."

"All you seem to need are your art supplies," said Isabella, teasing her older sister again. "How shall you find a husband with that particular skill, Elizabeth? I am sure any man would find a woman who paints far too dull to want to take her for his wife."

"Do you believe I am seeking a husband, Isabella?" Elizabeth asked with affectionate frustration as they began to walk down the elaborate staircase. The same conversation had been had rather often and the two sisters never seemed to agree on the outcome of it. "I am not sure that I am."

As usual, in response she heard Isabella laugh out loud.

"You may keep that desire from our mother and father, dear sister, but you do not hide it from me," Isabella said. "Worry not. I believe you shall soon find love, even if our parents do not go out of their way to find a suitable match for you."

Elizabeth felt startled by such an end to the conversation. She'd never actually told Isabella that she was ready to find love. Was she truly so easy to read?

8

The journey was underway. Sitting in the carriage with her family, Elizabeth began to feel the happiest she'd felt in a long while. As happy as she knew she should be in her life in her home, it was when the carriage left Chisholm Manor estate altogether that she felt her soul begin to soar.

She wasn't going anywhere new, but it was somewhere different from her day to day existence. She didn't know what could happen in Venice that couldn't happen in England, but she was certainly open to any possibility.

Looking across the carriage to where her mother, father and youngest sister sat, she caught her parents glance at one another. It was always easy to see their love for one another. She wasn't sure what it was that gave her the impression they loved each other so much. Perhaps it was the way that their eyes seemed to smile when their glances met. Perhaps it was the tone of their voices when they spoke to one another. Perhaps…

Elizabeth silently admitted to herself that she didn't know what it was that told her they had the kind of loving relationship that she wanted in her own life. She just knew that somewhere out there in the world beyond Chisholm Manor, there had to be a man who would love her the same way that her father loved her mother.

There had to be. Somewhere.

9

"Alessandra!" all heard called out after the long journey was over with and they'd finally arrived in Venice and entered the large home of Alessandra's aunt, Caterina. Despite her extreme exhaustion from such a long journey, when Alessandra heard her aunt's voice, she naturally turned and smiled.

"Hello, Aunt," she said as she was pulled into welcoming arms. "You look rather well, I am very pleased to see."

"Sì, certo!" Caterina replied. "I shall never die, as you well know," she added, laughing.

As Alessandra glanced at Edward she saw a very familiar expression of amusement on his face. He was trying to hide it, out of respect. He wasn't doing a very good job.

"Hello, Great Aunt," Elizabeth said when she could sense a moment of being able to seize the great woman's attention. She was grateful that her mother's aunt was well versed in speaking English, even if it did sound extremely odd with the strong, foreign accent.

"Benvenuta, Signorina Elizabeth," said Caterina before glancing around all of the young faces. "And you, Signorina Isabella. My, how you young ladies have grown since I last saw you both! Your madre and padre shall be kept busy during this time, fighting off no shortage of young men vying for your attention, I am sure! But who is this?" she asked as she focused on the youngest in the group.

"I am Florence!" Florence replied before attempting to curtsey. "It is a great pleasure to meet you, Great Aunt."

Caterina laughed softly but nodded.

"And it is equally my great honour to meet you, little Florence," she said. "But where is my great nephew? I did so enjoy his conversation when you all last visited."

"He was only three years of age, Aunt!" Alessandra said.

"Sì, but I could already see what a charmer your son was going to turn out to be, Alessandra!" Caterina said, making Alessandra grin.

"Charles is presently in London and did not travel with us," she said. "But he will join us in three days, so you shall see his happy face again."

"Very well," Caterina said, satisfied that her request had been at least partially met. "But let us not stand here for a moment longer. I am not yet on death's door, however my legs do not work as well as they used to. Come. The afternoon parlour shall be infinitely more pleasant for all of us."

Glancing at both of her parents, Elizabeth saw them exchange some kind of message with their eyes. She wasn't ever entirely sure what their messages said, but she was certain they'd both learned some kind of code that they each could use to say things, and to understand things, without either of them saying anything out loud. Would she ever find someone to be able to read her so well? Someone who could love her, and fully understand her? And if she didn't find someone like that herself, would she ever have the courage to tell her mother and father that she desired it, more than anything?

"We thank you for inviting us to come, Aunt," she heard her mother say. "We believed you might be…"

"Ready to depart this world?" Caterina teased her niece. "It was only a ploy. My health is not failing quite so much, however I am aging, of course. It has been my sincere wish to see all of my living relatives while I can - and for you all to see each other since so many of you have never met - so I thank you, Alessandra, for bringing your family all this way."

"Will other members of your family be visiting also, Caterina?" Edward dared to ask. He wasn't a sociable person day to day, but he'd been watching the faces of his children since they'd arrived in the large home. He didn't think he was ready to let any of his daughters enter into matrimony, but he could understand it might prove beneficial for them to at least be introduced to more social situations than they ever were a part of in England.

"Sì, Edward!" Caterina replied. "A great many! But worry not. You all have rooms here - one for you and your lovely wife to share, one for these beautiful signorine to share, and one for Charles when he arrives."

"That is very generous, Aunt," said Alessandra. "Thank you."

"Niente, Alessandra," said Caterina. "I am being entirely selfish, and when everyone is here, we will be holding a masked ball. It shall be the masquerade of the century for Venice, I am sure."

Alessandra grinned at her aunt's enthusiasm. For someone so old, she was certainly lively.

"A masked ball?" Elizabeth wondered in almost a whisper. She hadn't meant to voice her astonishment, and was regretful when she saw all faces turn toward her.

"Sì, indeed, Signorina Elizabeth," said Caterina, understanding perfectly the look on the young woman's face. Even as old as she was, Caterina could still remember her first masquerade. "In two days, my personal mask maker will be here. Then you shall each work with him to help him create the perfect mask for you."

"But will we not be able to see who is at the ball, Great Aunt?" Isabella asked.

"Not at all," said Caterina, always happy to encourage healthy imagination in the minds of those younger than her. "That is what makes a masked ball so very exciting, Signorina Isabella! Who will be there? Who will approach you? Who will talk to you? Who will wish to dance with you? Even when these things happen, you will not know who is behind the mask. Decadence! Intrigue! Mystery! You shall see, my great nieces - this will be nothing like you have ever experienced before."

Elizabeth smiled at her great aunt but said nothing more. Inside of her mind she could already imagine the gowns, the fashions, the masks ... and the gentlemen. Perhaps something could come of the night. Perhaps she might meet the man she was meant to meet. But if that was not to be the case, she could already imagine the vivid colours, the mask creations, and the wonderful paintings she would be able to later create out of her memory of it all.

10

That evening, in the quiet of the bed chamber they'd been assigned for the duration of their stay, Edward pulled his wife close.

"Should we be concerned about all this talk of a masked ball, Alessandra?" he asked. "It was mentioned to us on our previous visit that masquerades were no longer held here."

Alessandra looked at him in surprise. While she had heard such a thing said, she had not considered her aunt might be planning to do something wrong.

"You worry about this, Edward?" she asked. "Even if that is the case, my aunt has said she is holding the ball here, in her home. If such a ruling exists, I am sure it could not apply to what someone does in their own home."

"Yes, you are right," Edward said, smiling at her. "In full honesty, my lovely wife, I was teasing you," he added and saw Alessandra grin in response. "Our daughters at a masked ball. Should we allow all three to attend? Florence is only fifteen."

"She is plenty old enough to dance, Edward!" Alessandra said, loving how much of a caring father he was, and always had been. "Worry not. I shall keep her close to me on the evening."

"And if I desire to dance with you?" Edward asked.

Alessandra laughed at his attempt to look suggestive.

"Then you certainly shall, my lovely husband," she said. "Although, with masks on, perhaps I shall not know who is who, and who it is I dance with. What a fearful thought!"

Edward laughed at the look of concern on her face.

"You shall know it is me by the way that I pull you into my arms," he said as he pulled her closer to him.

"Indeed," said Alessandra before placing her lips on his. "Only one man will ever hold me the way that you do."

Mutually sinking into a loving embrace, neither thought about anyone else for a very long while.

11

"Today, you shall all go and see some sights," Caterina said as she glanced around all of the faces at her breakfast table the following morning.

"Oh?" Alessandra asked, surprised. "We did visit many sights last..."

"Sì, perhaps I spoke more delicately than I should," Caterina said, cutting her niece's words short with a smile. "I have further people arriving before midday. I would like to welcome them here without worrying about anyone else."

Alessandra smiled at her great aunt's bluntness. Most of the time, what she said made perfect sense, but that was not always the case. Regardless, Alessandra couldn't help but admire the elderly woman for her ability to be so straightforward in most of what she said.

"Of course, Aunt," she said. "We shall leave you directly."

"You shall leave after your family

have all eaten, Alessandra," Caterina said. "Even I would not let young women walk without sustenance."

Alessandra said nothing more as she processed how unique her aunt was, and how different she was from what Alessandra had known and could remember of her own mother.

"How goes your father?" she heard her aunt ask. "Is he well?"

"He is well," Alessandra replied. "He and Edward's mother still reside at Missinger Estate. They both appear very happy to be there, helping my brother, Nicholas, and his family."

"Ahh yes, Nicholas," Caterina said. "I still have not yet met my nephew. Will he be joining us also?"

"He did receive your invitation, Aunt," said Alessandra. "With his wife, Victoria, and their five children, he prefers to remain in his home and his work."

Caterina nodded but said nothing. Her nephew and his family weren't the only ones who'd been invited but wouldn't be attending. She understood. There were many things she wished she'd done differently in her life, including how many members of her family she'd made time for, but she understood about honour and dedication.

"I believe we are all finished, so we shall leave you now, Aunt," Alessandra said after glancing around the table, then prompting her family to stand.

"Grazie," Caterina said. She loved having people around her. Such instances had always needed to be offset by her having nobody around her. She'd never truly understood that aspect of herself, but she had learned that when she needed a moment alone, it worked rather well to simply tell everyone else to go away. "Return not long after midday and we shall all be able to dine together again."

Edward smiled. They'd just eaten. He couldn't imagine needing to eat again for a great many hours. That thought, he kept to himself.

"Come," he said as he and Alessandra shuffled their three offspring out the door. "Let us go."

As they exited the great home and stepped outside into the Venetian sunshine, Edward felt a moment of sadness. Whenever he walked outside of Chisholm Manor, there was green to be seen - trees, bushes and grasses spread out over the vast flat areas and tall hills. The main vistas he could see when he walked outside in Venice were those primarily of buildings and water. It was no less beautiful, but it certainly wasn't home.

"It will still be there when we get home, Edward," Alessandra said as she moved up behind him and took his hand in hers.

Edward naturally turned to her and smiled. Her ability to accurately interpret and understand his thoughts and his emotions had always impressed him. It was just one of the many things that he'd always been in awe about when it came to his wife.

"Shall we walk to where there are people?" Isabella asked in her usual don't-want-to-sit-still tone.

Alessandra chuckled at her second daughter. All of her children had their own personality traits - Elizabeth, with her serious but thoughtful manner; Charles, with his highly independent and jovial manner; and young Florence with her curious nature - but Isabella was by far the most outgoing and outspoken.

"Yes, let us do that," Alessandra said as she glanced at Edward and saw him nod in agreement. In truth, Alessandra didn't mind where they went. As far as she was aware, everyone in her family was healthy and content. That was more than she could ever wish for.

Strolling around the areas of Venice that most of them had visited before, little was said. Each had their own particular memories of different areas, and the things they'd done. As Elizabeth walked among her family, she tried not to focus on the way her father held her mother's hand as they walked, always wanting to be close by, as usual.

It was at that moment - in that very place and time - that Elizabeth Chisholm truly realized and admitted to herself just how lonely she was, and the extreme degree to which she longed for someone to come into her life and love her.

12

"Shall we walk back now?" Edward asked as he heard a large bell chime in the distance. It had been a pleasant walk, even though each of his family members had been unusually quiet. He hadn't minded that, although it did test his curiosity.

"Yes," Alessandra replied. "I must admit I am curious to see who will have now arrived at the home of my aunt."

"Someone related to you, perhaps, if I have correctly understood what Caterina said," Edward said, enjoying seeing the excitement growing on her face.

"Yes, that is what I, too, believe my aunt was implying," Alessandra said. "It is rather odd to not know who one is related to. I wonder what my mother was thinking by not coming back here after she married my father..." she began to ponder.

"Perhaps a long lost cousin waits to meet us," Isabella said, catching the end of her parents' conversation. "Someone who owns a great, haunted abbey in a mystery-laden area of land in an exotic location, and wishes for all of us to go and stay with them for some time."

Edward and Alessandra laughed together as they both turned and looked at their second daughter.

"I am quite sure that cannot be the situation, Isabella," said Alessandra, teasing. "And I am beginning to wonder if you might be reading far too many novels!"

As Elizabeth watched her sister laugh with their parents, she sighed inwardly. She wasn't as forward and loud as her younger sister. She wasn't loved like her mother was. She wasn't … anything. The thought left her saddened to another level.

As her aunt's home came into view, Alessandra felt her heart beat a little faster. Inside were more relatives, she was sure. It had taken much of her life to meet even her aunt and the few relatives she'd met in Venice on previous visits. Now she was going to be introduced to more relatives who had travelled from outside of Venice. Who were they? Where had they come from? And how were they related to her? She felt almost overwhelmed with intense anticipation of what was to come.

"All shall be revealed in the next few minutes, my love," she heard Edward say from beside her.

When she looked at him, she felt herself blush, just as she had a great many times over their long years of knowing one another. She knew his teasing didn't demand any response from her, other than the smile that she happily gave him.

Before entering the vast building, Elizabeth noticed a young man sitting from a vantage point, with an easel set up in front of him. Without thinking, she began to walk toward where he sat, keeping her distance as she moved in a circular path around behind him. As she tried to discretely see what he was drawing, she could see his head moving - looking up at the large home, then down at the paper set out before him. In the short time it took for her to walk closer, she saw his head repeat the action several times.

Too curious to consider how proper it might be for a young woman to approach a young man in such a way, she wasn't satisfied with trying to see his imagery from so far behind him. When she felt she just had to know what he was drawing, she began walking closer to him, subtly edging forward from behind where he sat.

Noticing her daughter wandering in a different direction, Alessandra turned and saw Elizabeth walking toward what looked to be a young artist. Alessandra said nothing to call her back. Instead, stopping where they were in front of the large home, she glanced at Edward. It was a glance that she knew he'd interpret correctly - one to indicate he could take a moment to discretely glance at their oldest daughter, but not disturb her.

13

"You draw a great likeness," Elizabeth said when she'd taken a couple of minutes to move close behind the young man and could finally see what was on the page. She held herself back far enough that her closeness wouldn't be impolite, so couldn't see the fine detail of the drawing, but was intrigued by what she *could* see.

There were few things that she'd ever considered herself good at, but drawing was something she did take pride in. Watching another's fingers moving across a page, creating, defining, and improving, was like watching a magician perform a magic trick.

As soon as she spoke, Elizabeth saw the young man jump, as if startled. Almost just as quickly, she saw him turn, see her, and stand to bow.

"Please forgive me," Elizabeth said,

feeling her face grow heated. It was something she'd always disliked about herself, but knew she could hardly do anything to control it. "I .. I did not mean to startle you."

"Aye, but you did startle me, Lass," the young man said, surprising Elizabeth with his strange accent. As she looked at his face, she thought she could see a look of amusement. She was relieved. If she'd accurately interpreted what he'd said, his words may have sounded like she was being scolded. His eyes told a different story altogether. "Dinna fash, however. I was far too absorbed in what I was doing. My mother always told me to stay aware of what is happening around me. She would not be happy to know that I was so absorbed in my drawing that I did not even notice you approaching me."

"You are drawing the home of my great aunt," Elizabeth said, disheartened that she hadn't understood most of whatever he'd just said. It had all been spoken with a dialect very different from the English one she was most used to, and just as different from the ones she'd so far heard in Venice. Not wanting to admit that she hadn't understood all of what he'd said, she tentatively moved even closer to see the image that was on the paper. "You are very talented."

"Thank ye. I do not know if I am *very* talented, but one day I hope to be. I am studying to be an architect," the young man said. "This is truly the home of your great aunt?"

"Yes," Elizabeth said, enjoying what looked like friendliness and amusement on the young man's face.

"Then you are a very fortunate young lass indeed," the young man said before bowing again and then moving to sit where he had been.

Elizabeth was left confused. She'd thought they were embarking on an easy going, friendly conversation. Had he just dismissed her when he'd sat down again? Feeling that to be the case, she began to walk way, her face heated. If she'd somehow offended him, she certainly hadn't intended to - nor could she identify *how* she possibly could have offended him. Even so, he'd bowed and he'd sat down, presenting his back to her. It seemed certain to Elizabeth that he had no desire to keep talking to her, and she was not welcome to linger close to him.

Seeing her family waiting for her on the steps of the great home, she walked swiftly to where they were. She expected reproach. She was relieved when nobody asked or said anything about her actions at all.

"Come, Elizabeth," Edward said as he watched his oldest daughter approach. He'd watched the interaction, and seen the abrupt separation of the two young people. He could also see the redness on his daughter's face. It was a sight he knew very well, having seen it on her mother for twenty years. "Let us move out of this sun."

Thankful for her father's discretion at not teasing her about her blushing, or her effort to talk to the young man, Elizabeth silently nodded and made her way indoors. She wanted to look back, to see the man she'd just interacted with. She fought not to. If interacting with young men was going to affect her so - or result in her feeling horrified at having been shunned - perhaps that was not something she should wish to do after all.

14

"And here is my niece and her famiglie!" all heard Caterina call out as they entered the morning parlour. "Alessandra. Edward. Please come and meet my grand-nephew. This is your … oh, cugino of sorts, I suppose … cousin … Gilberto Roselli."

"It is a great pleasure to meet you, Mia Cugina Alessandra," Gilberto said as he bowed to Alessandra and Edward. "My great aunt has long told me I have relations in England, however I have never before met any."

"It is a pleasure to meet you, Gilberto," Alessandra said. "This is my husband, Edward, and our daughters, Elizabeth, Isabella, and Florence."

Elizabeth watched and did as she knew was expected, curtseying when she was introduced. She smiled as she saw Gilberto take her hand in his and grin at her, but no words were spoken.

"And please allow me to introduce a close friend of mine - Lord Byron," Gilberto went on to say.

"I believe he is a close friend of *mine*, Gilberto!" Caterina said, making the two young men laugh.

"Indeed, Prozia," Gilberto said as he moved close to Caterina and kissed her cheek. "But you know that he is far too outrageous for you to be able to bear being around for very long, so I only do you the favour of keeping him away whenever I can."

"Do not pay any heed to such silliness, Miss Elizabeth," Elizabeth heard the lord say as he moved close to her and leaned down to kiss her hand. "In truth, I consider everybody to be my friend. After all, what kind of life can we be living if we do not have friends?"

Elizabeth felt her face blush, but only smiled and pulled her hand back, unable to think of any words that would suffice as a reply.

"You are both silly boys," Caterina

said, determined to look serious even though she was only ever amused by the young men.

Elizabeth watched as Gilberto and Lord Byron both laughed again but then appeared to remember their manners. They were both older than her by some years, but she couldn't deny she felt inspired to keep looking at both of them.

"I believe my great aunt intends to throw a masquerade, Mia Cugina," Gilberto said as he moved closer to Alessandra. "You and your family will attend, of course?"

Alessandra smiled at her newfound relative. He was much younger than her, but he and his friend appeared to equally be many years older than her daughters. For that, she felt surprisingly glad - and relieved.

"We shall attend," she replied. "None of us have ever been to a masked ball. Is there anything we must know?"

As Elizabeth watched, she saw Gilberto and his friend both throw back their heads and laugh heartily, as if they'd shared a great joke.

"The most important thing you must remember, Alessandra, is to be merry," Lord Byron said, grinning.

"That is not all, Lord Byron, and you know it," Caterina said. "And you shall address my niece as Mrs Chisholm!" she added with a stern tone in her voice. "Worry not, Alessandra. When you meet my mask maker, he will tell you much about such occasions."

"We shall all get our own masks made, Great Aunt?" Isabella asked, excited at the prospect.

"Sì, Isabella," Caterina replied. "It is a great honour to have your own mask, and it is very important to have one that represents who you are."

"But, Great Aunt, if everyone wears a mask that shows who they are, why wear a mask at all?" Florence asked, curious.

"That is a very valid question, Signorina Florence," Gilberto said, grinning at her. "But that is part of the fun of a masquerade. You cannot identify anyone by what they look like day to day. Instead, you must try and figure it out by the mask that they wear. It is like a pantomime that is designed to keep you guessing. I believe you shall greatly enjoy it."

"Yes," Florence said. "I do believe I shall."

"It is always a joy to see what kind of mask anyone wears to such an event," Lord Byron said as he faced everyone then settled his eyes on Elizabeth. "But the greatest joy of all is using what masks look like to ascertain who is who. It is quite the mystery!"

Elizabeth felt herself blush from the attention the lord appeared to be placing on her. Although he was obviously much older than her, she did regard him as very handsome. A part of her wished she could just keep looking at him. A glance she received from her mother reminded her that she absolutely should not.

As conversation moved on and all walked through to the grand dining room to dine, Edward felt his protective nature as a father show itself. He hadn't felt concerned about his oldest daughter approaching a young artist outside, but he most certainly had noticed her reaction to the suave gentleman kissing her hand. It wasn't something he wanted to worry about, so tried not to do so. His daughter was young, but of an age to be wed. She was also of a kind but intelligent mind. Her beauty was something he'd never given thought to, but realized it was time to start to consider that perhaps his daughter, in an environment comprised of many men, might turn out to be much like a flame, attracting a great many moths.

15

Sitting at the large table, Elizabeth quietly listened to the conversations happening around her. Although she'd been to Venice previously, she'd been only a child then, and there were things that newly intrigued her about the company she was among.

Her great aunt was as joyful as Elizabeth remembered her being on their previous visit. In many ways, Elizabeth could see a strong likeness between her sister, Isabella, and their great aunt. Even as she sat and watched people talking, she could see those two moving back and forth into a sync of words that she knew she'd never be able to replicate. Elizabeth was older than Isabella, but she knew she would never have the same level of blunt outspokenness that her younger sister had.

Glancing around, she accidentally

caught the eye of the lord seated opposite her. When she thought she saw him wink at her, she quickly diverted her attention, fearful of what colour her face might be transforming to. Her ability to go red with no effort at all had been something she'd disliked all of her life. That her father found the occurrence endearing in both Elizabeth and her mother did nothing to make Elizabeth feel any better about it.

Without conscious thought, despite her best effort, her attention drifted back to the handsome lord. To her relief, he'd turned and appeared to be sharing an intimate story of great amusement with Gilberto. It gave Elizabeth a moment to be able to look at both men without them giving her any notice. They were older than her, but not as old as her parents in age, and clearly not as old in maturity. Would they be of the age someone should be when they wed? Was that the age of man she should consider for marriage, if she was ever to be wed?

As she pondered the possibility of meeting more young men, she finally felt her spirit lighten. She'd been worrying about never finding love. Surely, if she was meant to find it anywhere, she was meant to find it in a romantic city such as Venice!

16

"You have been in this beautiful city before, I understand, Miss Elizabeth," she heard Lord Byron say as all left the grand dining room and made their way toward the back garden area.

Turning to face him, Elizabeth was initially startled by how close he was standing. Beyond him, she could see Gilberto happily striding as if in a hurry to get somewhere.

As excited as she was to be approached by a man as handsome as the lord, she was thankful that her parents and sisters were walking ahead but still well within reach if needed.

"Yes, we have stayed here with my great aunt previously but I do not fully remember it. I was only a child then, Lord Byron," she replied.

"Ah, but seeing the world through a child's eyes can only be the most wonderful way to see it, do you not agree?" Lord Byron said. "As we grow, we see so many things differently. Colours that were once vibrant, begin to seem faded and dull. Things that once seemed very big, start to seem not so big at all. Is it not preferred that we see things the way a child does, rather than how we do as we age?"

"You ... you sound like a poet," Elizabeth said. The loud laughter she received in reply stunned and perplexed her. "Forgive me, did ... did I say something wrong?"

Instead of hearing the man beside her reply, Elizabeth saw Gilberto look back and focus on her as he grinned at her and his friend.

"This rogue *is* a poet, Elizabeth," Gilberto said. "Watch out for him. He is very grand with words, but he is a rogue, and whatever he says most certainly should never be believed!"

Once more, Elizabeth saw a knowing glance pass between the men. She had no idea what it meant, but she'd watched the body language of her mother and father for all of her life. She was familiar enough with looks of intimacy to know that the two men must be very close friends indeed.

"Do you read, Mia Cugina Elizabeth?" Gilberto asked.

"Not as much as I wish to," Elizabeth replied. "But please, I do not speak the language that you use. What does Mia Cugina mean?"

"Fear not," Lord Byron said as he moved even closer to her in their approach to the exterior doorway. "It only means 'my cousin'. As your great aunt, Caterina, has not provided a detailed description of how you and Gilberto are related, he will call you, your mother and your sisters all Mia Cugina."

"Oh, I see," Elizabeth said, feeling silly for not knowing already. "Thank you."

Seeing her mother stop walking in the garden and then turn to look back at her, Elizabeth quickened her pace to catch up. She felt there could be much that she could talk to Gilberto and his friend about, but something about them made her wary of doing so too much.

"Seguimi, per favore! Come!" she heard Caterina call out to all. "We have shade here, and it is a wonderful afternoon to be outdoors. I cannot move as much now, but this is still a favourite place for me to sit."

Elizabeth smiled at her great aunt and followed the lead of her mother and father. As they all sat, she positioned herself so that she faced away from the men. From her brief moments of talking to both of them, she could feel a level of enthusiasm inside of her that excited her. It also frightened her.

"Worry not, Elizabeth. We do not need to worry about a mere cousin. You and I are to meet many others," she heard Isabella whisper to her. Although there was no specific context provided with the words, Elizabeth suspected she understood what Isabella was talking about. "Great Aunt says that even more people will be arriving over the next two days, and then we shall have the masked ball to attend, and a great many men to dance with! Are you as excited at the prospect as I am?"

Elizabeth smiled and nodded to reassure her sister, even though she wasn't certain if what she felt was excitement or apprehension. She was sure she might be as excited about the prospect of meeting potential suitors as her sister was. She was equally sure that she would do her best to never show it.

17

The following morning, Elizabeth felt exhausted. She'd gotten through her first full day in the grand home and met even more people who were distantly related to her. Although she constantly tried to look calm on the outside, she hadn't stopped feeling nervous on the inside. The unfortunate result had been a night of restless turning in her bed, instead of much needed sleep.

From where she sat, determined to appreciate the luxurious morning meal with most of the people she'd met the day before, she could see out the window. Once again there sat the young artist she'd noticed the previous day.

"Did the young man tell you what he is doing, Elizabeth?" Edward asked when he saw where her gaze rested. "Did what he draws inspire you to do some yourself?"

"Yes, Elizabeth, you did bring all of

your paints in your trunk," Isabella said, smiling at her sister. She had no time for drawing or painting, but she did love to tease Elizabeth about her love of it. "Perhaps you could draw with the young man," she dared to suggest before seeing a stern look from her father.

"He said that he is learning to be an architect," Elizabeth replied, speaking to her father while ignoring the not-so-discrete insinuation of her younger sister. "That is, I believe that is what he said. In truth, he spoke very strangely and I cannot be entirely certain that what I heard him say is what he did say."

Edward chuckled. His oldest daughter was often very quiet and very thoughtful. Sometimes when she spoke, however, he wondered if there wasn't a rose inside, simply waiting to sprout into full bloom.

"You enjoy drawing, Elizabeth, and have often said you wish to grow your skills in it," Alessandra said. "Perhaps

Isabella's idea is a good one. You could speak to the young man about it. It is rare for you to meet anyone who loves it as much as you do. He may offer you some guidance…"

"Are you suggesting our daughter go out there and just speak to that stranger…" Edward began to say in an effort to tease both his wife and his daughter.

Alessandra laughed.

"We shall be close by and able to observe, Edward, so yes," she said, greatly enjoying seeing the look on her husband's face. "What harm could it bring if you and I are able to view them from a distance?"

"I believe that might be entirely scandalous, Miss Elizabeth," Lord Byron said. "Perhaps what you should do today, if you have no other plans, is join me and Gilberto on an outing."

At the suggestion, Alessandra saw a very different expression flow over her husband's face. As bold as the invitation had been, she was glad that it had been made in front of her and Edward, and not offered to Elizabeth in private.

"Thank you, Lord Byron, however I believe Elizabeth shall remain here with us today," Alessandra said. She didn't often feel protective of her daughters when it came to the men they had contact with. The suggestion that her eighteen year old unwed daughter might go out with two men she hardly knew, and no other escort, was beyond what Alessandra would accept, even if one of them was a cousin of sorts.

"Yes," Elizabeth said, relieved at her mother's reply to the suggestion. "Thank you for your invitation, however I do wish to remain here today. There is much to see and do in this immediate area."

Glancing out the window again to look at the artist, she saw a familiar face stop and talk to him.

"Charles!" Elizabeth called out before standing and running from the room, all manners quite forgotten.

All stopped their eating to move and look out the window. As much as Alessandra wanted to run to her son, the look she exchanged with Edward said it was more than acceptable to remain just where she was.

18

"Charles!" Elizabeth said again as she ran out of the grand home entrance and straight to where he stood. He wasn't her next sibling in chronological age, but he was the one she'd always found easiest to talk to. Because he was away from their home much of the time, he was also the sibling she missed.

"Hello, Elizabeth," Charles Chisholm said when he saw his sister running toward him. When she reached him, he allowed her a rare instance of being able to briefly hug him. "Have you seen this chap's drawing?" Charles went on to ask as he pointed to the page before him. "Remarkable!"

Angus McKay grinned as he turned and looked at the young man who'd spoken.

"I'm not sure remarkable is accurate," he said. "I am only learning..."

"Learning. Yes," Charles said. "If that is the work of someone only learning, imagine how good he'll be when he is a master of architecture, Elizabeth!"

As Elizabeth smiled at the artist, she saw him glance at her briefly before returning to his work. Once again, he didn't seem inclined to want to speak to her. Understanding he'd already told Charles his name but hadn't introduced himself to her, pushed up her eagerness to not remain close to him.

Resolved that she may never know why he appeared so disinterested in conversing with her, she returned her focus to her brother again.

"Mother said you would not be here for another day or two," she said. "Why do you come so early?"

She watched as Charles threw his head back and laughed heartily in response to her question.

"My darling sister, sometimes I do wonder if you are aware of how the things you say - and the questions you ask - sound," he teased her. On seeing her begin to show regret and a deep remorse at having spoken, he stopped teasing her. "To answer your question, I had been wanting to stay in England a few days longer to complete a study assignment. I did expect it would take me that long to finish it. However, as you know, I am rather brilliant at my studies…"

Elizabeth laughed at him, finally realizing how much he was teasing about everything he was saying.

"Everyone will be eager to see you," she said. "Come."

"In a minute, Elizabeth," Charles said as he watched the artist resume his sketching. "This is far too intriguing to me, as I am sure it should be for you also since you are such a skilled artist yourself. See the way he uses charcoal to create this image. I have never seen it used in such a way, and do you not always use pencil and paint yourself? I must admit I find this rather intriguing."

Elizabeth wanted nothing more than to move away, but she indulged her brother and remained where she was. Even though the artist had resumed his sketching, he had at least responded to Charles talking to him. Elizabeth was resolved that there must simply be something he did not like about how she looked, to be so uninterested in speaking to her at all.

The silence felt uncomfortable as she and Charles stood behind the young man, watching him continue his sketching. She was sure it must have been making him uncomfortable, having two people watch as he drew. When she tried to imagine being in that position - drawing with an audience watching - she knew she'd be very uncomfortable indeed. She loved the activity and she believed she was skilled in it, but it was still something she didn't require others to see. When someone asked to see a finished piece of her work, she reluctantly showed them but, for the most part, her paintings were just for her.

"Mother is eager to see you," she finally said in a quiet voice. It was one more attempt to try and lure her brother away from the situation she was finding herself increasingly desperate to be away from.

Even though she could have just walked away herself, leaving Charles where he was, she was greatly relieved when he agreed, and they finally left to go inside together.

As twenty two year old Angus McKay sat and continued his assignment of applying strokes of charcoal to paper in the drawing of the large home, he'd listened with intent to the conversation that had been happening behind him. He supposed it would not be considered polite to do so, however since the two people who appeared set on talking about him seemed to want to do it right behind him, he felt it was only fair that he take note of everything they were saying.

He'd perceived that the two of them were siblings, and possibly close ones. That was something he'd never understood, being the only surviving child of his family in Scotland.

When he'd been very young, he could remember having had a brother and a sister. At some point, they'd stopped being around anymore. His mother had never said why, and he'd never asked. One minute they'd been there. The next, they hadn't. That was all he knew.

Growing up mostly without any other children around, he'd perfected the art of keeping himself occupied. In the woody area that he'd grown up in, he'd moved through stages of pretending to be a great Highlander warrior, and then on to other forms of role play. It hadn't bothered him then that he always had to play both sides of whatever battle he was pretending to be a part of.

As he'd grown, he had started to recognize that his childhood had been quite lonely. He'd also started to realize that his childhood had left him with few skills in interacting with others.

The previous instance of two people approaching him was a standard thing that happened with him. Many people were friendly enough. When anyone started to speak to him, he could always appear friendly enough for those first few minutes. After that, he shut down. He didn't know why. It was just part of who he was. Granted, it was a part that he wished he could change but, as yet, no matter how far he travelled or how many people he met, talking to people continued to be a hurdle he hadn't yet learned to overcome.

When he sensed the two young people finally walking away in their effort to approach and enter the very building he'd been sketching, he briefly stopped the movement of his charcoal. He was someone who liked to be kept busy, but now and then - not often, but certainly now and then - he found it rather necessary to stop whatever he was doing and simply contemplate where his life was at right at that moment.

There were things about him that he wanted to change. Over time, he would make sure that he did change. In the immediate moment, however, he knew he needed to focus on the present.

Thinking about where he was - the

beautiful city of Venice - and where he was from - a land very far away that was much greener and far more lush - he suddenly felt homesick. It had been a long time since he'd seen his mother - the one person who'd been constant in his life for as long as he could remember. He'd grown up loving her and knowing she was the person who possibly would always love him most. Even though he'd worried about no longer being around for her, it had been a great opportunity, being offered to travel with the architect who'd brought him to Venice, and learn from him. Although Angus hadn't been sure about leaving his mother, she'd been adamant in her eagerness for him to go. He was a young man. In her opinion, it was time for him to find his place in the world.

Determined to not dwell on the sadness that came from missing his mother and his home, Angus shook his head, focused on the great architecture before him, and began sketching again.

20

"È possibile? Can it be?" Caterina asked as she saw her great nephew enter the room. "No, I do not believe it! This cannot be the little Charles that I got to know so well before."

Charles grinned at the elderly woman. He'd only been three years old when he'd met her previously, but her happy and noisy personality had certainly remained in his memory.

"Hello, Great Aunt Caterina," he said with full formality. There appeared to be many people in the room aside from his immediate family. Not often nervous, he couldn't deny that seeing so many foreign faces all turn to look at him at the same time did affect him a little. "You are looking well. You haven't aged a bit since I was last here."

Caterina laughed loudly before indicating for him to move closer and give her a hug. She'd liked all of

Alessandra's children when they'd visited years earlier, but it was Charles who'd truly won her heart as a favourite out of all of her relations.

"I shall introduce you to all of your relatives here, Charles, however I do believe your madre over there is very eager to see you," Caterina said, grinning at Alessandra. "Go and say hello to her first."

Charles obediently obeyed the suggestion, taking his time to greet his parents and other two sisters.

"It is good to see you, Charles," he heard his father say as they greeted one another. Although he didn't consider himself anything like his father, he had grown up certainly respecting the man that he was.

"And you, Father," Charles replied.

As Elizabeth looked on, she felt content - not entirely happy, but certainly grateful for everyone in her family being with her, where they were, and as healthy as they all were.

Although she'd had many times when she wished she could be in the position that her brother was in - allowed to go away from the estate to study and meet many new people - she knew her life could never be like his.

She was a woman. Her role was to marry and become a mother, and that wasn't an existence she didn't want. She was also the heir to Chisholm Manor estate. One day, it would be up to her to manage all of the land, all of the tenants, and all of the people who worked in the manor house itself. Although she believed she had the wisdom to do what she would have to do when that time came, she did hope that by then she would have someone by her side, happy to support her in such a responsibility. She also hoped that by then she would know what it was like to be a mother.

Refocusing yet again on the present, she looked around the room. Her immediate family were by her side, as were a growing number of extended family. She knew that, beyond anything else, she must be grateful that she had so many people around her who loved and cared for her. As easily as she had always experienced life so far, her parents had ensured she knew how fortunate they were, and that there were many people in the world who had nothing and no-one.

21

Sitting back and waiting for her turn with her great aunt's master mask maker the following morning, Elizabeth watched how the gentleman took his time, looking at each face of her family, then asking a few questions. It intrigued her that such an exercise was useful in creating the perfect design of mask for those who were wealthy enough to be able to have them personally made and individualized. She was curious about the whole process, but equally excited about seeing the art works he was going to create.

"It is your turn, Elizabeth," she finally heard her mother say.

As she sat in front of the elderly man, she found herself wondering what his life had been like when he'd been her age. Her great aunt had already told her that he'd been designing and creating masks his entire life, and he was the only person anyone with the means to do so would get a mask made by.

The questions that came were few, but when she was asked what she wished her life to be like, she leaned in close to the man and whispered, "I wish to be loved." In response, she saw the man nod knowingly and then resume moving his pencil across the page that only he could see. He didn't ask her anything more. He didn't smile at her, or even look at her. The final question he'd asked, and the simple answer he'd received, appeared to be all that he needed to be able to create a design that would be only for her. That triggered Elizabeth's curiosity immensely.

With a look from her mother, Elizabeth was moved on and it was Florence's turn to talk to the man. Once again, Elizabeth saw that he very quietly asked her sister several questions, accepted her replies, and then dismissed her.

When all had gone through the process and the mask maker had shared some of his knowledge about the history of masquerades, the family left the room.

"I wasn't sure what that would be like when my aunt spoke of it, but now I feel I am even more intrigued about him as a mask creator," Alessandra said as she, Edward and their children walked through the passageway.

"Yes, I wonder how what he asked each of us will be interpreted by him, and how it will translate into the masks he makes for us," Edward agreed.

"I believe mine will make me look like a beautiful butterfly," Florence said.

"What makes you believe that, Florence?" Isabella asked as she chuckled. "Did you tell him you wanted that, or did he ask you if you felt like you're in a cocoon?"

"Do not be so silly, Isabella!" Florence said. "I simply hope that a butterfly will be the design."

Elizabeth watched and listened. The description of a butterfly, she regarded as something she'd never see herself as, but when Isabella had mentioned the word 'cocoon', she could relate to that. At times, she did indeed regard herself as being in a cocoon - and one that she had no idea how to break free from.

"Oh, but if you were to receive a mask that made you look like a butterfly, surely that would not completely look right unless you had a new gown to match," Isabella said.

Glancing at her sister in disbelief, Elizabeth couldn't help but giggle at what she considered an outrageous forwardness. Nobody had mentioned even the possibility of having new gowns made, and it was only days away till the masquerade was due to be held so highly unlikely to happen. Even so, Elizabeth admired her younger sister for being so bold in making the suggestion, even though it wasn't phrased as a direct request.

"Oh, a new gown, you say?" Edward asked, equally surprised but amused by his daughter's boldness. "It is fortunate then that your mother made such a suggestion before we arrived, and your great aunt has already employed her mantua maker to produce a gown for each of you."

"But we have not been measured for such a thing, Father," Isabella said, surprised. "How … when … how can this happen?"

Elizabeth heard her mother and father laugh as they all entered the afternoon parlour. Whatever news was to come about any possible new gowns she and her sisters might receive, she guessed she was going to have to wait to hear it.

"How wonderful to hear the sound of a family finding amusement together," she heard Lord Byron say upon their entry into the room.

"Sì, Lord Byron," Caterina said as

she grinned at Alessandra and her family.

"Our daughters have just not-so-discretely asked about new gowns, Aunt," Alessandra said.

"Oh, no," Caterina said, not hiding the surprise in her voice. "You have not told them?"

"We thought it might be a surprise for them," Edward said, chuckling.

"Alessandra! Edward!" Caterina said, beginning to pretend to scold them. "You have three beautiful daughters, all of whom will desire to be even more beautiful for my masquerade," she said before turning to face Elizabeth, Isabella and Florence. "Young ladies, this afternoon you shall meet my mantua maker. Before you arrived, I gave instructions for them to prepare gowns for each of you."

"It all seems rather extravagant, Aunt," Alessandra began to say.

"Not at all," said Caterina. "As I have already said, this shall be the masquerade of the year in Venice. Therefore, I must have control of what everyone looks like, including what they wear. Each of you will be called forth this afternoon to be fitted with the gown that has been designed for you. My mantua maker has assured me that once they have fitted the gowns to you, it shall only be a day before they shall be able to return them, ready to be worn."

"When is the masquerade to be held?" Elizabeth dared to ask. She'd heard reference to 'several days'. It seemed like several days had already passed since then. "If I may ask."

"Two days from now, Signorina Elizabeth," Caterina replied. "Later today, you'll be fitted for your gowns. Tomorrow morning, you shall be fitted with wigs…"

"Wigs?" Florence asked, her eyes wide in surprise.

"Indeed," said Caterina, laughing softly. "The hair colour of our family is too dark. No, I shall not have it! For our masquerade, all will wear wigs of white!"

"Then we truly will not know one another," Florence said in wonder. "We will not see faces, and we will not see true hair. How exciting, Great Aunt!"

Caterina grinned as she saw the expressions flow over the faces of the young women. Yes, it was good to be reminded of how life was in youth.

"And so the mystery of the night will deepen," Lord Byron said as his eyes danced across each of the sisters then settled on Elizabeth. "Indeed your great aunt is known to throw the greatest masquerades of all. I believe it shall be a night nobody shall ever forget."

As she watched him smile at her, Elizabeth felt herself blush. He was older but he was handsome, and he was looking at her in a way nobody ever had before.

"Your work is outstanding," Elizabeth later heard the now familiar voice of Lord Byron say. After her personal appointments with a mantua maker and a wig maker, she'd felt the need to escape into solitude. The items they'd selected and created for her had seemed too much for her.

When she'd tried on the gown, it had only been a little too loose, but the richness of the fabric had been like she'd never seen or felt before. The thought that her great aunt was doing so much for her had been overwhelming. As a result, at the first opportunity, Elizabeth had escaped to the outside world, and into her place of comfort.

When she heard the deep voice, she'd been out in the back garden for what seemed like hours, challenging herself to accurately capture the beauty of a particular flower she'd never seen before. It was something she regarded she should have been able to easily capture since it was one very small thing. The opposite was proving to be true.

"I thank you for saying so, Lord Byron, however I do not feel this is very outstanding at all," she replied as she tried unsuccessfully to shift her focus to the man standing far too close to her. "I know not why this one small thing is challenging me so."

"Perhaps you are looking at it too closely," Lord Byron replied as he pulled an extra seat closer and sat beside her. "In all things, I believe we can look at something too closely."

"Do we not see things more clearly if we study them?" Elizabeth asked as she finally shifted her view away from what she'd been attempting to draw, and turned to look at him.

As she turned, she realized just how closely he'd sat beside her. If the two of them had known each other more intimately, she imagined they were close enough to both lean forward and kiss. On recognizing where her thoughts had travelled to, she quickly focused on his eyes to divert herself.

"Sometimes, no," Lord Byron replied, not hiding his interest in her lips. "On occasion, one must step back and see the broader picture."

"But I only wish to paint a picture of this one flower," Elizabeth said.

She watched as he grinned broadly at her. The level of his handsomeness had continued to attract her since the moment she'd met him. Having overheard someone mention his age, she knew he was eleven years older than her. She suspected that was so much of an age difference that she'd never be regarded as someone for him to notice, but although she knew that logic, she couldn't help feeling that she was attracted to him, and he was paying particular attention to her.

"Do you see all of who I am when

you look at *me* so closely, Elizabeth?" he asked with a tone of intimacy that jolted her out of her thoughts.

"Oh! I ... I apologize," Elizabeth stammered. "I... please forgive me!"

"You are never required to ask for forgiveness, Miss Elizabeth," she heard him say. "Not with me."

Before she could even think of a reply, she watched him stare off into the distance as he started to speak in a way she hadn't heard before.

"Lo! where the Giant on the mountain stands,

His blood-red tresses deep'ning in the sun,

With death-shot glowing in his fiery hands,

And eye that scorcheth all it glares upon,

Restless it rolls, now fix'd, and now anon

Flashing afar,—and at his iron feet

Destruction cowers to mark what deeds are done;

For on this morn three potent Nations meet,
To shed before his Shrine the blood he deems most sweet."

Elizabeth studied his face as he spoke. On it, she saw thoughtfulness and sadness. It was a vibrant contrast to the happy outlook he'd presented previously. It was also a contrast that intrigued her.

"What does it mean?" she dared to ask, sure she would never understand the words he'd said, even if she sat and studied them for days.

"Does it mean anything?" Lord Byron asked as he turned to face her again. "I am not sure. Words come to me, just as scenes of natural beauty such as this come to you," he added as he pointed to the drawing in front of them. "But I suppose what these words reflect most to me is that no matter how far we travel in life, or what we experience, there can still remain a level of dissatisfaction that is constant."

"As if we are constantly seeking something more," Elizabeth whispered.

"Yes," Lord Byron said as he smiled sadly at her. "I do believe that sums it up very nicely. As a fellow poet has written, *The restless soul is driven abroad to roam*, but then, ultimately, *The restless soul is driven to ramble home*. Why? Because whatever we seek, we think we will find if we go looking for it. Most often, however, we do not, because it is not in the land or the sights or the experiences that we must find our true happiness. It is within us."

"Yes," Elizabeth said, feeling quite enraptured with the conversation taking place. Even though she didn't know how to reply, it felt more mature than any conversation she'd had before. "Have you travelled far and wide seeking something, Lord Byron?"

"I have," she saw him reply, again with that sad smile.

"And did you find what you seek?" Elizabeth asked.

"At times, I thought so," Lord Byron said. "But alas, in hindsight I believe I did not. I do enjoy Venice greatly, however. There is much peace to be had here. As the gondolas grace the waters, the history calms my soul."

Elizabeth studied his face. Being more thoughtful than her sisters, she liked that he appeared to be like her in that way. His facial expression didn't hide just how serious his thoughts appeared to have gone.

"You are very beautiful," she heard him say as he put on a smile again, then appeared to begin to reach out with his hand toward her face.

Startled, lost for words, and sure she was still far too close to the gentleman in her presence, Elizabeth was glad when, at that moment, she heard Charles call out to her from the exterior doorway of the large home.

"There you are!" Charles exclaimed. When he noticed the older gentleman sitting far too close to Elizabeth, he swiftly moved forward to where the two of them were seated.

"Is it I that you seek, Brother?" Elizabeth asked, feeling somewhat dazed but very glad of the distraction.

Thinking on his feet, Charles would have said anything to get her away from where she sat. The truth was that he'd heard in passing several things about Lord Byron that weren't entirely pure in subject. It wasn't something Charles would ever have taken notice of, except that he'd quickly noticed the attention the lord was giving to Elizabeth. There might be nothing in it, he knew. He also knew that Lord Byron was reported to have created such a scandalous reputation throughout London and Venice that anyone associated with him could be put into disrepute just by spending time with him.

"It is," he said. "Mother and Father wish to speak to us all. Will you come now?"

As he spoke, he snuck a glance at

the lord. Curiosity took over as he noticed the way that not only did Lord Byron look at Elizabeth, but was also looking at him.

"Yes, of course," Elizabeth said, feeling the need to be away from the handsome older man in her presence. "Excuse me, Lord Byron," she added, curtseying before seeing him bow his head from where he sat.

23

"You wished to see all of us?" Elizabeth asked when she and Charles entered the small parlour that her parents and sisters were in. She'd felt confused by the attentions of the older man outside, so was highly relieved when Charles had come to summon her. Now that she was away from Lord Byron, she was curious about what was happening that would have demanded she be summoned at all.

"Yes," Edward replied as he watched Elizabeth and Charles enter the room.

"Is something wrong, Father?" Isabella asked.

"No, not at all, Isabella," Edward replied. "Your mother and I have received an invitation for all of us to attend the opera this evening."

"Oh?" Elizabeth asked, still uncertain. "All of us? Everyone currently staying with our great aunt?"

"No, just us for this evening," Alessandra said. "Do you all wish to go?"

"Yes!" she heard a unanimous reply flow back to her, making her grin at each of her children's responses.

"But our great aunt will be joining us?" asked Charles, feeling surprisingly attached to the elderly woman he hardly knew.

"She has said that she is weary today," said Alessandra. "We shall go out and let her have her peace."

"But who invited us, Mother?" Florence asked.

"Lord Byron is responsible for our invitation," Edward replied. As he said the words, he watched his oldest daughter's face. It was easy for him to see her face change on hearing the lord's name, but he said nothing to her about it.

"Well, that's all settled then," Elizabeth heard her mother say. Why they'd all been summoned into the room for such a mild conversation, she had no idea. She was just glad that it had happened. If it hadn't - if she'd remained sitting outside, close to Lord Byron, for any longer - she wasn't sure what might have happened.

24

"Do you enjoy the opera, Miss Elizabeth?" she heard Lord Byron say as she later made her way out toward the back garden again to retrieve her art supplies. Nothing in his voice betrayed they'd recently spoken intimately at all.

"I have never before seen an opera, Lord Byron," she mumbled, trying to be polite. The more she'd talked to him, the more she'd grown certain that she was developing feelings for him. The difficulty came from not knowing if he felt the same way about her. Not wanting to do anything that might result in her looking silly, she wasn't sure she should keep talking to him but her lack of conversation didn't seem to influence him to stop speaking to her at all.

"Then I am hopeful you accepted my invitation to attend this evening," he said in a quieter voice as he moved closer.

"I believe my mother and father have

accepted your invitation," Elizabeth said, feeling her face begin to redden.

"Indeed," he said as a broad grin spread over his face. "But, I do believe you may be a young woman who might protest if you do not wish to do something."

Elizabeth stopped walking and looked at him in surprise. No matter how she replayed his words in her head, she couldn't think of any way to reply that would be satisfactory.

"This evening you shall see Teatro La Fenice. It is one of the greatest places I have ever watched the opera. Do you know why I am drawn to such a great theatre, Miss Elizabeth?" he continued, moving closer still. "It was built to replace its predecessor, which burned down, you know. Now that La Fenice has been constructed, it provides us with the opportunity to see operas somewhere even more magnificent than we could have before."

Not wanting to rush to reply,

Elizabeth resumed her walking toward where her easel still stood. After the brief meeting with her parents, she'd tried to remain indoors for enough time for Lord Byron to have left the outdoors area, and perhaps have gone out of the house altogether. It wasn't because she didn't enjoy his attentions. It was because she enjoyed them too much.

To know that he was still close by, perhaps having waited patiently for her to return, was confusing for her. She wanted to scream out the most obvious question to him - what do you want from me? She knew she could never ask such a question to him, or anyone else.

Determined to do what she had to do, and not be swayed by something that might not even be real, Elizabeth swiftly gathered up her art supplies and easel in one hand, and her painting in the other. She could see the handsome older man continuing to walk beside her, but he said nothing more. For that, Elizabeth was very grateful.

25

As Elizabeth entered the grand theatre that evening, she was struck by the beauty and grandeur of the foyer. What Lord Byron had told her about the theatre having been so recently built, to be more magnificent than the theatre people had most attended before, left her wondering what the previous theatre had looked like. She'd thought her aunt's home was the ultimate height of luxury. Even that didn't compare to the building she currently stood in.

"Come, Elizabeth," she heard her father call out to her when she'd stopped walking to absorb the splendour of the interior of the building. "We do not want to miss the opening."

"No indeed," she heard Lord Byron say as he approached from behind. "There is always much to be amazed by when you see an opera, Miss Elizabeth, but the one aspect of magnificence that crosses all operas is the moment the rich velvet curtain opens and the opera begins. That is the moment that I find most satisfaction in. Come. Let us find our seats."

Elizabeth quickened her steps as she followed the lord and her family up the levels of the grand staircase, and followed them through to a small area containing only eight seats.

Glancing around from the curtained box that her family had walked into and were being seated in, Elizabeth cast her eyes over the masses of people she could see below, and the long stage with its lush red curtain.

"When people talk about Teatro La Fenice having replaced the San Benedetto Theatre, I have heard it said that opera in Venice truly is a phoenix that has risen from the ashes," Lord Byron whispered to her as he sat in the seat beside her, a row back from where her parents and siblings had sat. "Sometimes I feel like that applies to who I am as well. I wonder if you ever feel that? Like you are sometimes changing, and wonder if it might be possible to change so much that you end up being a completely different person?"

"I believe… " Elizabeth started to reply as the illumination of the theatre began to dim. Lowering her voice, she whispered what she thought might summarize what she thought about his question. "I sometimes feel like nothing ever changes at all."

The final expression she saw on the handsome face before the theatre went completely dark, was one of surprise.

26

Watching the larger than life happenings on the grand stage before her, Elizabeth felt enraptured. Everything about the evening felt magical - the costumes, the opera singers, the music, and the theatre itself. Although she couldn't understand any of the words that she heard throughout the performance, she felt deep emotion at the way they were expressed. It was unlike anything she had ever experienced before.

Throughout the performance, she could now and then sense Lord Byron leaning closer toward her. As quickly as she thought that was happening, he then seemed to withdraw and pull away. Although confused by whether he was implying anything, or she was simply reading everything incorrectly, Elizabeth was grateful that for most of the performance, she was able to maintain her concentration on the stage.

When the performers made their final bow and the theatre was illuminated once more, she felt like she was woken from a dream. Glancing around her, she saw her parents each cast their eyes over to where she and Lord Byron sat, but only smile at her. She took her time before she finally turned and looked at him. When she did, she saw his attention lay in the crowd and not on her at all. She was both relieved and saddened at the same time.

Looking down over the crowds of people below, she took her time to study how the women were dressed, and how they wore their hair. Fashion had never been of any interest to Elizabeth, but she could appreciate the beauty of the gowns, and the ways that some of the women painted their faces.

"Come, Elizabeth," she heard her father call out. "It is time we all returned."

"Or perhaps Miss Elizabeth would

like to join me and Gilberto on a walk around the calli?" Elizabeth heard Lord Byron ask.

As much as her emotions felt activated further by his invitation, Elizabeth knew what the right answer was for her, even before her father had an opportunity to speak.

"I thank you, Lord Byron, however I shall return with my family," she said. "I do feel weary, and I look forward to returning to my great aunt's home."

Glancing at her father, Elizabeth saw relief on his face. It reflected the relief she felt at being able to not see the lord any more for that evening. Without having said anything directly, she felt like he'd played with her emotions a little throughout the entire day. Whether he'd intended to or not was irrelevant to her. All that mattered was that he had, and she wasn't sure if she wanted that to continue or not. If he had some serious design on her, perhaps. If he found joy from securing her attention and turning her head and her heart, with full knowledge that nothing would ever come from it, definitely not.

Before leaving the box, she allowed herself one more glance over the crowds below. So many people. So many gowns. So many different looks that everyone had. She couldn't help but wonder if she would ever see such a glorious sight again. She certainly hoped so.

27

"What a surprise!" Elizabeth heard her brother, Charles, exclaim as they made their way down the grand staircase to the exit level.

Looking at him, she saw a smile on his face. It was only when she followed his line of sight that she saw another familiar face.

"Mother, Father, this is the young man I have seen sketching my great aunt's home!" Charles said, summoning all of his family over to where the young man stood with an older gentleman. "I am so sorry. I have not even introduced myself, even though I have admired your work. Charles Chisholm," he added before bowing.

As Elizabeth watched and realized who she was facing, she felt an invisible wall build around her. The young man had chosen not to be friendly toward her not once but twice. She was wary of attempting to be friendly toward him a third time.

"Guid evenin," the older gentleman beside him said as he bowed toward Elizabeth's father. "I see ye have met my apprentice. Please allow me to introduce myself. I am Archibald Elliot, and this is Angus McKay - my apprentice."

"Edward Chisholm," Edward replied. "And this is my wife, Alessandra; my daughters, Elizabeth, Isabella and Florence; and my son, Charles. We have seen you sketching outside of the home that we currently stay in," he added, turning to face the young man.

"Aye, he doesn't say much, this one," Mr Elliot said before Angus could say anything himself. "But he has great talent. Don't ye lad?!"

As Elizabeth watched the older man slap his hand on the back of the young man, she saw a similar glimmer of expression of amusement that she'd thought she'd seen on the first day she noticed him. The expression was such a joy to watch that she wished he would match her gaze and look at her so she could say hello. With the sadness of realization, she could see that he was looking at everyone except her.

"He's far more handsome close up, Elizabeth," she heard Isabella whisper in her ear from behind. "Did you not consider taking my advice and going to speak to him when he was drawing?"

"Shh, Isabella!" Elizabeth said, scolding her sister. She felt bad enough that she'd twice talked to a man who clearly didn't want to know her. She didn't need things to be made even worse by him hearing Isabella's comments.

"Do you take a particular interest in my aunt's home, Mr Elliot?" Alessandra asked, mostly out of simple curiosity. As far as she was aware, her aunt hadn't mentioned having asked for her palatial home to have been drawn.

"Oh, no, no, no!" Mr Elliot replied as

he glanced back at Angus and then smiled at Alessandra. "I am here in Venice on a mission of gathering ideas for structures being planned in my home of Edinburgh. While here, this young lad has offered to pick out and draw a select few properties with features he feels might represent what we could suggest for some new Scottish buildings. He has been quite left to his own decisions, with the freedom to choose whatever buildings he is attracted to. Whatever he draws, it may help with designing buildings in Edinburgh, but will certainly help with his future as an architect. This would be the one ye submitted to me this morning?" he turned and asked Angus and saw him nod his reply. "Aye, it is a beautiful structure indeed."

"It is," said Edward. "But you sound Scottish, Sir. What could have brought you and young Angus here to Venice? Do you also have work commissioned here?"

All watched as Mr Elliot chuckled,

having found the idea amusing.

"No, not I, although this certainly would be a wonderful city to make a contribution to," he said as he looked around the foyer they stood in. "Alas, architecture such as this is something I've never delved into. No, Angus and I are here simply to look and to draw. The architecture of our homeland is very different from this, but there are certainly aspects that I appreciate may contribute to a new style in Scotland."

"It is your choice to draw my great aunt's home then?" Charles asked the young man who continued to be oddly quiet.

"Aye," Angus said as he moved forward. "I hope I have not been too intrusive, sitting in front of yer family home for these past days. It is a very beautiful structure indeed. That particular sketch is now complete so I shall be moving on to another location tomorrow."

"It has not felt like you have been

intrusive at all," Alessandra said to the young man. "I am sure my aunt would love to see the finished likeness of her home, if you would like to share it with her."

"Oh, I do not think it is good enough…"

"Nonsense!" Charles said, smiling. "I am sure you will agree, Mr Elliot, that Mr McKay's drawing ability is outstanding."

"Aye, he has many skills, I cannot deny," said the older man. "For now, however, we must away. We are due to travel to Rome in one week, and we must finish the drawing of more structures here in Venice before we go. I fear I must bid ye farewell, Mr Chisholm and all of yer family."

"Of course," Edward said before giving a polite bow and seeing both men begin to walk out.

As Elizabeth watched the young man walk past her, her eyes followed him. She'd hoped that he would see her and at least have the manners to say hello to her. That he didn't even regard her highly enough to be so polite stung her deeply.

"You did not greet him, Elizabeth," she heard Isabella say quietly. "Why ever not? He has had your attention each time you have noticed him sitting outside of our great aunt's home."

Elizabeth turned to face her sister. Usually she forced herself to smile and seem happier than she felt. At that moment, she felt almost defeated. She'd never had opportunity to make many new friends. Now that she was in a new place, with many new people to meet, it seemed it might not have been her location that had always been a problem, but something about herself instead. The realization made her unwilling to try to present a façade different from how she truly felt.

"I do not think he regards me as worthy of investing his time, Isabella," she said. "That is all there is to say about that."

She watched Isabella's face change from sly, as if about to tease her sister, to serious.

"I beg you to not feel that way, Sister!" Isabella said as they began to follow their mother and father out of the foyer. "I am sure that is not what he thinks at all."

"Then why does he not even say hello, when he knows that I did so to him on the first day that I saw him?" Elizabeth said, feeling a tear threaten. Why she felt so sure she'd like the attention of the young man, she didn't know. He hadn't done anything to inspire her to speak to him. All he'd done since she first saw him was sit and draw. He hadn't sought her out to speak to, and he'd hardly replied to the few conversations she'd tried to initiate with him. It made no sense that she should even care.

"I hope the opera was up to your expectation?" she heard Lord Byron ask. When she looked at him, she saw that he was, thankfully, addressing their entire group and not just her.

"It has been a lovely evening, Lord Byron," Alessandra replied. "Thank you for inviting us. Shall we see you again at my aunt's home?"

As Elizabeth focused on her mother's words to Lord Byron, she felt she'd experienced a small level of intimacy with the lord, but knew that at another level, she'd learned absolutely nothing about him at all.

"Indeed you shall, Mia Cugina Alessandra," Gilberto said, grinning. "If not before the masked ball, then you shall see both of us on that evening."

"Of course, whether you will know it is us or not, I cannot say," Lord Byron said, smiling at Alessandra and then diverting his gaze to Elizabeth. "Perhaps you shall know me, or perhaps you shall *think* you know me, when you have the wrong person entirely!"

"You do talk in riddles sometimes, Lord Byron," Florence said, making the young men grin.

"Because that is what life sometimes *is*, Miss Florence," Lord Byron replied as he smiled at her. "Just one big riddle, created to keep us entertained by trying to solve it! But we shall leave you all now, and bid you goodnight."

"We hope to see both of you at the masquerade," Edward said when he saw gondolas approach for their transport back to Caterina's home. The gondolas were a welcome distraction from the growing concern he felt about the attention the suave gentleman kept paying to his oldest daughter. "Good evening, Gentlemen."

28

As the family settled in for their short journey back to the grand home, Elizabeth felt Isabella sit close to her and take her hand. It wasn't common for the siblings to share affection, but Elizabeth couldn't deny it felt nice to have her sister beside her. Isabella was always more outgoing, but when it mattered, she had always also shown Elizabeth a very caring side as well. She could be loud and she could be funny, but she also knew when something wasn't quite right.

Turning toward Isabella, Elizabeth received a sad smile and returned it. Close by, she could see her mother and father, and Florence and Charles. All looked happy and excited by the evening they'd had. When Elizabeth focused on that, she determined to at least force herself to appear happier. Before that moment when she'd seen the young artist, she had been in awe of the theatre that she'd heard described as 'magnificent'. Casting her mind back to what the interior had looked like, and what the people had looked like, she agreed with the description. When she focused on the evening, she could still see the lushness of different fabrics, and the bright and dark colours that had contrasted beautifully against each other. So absorbed she was in remembering the imagery of the theatre that she hardly noticed when their journey was complete.

"It is late," she heard her mother say when they reached their destination. "Let us all say goodnight."

"Yes, Mother," Elizabeth's siblings all replied obediently before heading to their respective bed chambers.

Once in their room and settled in for the night, Elizabeth found it difficult to sleep. Across the room from her was Florence, already making sounds that indicated she'd quickly and easily found sleep. Next to her, Elizabeth saw Isabella was also awake.

"Do not be sad, Elizabeth," Isabella said. "What does the opinion of such a young man matter when you have an exceptionally handsome man chasing you?"

Elizabeth was surprised, and showed it.

"Who do you mean?" she asked, trying not to portray that she'd wondered if that was what was happening between her and Lord Byron.

"Do not act coy, Sister," Isabella said. "It has been noted by everyone that Lord Byron has been paying particular attention to you since we arrived in Venice."

"Lord Byron is eleven years older than me, Isabella!" Elizabeth exclaimed. She knew it wasn't a valid reason for her to dismiss anything that had happened. Young women wed much older men all the time. Even so, she wasn't sure her parents would agree to her marrying a man of such an age.

"That may be so, but his age does not seem to limit him in his efforts to get to know you," Isabella whispered. "If he declared his love for you, would you accept him?"

The question prompted Elizabeth to sit up in her bed, stunned. She'd been wondering if the handsome lord had some particular interest in her, but any possibility of such a declaration wasn't something she'd considered.

"Why would you ask such a thing, Isabella?" she asked, desperately hoping Florence wouldn't wake up while the current conversation was taking place.

"I believe many people are wondering, Elizabeth," Isabella said. "I do not see how you can not have considered this as a possibility."

"I cannot have considered it because the idea … the idea is preposterous," Elizabeth replied. "I concede that Lord Byron has paid me some attention, but there is nothing in it, I assure you, Isabella."

"We shall see," Isabella said before making a strong display of turning over to go to sleep. "Sleep well, Sister."

Elizabeth remained quiet as she played through the idea in her head. Lord Byron making a declaration to her? Why would Isabella even have dreamed up such an idea?

Knowing she couldn't know what was real and what was just the imagination of her sister, Elizabeth lay back on her bed, closed her eyes, and waited for whenever sleep would finally come.

29

"I would like to commission a painting from you, Miss Elizabeth," Caterina said the following morning at breakfast.

"Oh?" Elizabeth asked, surprised. "I fear my painting ability may not be quite up to the standard you are used to, Great Aunt. The artworks you have here," she said as she waved her hand around the walls of the grand dining room. "They are truly outstanding."

"Do not be modest, Signorina," Caterina said, smiling at her great niece. "I would never expect a young person such as yourself to produce the same calibre as these paintings, as they were completed by masters, however I have heard that you paint well, and I am willing to pay you…"

"You shall not!" Edward exclaimed before realizing just how sharply he'd spoken to the elderly woman. "Forgive me, Caterina, but if you wish for

Elizabeth to paint something for you, she may, but she will not be paid for it."

"Perchè no?" Caterina asked, somewhat surprised and amused by the reaction she'd inspired from her niece's usually-quiet husband. "Why not?"

"Aunt," Alessandra said. "You have welcomed us into your home and provided us with beds, warmth, food and wine. I believe it is us that owe you, not the other way around."

"Yes, Great Aunt, I could not possibly accept payment from you," said Elizabeth. "However, if you are accepting that my work may not be up to a high standard, I shall gladly do what you ask. Is there a particular subject you wish for me to paint?"

"There is," Caterina replied, grinning. "The Rialto Bridge, over the Grand Canal. It is a scene that I do not see very often now that I am more housebound, but I remember it vividly in my mind. The artists that I know prefer to paint people, but I believe you have the skills to do landscapes and buildings. Correct?"

"That is certainly my preferred subject," Elizabeth said. "I do not feel my skills extend to people."

"Yet," Isabella said quietly. "But Great Aunt, Elizabeth is very good at whatever she draws and paints. I do believe this is a wonderful idea."

"Then that is settled," Caterina said.

"You will need someone to escort you to that location, Elizabeth," Alessandra said.

"I shall happily go," Charles offered. When he saw all members of his immediate family look at him in surprise, he grinned. "I have not visited that part of Venice so far, but I have heard much about it. If we can get directions to go there, I am happy to help my sister do as you have requested of her."

"I expect it would be very boring for you, Charles," Elizabeth said. "It could take me many hours just to draw what I see, even before I paint."

"And? What of it? It is early now," Charles said. "Let us eat, then pack up your things and be off. That will give us plenty of time to get to the Rialto, and still give you plenty of time to find the right spot to draw."

"Are you sure, Charles?" Edward asked. "All of us could go…"

"Not necessary, Father," Charles said, having an ulterior motive for wanting to be around his sister when no other members of their family could hear their conversation. Some things had reached him that he'd considered sharing with Elizabeth. Whether he would be bold enough to share them or not, he wasn't yet certain, but he liked the idea of at least having the opportunity to. "Please allow me to do this. If it turns out to be frightfully boring, I would rather not all of you suffer."

Elizabeth grinned at his impertinence but was silently thankful for him offering to support her in such a way. She'd been thoughtful well into the night but, before finding sleep, had finally felt happier again. She'd been momentarily confused by Lord Byron's attention, especially after comments her sister had made, but she knew there was nothing behind it. Fully understanding and accepting that, she'd slept well and woken in a much better mood. The thought of going to a new location and drawing something new pushed her happiness even higher.

30

After much back and forth of packing what she needed to be able to work on her planned artwork, Elizabeth was satisfied she finally had everything ready to go.

"Are you sure, Sister?" Charles teased her.

"Yes!" Elizabeth replied, laughing softly. Usually it wasn't important if she had everything with her because her pictures were only for her and she was usually at home, close to her belongings. Packing things up for drawing in a different location felt like a new adventure in itself was about to be embarked upon.

"Then let us depart!" Charles said.

"Look after your sister, Charles," Alessandra said, smiling at her children.

"Mother, I am sure you are aware that Elizabeth is two years older than me," said Charles. "Surely that would mean that *she* should look after *me*!"

"He has you there, Alessandra!" Caterina said as she laughed at the banter happening before her.

"Be off with both of you," said Edward. "You know the hour your great aunt dines. Do not remain too late."

"We shall not be too long, Father," Elizabeth said. "Once I have a drawing that I am happy with, I will be able to paint from here if need be."

"Grazie," said Caterina. "Thank you for doing this for me, Signorina Elizabeth."

Hearing a sliver of melancholy in her great aunt's voice, Elizabeth moved close to Caterina, leaned down, and kissed her cheek.

"It is my pleasure, Great Aunt," she said before turning to face Charles. "Let us go, Brother! The day does not wait for us!"

With a smile to all, both walked out, eager to begin their small journey, and for quite different reasons.

"Are you sure this is the right spot for your selection, Elizabeth?" Charles teased her when they'd reached the right location and angle that Elizabeth felt suited her needs. She'd already chosen several spots, only to then see a different one and wonder if that might be much better.

"Yes, I believe so … although…" she started to say before smiling at her brother to show she was only teasing him back. "No, from the few things that our great aunt has shared with me about her memories of the Grand Canal and the Rialto Bridge, I believe this is the angle she has the strongest memory of. It will certainly do for a start. I know not even if I can reproduce this accurately or with skill!"

"Did you not say you painted a scene like this before you even left England?" asked Charles.

"I did," Elizabeth said. "But it was purely from some corner of my childhood memory. As I look at the canal now, I can see that I painted it without any accuracy at all. It was a pleasant-enough picture, but it did not portray what is truly here in front of us. With our great aunt having lived here for her entire life, I certainly must do better with the painting she wishes me to complete for her!"

Charles didn't try to persuade her to re-think the quality of her artistic skills. He'd given that up years earlier. In his opinion, everything he'd ever seen her draw or paint had been impressive. No matter how good something was, however, he knew she rarely allowed herself to fully believe quite how wonderful her work was.

Once both were seated at the finally-perfect vantage point, he remained quiet as he watched her begin to draw. He knew he'd be happy to remain right where he was for many hours if need be, with the amount of people passing by, this way and that. Although he knew other people were most interested in making acquaintance with new people - and the right people - he found it far more intriguing to sit and simply watch people. Everybody had a story to tell - a story they possibly never would. Charles gained great joy from looking at someone and wondering where they'd come from, what path they were presently on, and who they truly were.

"I do hope nobody considers me not worthy of being here to draw such a beautiful sight," Elizabeth said quietly as her pencil began to move over the page in front of her.

"Why would you say such a thing, Elizabeth?" Charles asked. "Why should anybody not consider you worthy of drawing?"

"I feel very exposed here," Elizabeth replied, stopping for a moment to look up, and then look around her.

"You must not worry about such

things," said Charles. "You are an artist. Look. There are other artists also with easels set up over there. Do you feel compelled to stare at them?"

"Oh, no, of course not," Elizabeth said. "I had not even noticed them until you pointed them out."

"Exactly!" Charles said. "And nobody will have noticed you here either. Now stop finding excuses to not draw the brilliant scene you are going to."

"Yes, Brother!" Elizabeth replied. She knew he was right. She wasn't looking at anyone in particular, so nobody was likely to be looking at her.

Except, in that, both Elizabeth and Charles were quite wrong.

32

From across the canal, Angus McKay stood in a corner shaded by the high building beside him. He'd only been out for a stroll, taking in the beauty of a part of Venice he hadn't yet visited, when he'd noticed the brother and sister who'd spoken to him before.

He suspected that if he was someone else, with a different kind of confidence, he wouldn't hesitate in walking up to the two of them and simply wishing them a good morning. It seemed an easy thing to do for anyone else. For him, it wasn't so easy.

With his mind indecisive, he found he did want to go and greet them. They'd both seemed friendly enough and there was nothing about them that told him they were not good people to know. Regardless, he couldn't bring himself to do it. He just couldn't.

For quite some time he watched the

two of them talk and laugh together. It seemed as if the young woman was trying to find somewhere to set up the easel that her brother carried for her. How that felt - having a sibling that one got on so well with - Angus couldn't imagine. He could hardly imagine even having a sibling in his life, let alone one he could laugh and talk with.

Pondering his life to date, and his current options, he felt sadness as he watched the two of them move this way and that and then finally settle in the spot that he could see was a good point to paint the well-known bridge.

In addition to his sadness, however, he also felt a sliver of joy. Watching artists had always provided inspiration to him. He didn't consider himself one since he only ever sketched likenesses of buildings, but he loved seeing the work of true artists. Landscapes, animals, people - whatever artists wanted to capture a likeness to, they seemed able to do it with so much ease.

He knew he didn't have that talent, even though on occasion he enjoyed trying to recreate such imagery anyway. Those images he'd never show anyone, but it had been an enjoyable enough pursuit to try to do them all the same.

Once he saw the young woman set up her tools and her easel, and the brother and sister sit down and relax, Angus was absorbed. He was a distance away but he knew the stance. The young woman was comfortable, and she had just begun to apply pencil to paper. He was curious to see how she worked, especially so since she'd seen him work more than once.

Not in any hurry to get on and begin the next project he was supposed to be doing that day, Angus relaxed back, remaining in the shade, and just watched. The young woman looked intent on what she was doing, and he understood that fully. He also couldn't deny that the young woman was beautiful to look at, especially when she was deep in concentration and focused on what she wanted to capture the beauty of.

Beauty. It was something that Angus, with an appreciation for the visual, could identify and appreciate, but external beauty of a person was also something that didn't drive him to want to know someone. In his travels with his mentor, he'd grown to realize that there were a great many people who looked beautiful on the outside. Only a portion of them were beautiful on the inside.

He remained where he was for a long time, captivated by watching the young woman drawing, and her brother next to her, seeming to be there only as a companion. Angus was envious of them both. He missed his mother - the only family he had left. He looked forward to returning to Scotland and seeing her again.

With a sigh, he prepared to leave. He could stand in the shade where he was, watching the young woman and her brother for hours, but he had a job to do. He would be starting to sketch another building, in another part of Venice. As he refocused on that, he felt his excitement begin to grow. There was still much for Angus McKay to learn before he could become an architect himself, but he was learning from one of the best, and he was on his way to living the dream he'd long wanted.

33

"It looks fine indeed, Sister," Charles said as he saw Elizabeth sit back from her work, appear to study it, and sigh. "You have captured the bridge, the buildings, the water, and the people very well."

Elizabeth took her time, glancing from the paper in front of her to the vista. It certainly wasn't the greatest picture she'd drawn but she was happy enough. She'd told her great aunt that she wasn't as talented as many other artists, and her great aunt had reassured her that perfection was not needed. Knowing that, Elizabeth allowed herself the permission to enjoy the process and simply do the best she could do.

"Hmm ... it is not quite ... that is, I believe it may suffice, although these windows do not look quite right," she said as she focused on one building in the background behind the bridge.

As she began to alter some lines on the page, Charles smiled to himself. She was absorbed in her project. In some ways, he was envious of that. He loved being at school, and all of the learning that he got to do there. When he was outside of the classroom, however, he did feel a strong restlessness. He was studying for a career, but he wasn't sure that was what he wanted.

Several of his friends at school had shared with him that they would be inheriting estates when their parents passed. They'd assumed the same would be true of Charles, knowing he was the only male blood of his parents. Whenever that topic of conversation had happened to come up, he'd managed to divert it to another topic altogether. He hadn't lied and said he *was* the heir to Chisholm Manor estate. He just hadn't corrected them in their assumptions and told them he *wasn't* the Chisholm Manor heir at all.

Glancing at Elizabeth again, he knew that was part of what drove a degree of desperation in him to succeed in something away from the estate. It wasn't his chosen path of study that drove him on. It was his need to be good at something when his sister became ruler of the small empire that was their home estate. The thought of her taking over the tiny realm, while he had no achievements at all, played with his emotions frequently.

Where his thinking had gone, Charles was unhappy with. It was unfair to not be happy for Elizabeth and the role she would play in their family in the future. It wasn't her fault she'd been born first, and Charles equally didn't hold any ill feeling toward his father for choosing to make his firstborn the heir, instead of his first son. Life was changing that way. Society was changing. Things that were before, weren't going to necessarily be in the future and Charles agreed with that sentiment. Old ways were gone. New ways lay ahead and the young were the future.

"Are you well, Charles?" he heard Elizabeth ask, without turning her head away from her page. "You do sigh a great deal today."

Charles chuckled. He'd been in thought that had been far too serious. He'd been raised to appreciate all that he had, and he did. Pondering a different life would never serve him any good.

"I thank you for asking, Elizabeth, but I am well," he replied. "I am merely enjoying watching you work."

Elizabeth smiled to herself. She could hear discontent in her brother's voice but she didn't question him about it. After all, discontent was something she fully understood herself.

34

After finding satisfaction with the drawn outline of the picture she wished to paint, Elizabeth spent time mixing and applying colour to the paper in front of her. Doing so made her feel elated. There were many challenges that she faced with each painting she did, but one of the most joyous was getting colours in her paint to match as closely as possible to the colours of what she was seeing.

When she started to see everything come to life in colour, her happiness grew. She was generally happy with her work, but she wanted that particular painting to be the absolute best that she could do. Even though her great aunt was an elderly woman, there was something about her that Elizabeth greatly admired.

Even when her parents had taken her to Venice when she was a child,

Elizabeth had noticed her aunt had no husband living with her. She'd never been told why that was, and Elizabeth had never asked. She'd also never seen or heard of any children. Why was that? Caterina was an elderly woman. She must have had marriage in her life - mustn't she?

These were some of the questions that had almost pushed Elizabeth to ask about things she knew a young woman need not know. Of course she'd held back. As much as she wanted to know the answers, even just thinking about asking someone such intimate questions was enough to make Elizabeth's face go red.

As the paint colours expanded and were perfected in her painting, Elizabeth worked so hard to keep her thoughts in check that she forgot about the people around her, not noticing if anyone was looking at her or not. Sometimes it was like that for her - her mind either working far too hard, thinking about things that she believed she should never think about, or her mind shutting down as her creative side took over. Given a choice, she knew she'd most prefer the latter. The former could surely only lead to discomfort, and that would not be pleasant at all.

When she was sure she'd captured the imagery as best she could for the moment, she turned to look at her brother. She could see Charles looking everywhere, turning his head this way and that. Before he noticed her, she felt grateful toward him, thinking it must have been the most unpleasant way to spend the few hours they'd been in the same spot.

"I say, Elizabeth, that is looking very smart," she heard Charles say as he looked at her. "I am sure our great aunt will be extremely pleased with what you have done."

"Thank you, Charles. I do believe I am now happy with where it is at," Elizabeth replied. "Shall we depart?

Now that I have the outline and the most important colours accurately represented, I shall be able to finish it back at our great aunt's home."

"Are you sure?" Charles asked. "Do not say you wish to leave, just because you believe I wish to."

"Oh, no, Charles," Elizabeth said, smiling at him before glancing at her work in progress one more time. "I do feel this is accurate enough for now, and I tire of sitting for this amount of time. I must move!"

"Very well," Charles said. "Let us pack all of this up and begin our journey back."

After gathering up her art tools and allowing Charles to carefully carry the painting, they set off.

"I wonder who shall be there when we return today," Charles said as they walked toward a line of waiting gondolas. "More relatives, do you think?"

"It has seemed odd to me that we

have so many relatives at all!" said Elizabeth. "Although our mother has always told us our grandmother was from Venice, I do not remember being told just how far and wide we have relations."

"I am not sure that our mother was aware of there being this many," said Charles. "It seems we are far more fortunate than our dear mother when it comes to this unique place. Our parents have brought you and I here twice now. Her mother never brought her or Uncle Nicholas here, even when they were young."

"Yes," Elizabeth said. "I wonder why that was."

"Perhaps due to the simplicity of money, Sister," Charles said. "I am not sure Mother's family lived to quite the lifestyle that our parents do."

As Elizabeth pondered the last sentence he'd said, she considered the stark contrast to the idea that her mother hadn't grown up wealthy, but yet her aunt, Caterina, seemed to live in a home that Elizabeth considered palatial.

Despite her curiosity on the subject, she could feel they were moving dangerously close to a subject she preferred to avoid.

Although Charles had never said anything to her about her being the estate's heir, she did know it was traditionally the oldest son who inherited property. She didn't know his views on the way things were going to be when their parents passed, and she didn't want to know. Her father had made the decision when she'd first been born. It was a decision that Elizabeth hadn't influenced in any way and, no matter how she felt about it, it was a decision she would honour and not question.

Without hesitation, she changed the subject entirely, not giving it any chance to move in a direction that she didn't want it to.

35

"And there is my great niece and great nephew!" Caterina called out when she saw Elizabeth and Charles enter the afternoon parlour. "They have been fulfilling my wish to have the Rialto Bridge captured in paint. And what timing you have!"

"Oh?" Charles asked. "Did we miss something of great import, Great Aunt?"

"Almost!" Caterina replied. "Gowns, wigs and masks for everyone have arrived. Elizabeth, yours are up in the bed chamber you share with Isabella and Florence…"

"Yes, Elizabeth," Florence said. "Wait till you see what has been created for us!"

"Sì, you must try it all on, per favore," Caterina said. "You also, Charles. In your room waits all the pieces of your disguise," she continued, adding a tone of mystery and intrigue into her voice.

Elizabeth looked around the room until she could see her parents. With a knowing nod from her mother, she felt her pulse increase at the prospect of the masquerade getting closer. She'd never attended such a thing. What could such a night bring into her life of tranquility?

"Come, Elizabeth," she heard Isabella say. "I shall come with you to help you try your costume on."

Elizabeth smiled at her mother, father and great aunt before starting to follow Isabella out of the door. No words were spoken between the sisters until they were in their bed chamber and the door was closed behind them.

"Lord Byron was here with Gilberto earlier," Isabella said quietly when she was sure they were alone.

"Oh?" Elizabeth asked, only then noticing she hadn't given much thought to the handsome lord all morning. "That is not out of the ordinary, is it?"

"No, of course not, but he *was* asking where *you* were," Isabella said.

As Elizabeth felt surprise flow over her, she walked toward her bed. On it were laid out the gown she'd previously tried on, a tall pale wig of what looked like a lavish design of light coloured hair, and the mask that had been created for her.

"Oh!" she exclaimed when she saw the design and the workmanship that had gone into the mask. Without hesitation she moved forward and picked it up, turning it over to view it from one angle then another.

"Oh?" Isabella asked. "Did you hear me, Sister? You seem more interested in that mask than what I just said!"

Elizabeth turned to face her sister. The mention of Lord Byron had made her heart beat faster, but she wasn't sure she wanted it to. Was he intending to make an offer to her? Did he want to take her for his wife? She knew he was from England. Did he wish to return there, with her by his side?

Although there had been times when

he'd seemed to speak to her with a surprising level of intimacy, she didn't want to lose sight of the fact that he hadn't said anything to make her think he had intentions for her. Surely he was just some kind of flirt who did the same thing to many women, like some of the men Elizabeth had read about in the novels she'd read. Wasn't he?

"I am not sure his visiting today has anything to do with me, Isabella," she replied. "You know that Lord Byron is a friend of our great aunt. He appears to visit here often."

"Yes, but he was asking about *you*!" Isabella said. "Do you not see, Sister? He must wish to pursue you - to court you."

"I see," Elizabeth said as she moved toward the small looking glass on the room dresser, then held the mask up to her face. It was only a ploy to try and make herself look less excited than she felt. In truth, on hearing Isabella's insistence on the subject, Elizabeth's heart had increased its pounding in her chest again - so much so that she began to wonder if she might faint.

"Do you love him, Elizabeth?" she heard Isabella ask quietly as she walked right up to where Elizabeth stood, moving her head this way and that while studying how she looked in the mask.

"Isabella, Lord Byron has made no declaration to me, and I do not think it is wise to expect he will…"

"But the way he looks at you…"

"Please do not keep saying what you think you see," Elizabeth continued, cutting short the argument she knew her sister was preparing to force upon her. "I find him very handsome to look at, and the few conversations I have had with him have been very … interesting … however I do not wish to expect anything from him."

She watched as Isabella turned away quickly and moved to her bed to lie down.

"I do not understand you at all,"

Isabella said. "Lord Byron is an extremely handsome man, and he has been paying you much attention. If I were in your position…"

"If you were in my position, you would … what exactly?" Elizabeth asked, her patience with her sister beginning to be tested.

"I know not," Isabella admitted. "You know I have no experience in such things."

"And you know that *I* have no experience in such things!" said Elizabeth, exasperated. Seeing her usually-outgoing sister begin to look forlorn, she moved to the bed to sit beside her. "You and I are both of an age where many other young women are either already wed, or betrothed to be wed."

"Yes, but neither Father nor Mother have ever spoken of such an idea to me," Isabella said. "Have they to you?"

"No," Elizabeth replied. "Never."

"Do they wish for you and I both to

never be wed?" Isabella asked. "Shall we be spinsters forever, living together at Chisholm Manor for the rest of our lives, never to find out what it must feel like to be in love?"

"I know not," said Elizabeth. The questions her sister asked sounded extreme and silly and yet they weren't dissimilar to questions she'd been asking herself in recent times.

"We could just ask…"

"No, Isabella, we must not do that," Elizabeth said. "The idea of broaching such a subject with Father does not appeal…"

"But with Mother!" said Isabella. "I believe she would be far more approachable about this. She was a young woman once, you know! She must know love and marriage is on our minds."

"Is it? On your mind?" Elizabeth asked. "You have always seemed very happy with how things are. I did not know you sought marriage at all."

"It is something I have not wanted to portray - a woman dreaming of love," Isabella said. "But of course I do, Elizabeth. Do we not all wish for that? Should we all not have a husband who loves us, and children that we can love?"

Elizabeth was surprised by her sister's declaration. She'd never thought it was on Isabella's mind at all, to be a wife and a mother.

"It is a fine idea," she said as she pulled her sister into a rare embrace. "If it is meant to be for us, Isabella, I am sure it will happen."

"And if it doesn't?" Isabella asked.

"It will," Elizabeth said, finishing the conversation. "Now! How do we possibly wear these?" she asked as she reached out and picked up her extravagant blonde wig.

She was rewarded by Isabella sitting up and starting to giggle.

"It must go on like this," Isabella said as she grabbed her sister's wig and placed it on her head. Seeing the haphazardly way it sat, she giggled more.

Elizabeth laughed. It was good to see her sister happier again, and it was good to not dwell on such serious subjects. They were both old enough to wed, and they both knew it. They also knew that sometimes laughter was the best medicine for anything.

36

"How does your gown fit, Elizabeth?" Alessandra asked when she saw her two oldest daughters enter the afternoon parlour again.

"It fits very well, Mother," Elizabeth said before turning to face Caterina. "The mask is also very beautiful, thank you Great Aunt."

"There is nothing to thank me for, Miss Elizabeth," Caterina replied. "I take great pleasure in the masquerades I hold. Rest assured - my providing such pretty things for you to wear is purely for my own benefit."

"Of course," Elizabeth replied, not sure if her great aunt was teasing her or not, and desperately not wanting to offend.

"You did not show me your painting when you came in," she then heard Caterina say. "I shall not have to wait long to see it, I hope?"

"Oh, Great Aunt, there is a great deal more for me to do before it will be finished," Elizabeth said. "I hope you are not displeased. I shall be happy to reveal it to you once it is completed."

"It is going to be a very fine painting, I believe, Great Aunt," Charles said. He'd just tried on his mask and wig. They'd both seemed odd things to wear, but he did enjoy trying new things and he did also love social occasions. More people to meet could only be a good thing in his opinion.

"It is kind of you to be so supportive of your sister, Charles," Caterina said.

"I only speak the simple truth," Charles said, smiling at her. "My sister has a level of artistic talent that she does not always believe in, but I do."

"Then I greatly look forward to seeing the finished work," Caterina said as she turned and faced Elizabeth once again.

Elizabeth smiled but didn't reply. She'd thought the painting was going fairly well. Hearing her great aunt express such a high degree of expectation made her again feel nervous and unsure if she had the talent to please with her art. It took all of her internal might to smile hard enough until the smile transformed from one of pretend, to one of authenticity.

37

As the evening wore on, Elizabeth and her family relaxed in the presence of the few relations also staying in the palatial home. Being among them all in the large room with its many larger than life sized portraits around the walls, the paintings inspired her to wonder what the lives of those people had been like.

"Would you like to paint like that one day?" she heard a voice say quietly from behind her as she was taking a turn of the room. On hearing it, she felt her heart begin to pound. She hadn't been familiar with the voice for very long but she felt she already knew it very well. A part of her had hoped she might not hear it again, with all the confusion that it caused.

When she stopped walking and turned to greet the handsome face, her breath held. It was no news that Lord Byron was fine-looking to most, and especially to her, and yet she still was captivated by the intensity of his eyes as they moved over her face and settled on her lips.

Aware there were others in close vicinity to where they stood, Elizabeth began walking again, taking one slow step at a time while trying to calm the nervousness she felt.

"To be able to paint in such a way," she started to say as her eyes drifted up to the large frames on the wall. "Oh, I could only dream of having such talent, Lord Byron. I fear I am nowhere in the league of such artists."

"Do you truly believe that?" Lord Byron asked.

"Yes," said Elizabeth. "I believe I do have skills in drawing and painting, but I have much to learn."

"And will you? Learn?" asked Lord Byron.

"I shall not study formally, but I shall certainly continue to practice, and try to get better," Elizabeth replied. "Is that not all most of us can do in life?"

"Practice?" Lord Byron asked. When he saw her nod, he was thoughtful for a long while. "But practice for what? How do we know what is good, what is better, and what is bad?"

"I do believe, Lord Byron, that these portraits are good – even better than good, in fact, and certainly not bad," Elizabeth said, prompting a loud laugh from the lord.

"You did that rather well, using all three of my descriptions – so much so that I begin to wonder if you also are as much of a wordsmith as people believe I am," Lord Byron said, delivering a surprisingly sly smile. "But what if I said that I do not like that particular portrait there?" he added, pointing to one. "Does that mean it is not good?"

"Not at all," said Elizabeth. "Surely there is a difference between something being good, and something not being liked by any one of us."

"You have a very mature mind for

someone so young," Lord Byron said, his eyes falling to her lips once again. "And yes, it is true. When many smell a rose, they say it smells magnificent. When I smell a rose, I do not enjoy the scent at all. Some of us will say that we just do not like that smell. Others will say that the rose itself is unpleasant. Who is right?"

"But ... everybody is!" Elizabeth exclaimed.

"Do we smell roses differently?"

"No ... yes ... I am sure that you talk this way to confuse me, Lord Byron!" Elizabeth said.

"Yes, I have been told many times *that* is what *my* skill is," Lord Byron replied.

Elizabeth stopped walking and looked at him. She'd thought he was being serious. His eyes told her he was enjoying the conversation, but only at a light-hearted level.

"I am beginning to believe that you like to provoke and tease me," she said quietly. The initial response she received was Lord Byron throwing his head back and laughing out loud.

"I admit I do take great pleasure in conversing with you," he said after his laughter faded. "But tell me this, Miss Elizabeth - do you approve of such actions on my part?"

"Do I approve of you teasing me so?" Elizabeth asked and saw him nod while delivering a smile to her that could only be described as glorious. "I feel I must insist on taking some time to consider that question, Lord Byron."

"And rightly so, too," Lord Byron said to her. "I hear that your great aunt has commissioned you to paint the Rialto Bridge."

"Yes," Elizabeth replied. "Do you enjoy the beauty of that location?"

"I love all of the Grand Canal," Lord Byron said. "So much so that one day I fully intend to swim in it!"

For a long moment, the two of them stood still, appraising each other, before

Gilberto appeared by their side.

"You two look far too intimate," he said. "What information am I missing out on?"

Although Elizabeth sensed he was teasing and his words were not to be taken seriously, what he said did prompt her to bow her head, take a step back from the lord, and then turn to find and approach the safety of Isabella instead.

"That looked very intimate, Sister," Isabella said, unknowingly repeating the comment Elizabeth had just heard from another. "Mother and Father have both been watching the two of you."

"I am relieved," Elizabeth said.

"Why would you be?" asked Isabella. "Surely you do not wish our parents to see everything that you do!"

Elizabeth grinned at her sister. Although they accepted who each other was, there were times when she could see they'd never be alike, in far too many ways.

"Are you excited about tomorrow

evening?" she asked for diversion.

"I see what you are doing, Elizabeth," said Isabella, grinning.

"And what, exactly, am I doing?"

"Changing what we are speaking of," Isabella said, laughing softly. "However, I shall allow it this time, as I am indeed excited about tomorrow evening. Great Aunt has said that in addition to the many people who are staying here in her home, many more people from Venice and beyond will also be attending. We shall get to see a great number of new people, Elizabeth!"

The thought of so many different people momentarily made Elizabeth apprehensive. She'd been smiling and responding how she should to many different relatives in preceding days. The thought of having to do it on an even larger scale was not a pleasant thought at all.

"Elizabeth and Isabella!" she heard Charles call out. "Do come and join us for this game of whist. I am sure that

Florence is deceiving me."

"What a horrid thing to say, Charles!" Florence said with defiance in her voice.

Shifting her view to the small card table where her two siblings sat, Elizabeth's eyes unintentionally met Lord Byron's. When they did, she felt her face heat up. Inside she sighed, knowing that it would be a moment when he saw her blush deeply. In an effort to not dwell on the discomfort she felt, she smiled at Charles.

"Florence is certainly known to deceive all of us when she plays cards," she said as she and Isabella moved toward the table.

"That is not a very nice thing for you to say, Elizabeth!" she heard Florence say in objection, before then hearing her giggle.

"Nor a very nice thing for you to *do*, Florence!" Elizabeth counter argued. "Now there are three of us here, and we shall all be watching you! Deal the cards, Charles."

As the four siblings laughed together and began a round of the game they'd played most for as long as any of them could remember, all around them conversation moved on.

Now and then, Elizabeth thought she could feel eyes on her. In those moments, the desire to turn and look was almost unbearable, but she was determined. She thought the lord was handsome, and she found his conversation intriguing, but she could also recognize that she knew absolutely nothing about men and women relationships, and was too shy to ask anyone with knowledge about them.

As the evening wore on, her concentration more easily sat with her siblings, her mother and father, and her great aunt. Other relatives came and spoke to the small group, and then went away. It was a level of interaction that slowly but surely enabled her to forget one particular person in the room - at least for a while.

38

By the time Elizabeth heard her great aunt instruct everyone to turn in for the night, she'd successfully diverted her thoughts completely. As she, Isabella and Florence passed through the passageways, a plea from Florence for Isabella to escort her to the kitchen to ask for something to eat was met with a smile between Isabella and Elizabeth.

"How can you possibly still be hungry?" Isabella teased her younger sister.

"How can I?" Florence asked as she rubbed her belly. "It's been *hours* since we dined!"

"But you shall be asleep soon enough," said Isabella.

"Isabella, you know that I will not go to sleep if I feel this hungry!" Florence exclaimed, prompting Isabella to laugh.

"I will take her down to the kitchen," Isabella said to Elizabeth. "We shall see you in our room."

Elizabeth smiled and nodded before watching the two of them deviate from the main passageway and walk toward the back staircase.

"Miss Elizabeth," she heard the familiar voice say in almost a whisper. Turning around, she saw Lord Byron lazily leaning against the passageway wall while seeming to assess her intimately from head to toe.

"Lord Byron," Elizabeth said, feeling nervous. "You find me all alone."

"Yes, that is quite what I was hoping for," she heard him say as she watched him begin to walk toward her. "I do so enjoy my conversations with you," he continued as he reached where she stood and extended both of his hands to take both of hers in his. "It has quickly become a highlight of any day - seeing and talking to you."

Elizabeth felt stunned. She'd been aware of his close proximity to her on several occasions but he'd never before actually touched her. Although they'd been alone together before, she felt a different kind of concern at being alone with him at night, in the dimness of the vast passageway. The home had many rooms, and many people staying in them, but it was also very spread out. The area she and Lord Byron were immediately standing in was not near any of the bed chambers.

"I thank you for paying me such a compliment, Lord Byron," she said as she tried to push concerns out of her mind. Why she was even worried, she didn't know. For days she'd been in the company of people who knew the handsome man in front of her. In that time, nobody had said anything negative about him. Granted, they hadn't said anything at all about him, but surely the importance of that must have been that they'd had nothing bad to report or warn her about.

"I only speak the simple truth, dear Elizabeth," she heard him say in a tone that was different from how he normally sounded. "I shan't keep you long from your bed, but I do wish to ask you if your affections are already engaged."

"My … affections?" Elizabeth asked, surprised to another level.

She watched as Lord Byron moved even closer, until his chest almost touched hers. Looking up into his eyes, she felt dismayed to realize that she felt strongly attracted to him not only in what she saw, but also in how her body felt.

"Yes," he replied, grinning. "Your affections. I have not wished to enquire about your status to your great aunt as, since I have been living here in Venice, she has become a very dear friend of mine," he said. "However I do take great pleasure in seeing you and talking to you. I sense you see the world through a different lens than I ever could."

"Why do you suppose such a thing of me?" asked Elizabeth before seeing one of his hands let go of her own and then rise toward her face.

"You appear to be at ease with the world," Lord Byron replied, reaching out to softly run one fingertip down her cheek from ear to jaw. "I have travelled to many places, Elizabeth, but I have not met many who are like you. Since meeting you I have started to wonder how one can be so at peace in one's own skin."

Elizabeth felt uncertain what to do. With every word he said, she felt her heart wanting to give itself to him. In the back of her mind, she wondered if that would be a good idea. The combination of his words he said, and the tone they were being delivered with, all played on Elizabeth's senses.

"You have a wonderful way with words," she said as she found some strength and took one step backward. Pulling her hand out of his, the connection was broken, leaving her feeling saddened but also surprisingly empowered.

"I am only a poet," Lord Byron said,

delivering her the same sad smile she'd seen before. When he smiled like that, she felt sympathy for him. It confused her. As handsome as he was, he could have the love of any woman he desired. Why would he inspire sympathy? "There is little I could ever offer you, but…"

Elizabeth was wholly invested when she heard the start of that sentence. That was before the words were interrupted.

39

As Charles walked away from his family to make his way to his bed chamber, he sensed someone walking behind him. Each time he turned around, there was nobody there. With each successive discovery, he grew more amused with himself. He usually felt confident in his gut feeling. Obviously, at that moment, his gut feeling wasn't accurate at all.

The emptiness of the long, grand passageway forced him to acknowledge just how great a home he was staying in. It was his great aunt's home, but had it been his grandmother's family home? He didn't know the answer to that, but didn't mind imagining that it had been. Sometimes he did things like that - got caught up in his imagination.

With the home being so palatial, it was easy for him to enter into a dreamlike state, wondering if it would now be his home if his mother's aunt hadn't outlived his mother's mother. Although he knew it would surely be regarded as a wicked thing to even think about in the silence of his mind, he enjoyed the falsehood and all of the luxuries it could provide to him if it had been real.

So intense he was in his thoughts and stories of imagination that when he rounded a corner, he almost walked into Elizabeth and Lord Byron talking together.

"I am only a poet," he heard Lord Byron say. "There is little I could ever offer you, but…"

"Elizabeth!" Charles said louder than usual in an effort to make sure his presence was noticed. "I have been looking for you. There is something I absolutely must discuss with you at once. May I have a word while I walk you to your room?"

As intrigued as Elizabeth had been to hear whatever Lord Byron was about to say to her, she was also relieved to hear her brother's voice interrupt the conversation. She wanted to be a wife and a mother, and she wanted to be loved, and to love. She just wasn't sure she wanted to do any of that with a man who would demand her attention without supervision in the quiet darkness of such a passageway.

"Thank you, Charles," she said. "Of course I am here for you. Please excuse me, Lord Byron," she added as she curtseyed and then began to walk away with her brother. "What plagues your mind?"

There was silence between the two of them until they reached the far end of the passageway and could see the older man hadn't followed them.

"Are you well, Brother?" Elizabeth asked. She'd wondered if he'd used needing to talk to her only as an excuse to allow her to move away from the situation she'd just found herself in. When he spoke, her suspicion was confirmed.

"I am not as old as you, Elizabeth, however I am old enough to know that it is not seemly for any young lady to be standing with a man, sharing such intimacy as I just saw," Charles said, feeling oddly protective of his oldest sister. "I had no need to speak to you. I simply felt … that is, I thought I should do something to assist you."

Elizabeth smiled at him. He was two years younger than her but she knew that, in many ways, he was far more worldly. Most of the year, he was away from the cocoon of the estate, living a life that encompassed meeting many people, and learning many things about his particular study and the world at large.

Since the day he'd first left to go off to school, she'd felt some envy at his opportunity. As she looked at him in his present role of a brother prepared to defend and protect his sibling, she was newly appreciative of what kind of man he was growing into.

"I have no need of your protection, Charles," she said. "I had the situation in hand, but I am thankful all the same. I do not believe I was in any danger from Lord Byron…"

"Perhaps not physical danger, Sister, but what about danger to your heart?" Charles asked. "There are things I have heard…"

"Perhaps there are," said Elizabeth. "This time of night, however, is not the right time for you to share them with me. Here is my room. Thank you for escorting me here. If you wish to speak more about this, may we do so tomorrow?"

"Of course," Charles replied before watching her enter her bed chamber and then once again resuming his journey to his own.

Alone in his room, he pondered the situation with the lord. Through two small walks Charles had made around the canal on his own since he'd arrived in Venice, he'd heard Lord Byron's name several times in passing. Out of politeness, he hadn't been able to stop and hear any ongoing conversation about the handsome older man, but the few snippets he'd heard had been enough for him to be concerned.

Debts. Women. Men. Children who he didn't appear to want to be an active father to. Any of those things alone might have been concerning. All of them together made Charles feel particularly protective over his older sister being, in any way, pursued by such a man.

Climbing into bed, his mind continued to be active. Why he should be so worried about his oldest sister having the attention of the lord, he didn't know or understand. He just knew that he was, and it was up to him to keep a closer eye out for anything more happening that he knew would be frowned upon by his mother, his father, and society as a whole.

Along the passageway, Elizabeth's

mind was also active as the somewhat intimate conversation she'd just had with the lord was replayed in her mind. Had she heard correctly? He'd said he could offer her little, but. What had the 'but' meant? Had he been about to make an offer to her? Had he been about to tell her that he wanted to court her, and declare to everyone that he wanted her for his wife?

Recognizing that she could not know how he felt about her, or what he'd been thinking, or if he had any plans at all for her, Elizabeth scoffed softly to herself. There was nothing she could do at that moment to resolve an unfinished conversation, and the following evening would be the masked ball. She assumed he would be there, but even if he was, with everyone wearing wigs and masks, would she know?

40

The day had arrived. As Elizabeth sat with her immediate family, her great aunt, and other relatives around the grand dining table in the morning, she couldn't ignore the ongoing feeling of uncertainty flowing through her.

As they dined, across the table from her sat her brother. Now and then she saw him look at her as if the brief concern she'd seen on his face the night before had grown and deepened through the night. Despite her smiling at him to reassure him she was well and there was nothing for him to worry about, she could see the concern continue. While she was thankful for having a younger brother who cared so much about her reputation, she did wish he'd worry only about himself.

"Are you excited, Elizabeth?" Isabella asked quietly from beside her.

Turning to face her younger sister,

Elizabeth smiled and nodded. Despite any confusion she'd been feeling, when she considered she was going to be attending a masked ball that evening, she did allow herself to feel excitement at the prospect.

"Of course," she replied. "Even the thought of us preparing to go to the masquerade is exciting."

"Yes, although hopefully we shall be able to get our wigs centred correctly this evening!" Isabella said as she remembered trying on each of the wigs that had been designed for her and her sisters.

On being reminded of seeing Isabella trying on a wig, Elizabeth chuckled. Her sister wasn't as outgoing as some young women, but when the moment fitted, she was usually able to do something to make people laugh and be happy. It was a skill that Elizabeth had appreciated many times over their years, even though when they'd been much younger it had sometimes driven her to distraction on occasions when she'd tried to be serious and 'more grown up', and Isabella had done something silly to not let her be.

"You shall all look very beautiful - moto bella!" they heard Caterina say. "It is impossible not to at a masked ball. The gowns will be like none you have ever seen before. The masks will all be beautiful and exotic, making you wonder what secrets lie behind them. The wigs…"

"Will be very funny, Great Aunt," Charles said cheekily, making most at the table have to stifle a laugh.

"That will be enough cheek from you, Grande Nipote!" Caterina said, grinning while pretending to scold him, all knowing she was only ever amused by him. "We shall begin getting ready after our afternoon meal."

"But Great Aunt," Florence began to ask. "Please forgive me for not understanding but if we are all getting ready here, and we are all attending here, how can it possibly be a surprise who is who once the ball begins?"

Elizabeth watched their great aunt smile and wink at Florence. The elderly woman appeared, to Elizabeth, to have gotten younger since members of her family had started arriving from far and wide. It was quite something to see.

"It will be an evening of mystery, young Florence - or as the French say, mystique!" Caterina said, enjoying the creation and delivery of suspense and intrigue. "All you need worry about is making yourself as elusive as you can."

On Florence's face, Elizabeth could see she didn't understand what their great aunt was trying to tell her. Elizabeth understood why. The question had been valid - as far as she knew, most of the people attending the ball were staying in the home. She'd already gotten to recognize many faces, and the way those people walked and talked. How could it be any surprise who was who on the evening, even behind the pretence of wigs, masks and costumes?

"I shall certainly try," Florence said.

"And that is all any of us can do in life, Signorina," Caterina replied. "Now, if there are no objections, I shall take my leave of you all to go and rest."

"Are you well, Aunt?" Alessandra asked as she stood and began to move toward the elderly woman.

"Sì, do not fuss, Alessandra," Caterina said. "Sto bene. At my age, it sometimes feels better to lie down than to sit. It is odd, but I have long ago accepted this truth."

All watched as she allowed her assistant to help her out of her chair and the two of them moved toward the door of the large dining room.

"I shall see you all at our afternoon meal," she added before leaving the room entirely.

"Oh dear," Alessandra said when she sat down again. "I do hope my aunt is well enough for this evening. She has so been looking forward to it."

She felt comfort as Edward reached out and took her hand in his.

"I am sure she knows what she is well enough for, and what she isn't, my love," he said. "She has her assistant with her. She must know Caterina better than anyone else, and she will know what to do if things are not as positive as we hope."

"Yes, I know you are right, Edward," Elizabeth saw her mother say. "I am sure that even if she has little energy at present, that will change when she sees her masquerade underway."

"Are you looking forward to wearing your wig, mask and new gown in costume tonight, Mother?" Charles asked.

Alessandra smiled at her son. In truth, she felt somewhat apprehensive about the evening ahead, but she was determined to not let her children know that.

"It shall be an evening of delight for all of us, I am sure, Charles," she replied.

As Elizabeth looked around the large room of people, she hoped that would be true. Around her were many 'cousins of a sort', as Caterina had described them. She'd met and spoken to many, but not all. Some were around her age but many were much older. Whoever had approached and spoken to her, she'd been happy to speak to. Some, she'd understood easily when they'd talked. Others, she'd just had to smile and nod at, hoping that whatever it was they'd just said to her in their odd styles of talking had rightly deserved a smile and a nod.

Contemplating the people she could see, her mind then rebelliously shifted back to the memory of the evening before. Lord Byron and Gilberto weren't currently at the large table. Although they'd spent a bit of time in Caterina's home, they seemed to more often be out, staying elsewhere.

It was yet another unknown about

the handsome lord - where did he go in Venice? Where did he stay? He'd seemed as comfortable in the large home as Gilberto had, and Caterina seemed to know both of them very well, and yet they did not have rooms there. Should Elizabeth have asked, much earlier, about where they resided?

There were so many questions that she had no answer to, but did it truly matter if she knew nothing about the lord? He'd seemed to want to see her and spend time with her, but he hadn't made any firm declaration to her. What was she to think of it all?

"You are very thoughtful, Sister," she heard Isabella whisper in an attempt to not bring attention to the two of them. "What - or perhaps I should ask, *who* - is on your mind?"

"I am only eager to see the beauty of what everyone shall look like tonight, Isabella," Elizabeth replied. "Can you imagine what I shall be able to paint after the evening is over with?"

"You can say such things, Elizabeth, but you do not fool me," Isabella said in her hushed voice. "How could you not think about a certain someone and what he will look like? I cannot see how he could look any more handsome than he does day to day. Can you?"

Elizabeth sighed but didn't reply. Silently she had to acknowledge she'd been wondering the very same thing herself.

41

After dining with his extended family, Charles felt compelled to move. At times, he liked to ask at least one of his sisters to walk with him, no matter where they were. At that moment, he felt the need to be alone.

So far it had been wonderful meeting so many members of extended family, but it also felt stifling. The number of people wasn't as great as he experienced when he was away studying, but even then there were fewer people in his classrooms than there were in his great aunt's dining room. He was someone who liked to be around people, but sometimes he did need solitude.

Since arriving in Venice, he'd taken several walks by himself. Unlike where he studied in London, with its busyness and almost constant noise, Venice had a unique kind of tranquil peace about it.

He liked that. There were people out and about but everything still seemed quiet. It was an odd landscape to be a part of, especially compared to London and its large population, and equally compared to his home of Chisholm Manor estate, with all of its green and lush landscape. Venice held neither, making him appreciate it for not only its unique look, but also its unique feel.

Stepping outside of the large home, he began to feel invigorated as he looked around. He could stay on the land and walk from where he was, or he could take a gondola to another part of the strange city. It took only moments to decide that on the water was where he wanted to be. He didn't care where the gondola would take him. For that moment, the idea of feeling the smoothness of the boat gliding through the water, combined with the soft sound of the water's movement, was what appealed to him most of all.

Once settled into the small boat, he

sat back, relaxed and closed his eyes. He'd told the gondolier that he simply wanted to be in peace. He trusted the result would be the gondolier guiding the gondola away from the Grand Canal and instead moving along some of the smaller, narrower waterways.

Breathing in the cool, fresh air and appreciating each sliver of sunlight that hit his face when the direction of the gondola allowed it among the buildings, his mind eventually moved back to his oldest sister and the man he'd seen her huddling with the night before. He supposed it wasn't something for him to worry about, especially since she was older than him, but he was worried. Uncertainty lay in whether he should mention anything about it to their mother or father. If Charles said something, how could he know that his worries were truly justified? And if they weren't truly justified, would he be creating a situation that was uncomfortable for several people, when everything would have been suitably calm without his intrusion?

Regarding that particular subject, the argument inside of his head swayed this way and that. He wouldn't rush to speak to either of his parents. There was nothing about the lord that he knew to be fact. His worries had been instilled only by small amounts of information that he'd overheard, and he couldn't know for sure were true. He didn't know the people he'd heard the worrisome details from, so couldn't know if they were being truthful.

After much thought, he was resolved there was nothing he could do. Although he had heard some members of his extended family murmur, openly wondering if Elizabeth had captured the heart of the handsome Lord Byron, Charles also believed his sister's reputation was preserved and there was nothing to worry about.

Happy that he'd considered options and come to a decision to remain quiet, he sat up, feeling more invigorated. With nothing to worry about regarding Elizabeth, he could concentrate only on the evening ahead.

A masquerade. He'd never attended anything like that before. In his life, he'd not even attended any balls. While the other young men at school were a pleasure to spend time with, in and out of the classroom, only a few of his acquaintances had sisters that he'd gotten to meet. Once or twice, he'd enjoyed the idea of getting to know those young ladies. The thought of a friendship being ruined over that had made the idea less desirable in Charles's mind, but he was only sixteen. He knew he had plenty of time to discover the world of feminine delight.

As the gondola veered into a slightly wider waterway, Charles was able to see more people standing around or walking. He took his time to watch all. Some looked happy, with their smiles and their laughter. Some looked far more serious.

He found it easy to wonder what was happening in other people's lives. What made them so happy? What made them so sad? Trying to guess was a pointless exercise, he knew, but watching people was something he'd learned to enjoy early in life.

When he saw some artists along the edge of the waterway, he was reminded of his sister again. For a fleeting moment, his thoughts almost travelled back to where they'd been earlier. On seeing one person in particular - someone he recognized - he called out to the gondolier, asking him to stop at the nearest place possible.

"Good afternoon!" he called out after exiting the boat and beginning to walk back to where the young man had his easel set up. "What a pleasant surprise, seeing you here!"

Angus McKay was startled when he looked up and saw the familiar young man approaching him. Glancing behind where he sat, Angus considered the young man might be addressing someone else.

"Mr McKay!" he then heard called out, forcing him to look forward again. "What do you draw today? May I see?"

Before Angus could say anything, he saw Charles walk around and behind him.

"I have chosen this structure to draw as one of my final submissions for Mr Elliot before we leave for Rome," Angus said. "It is rather unique, do ye not think?"

"I do indeed," said Charles as he glanced up at the building being drawn. "I now wish I'd brought Elizabeth with me today. She would have loved to see what you are now drawing."

"That is yer sister?" Angus asked, feeling his usual discomfort at the prospect of talking to someone. It was a discomfort he was eager to at least try and push through and, although he'd already believed the young man and woman were siblings, asking such a question seemed an easy way to find out more without having to ask anything too directly.

"Oh, yes," said Charles. "Do forgive me. Yes, my sister, who you have spoken to previously, is Elizabeth."

Angus took note of the name but didn't correct the young man who seemed to think Angus had embarked upon an actual conversation with his sister.

"It is a pleasure to be able to speak in a more relaxed setting," Angus said.

"Oh, yes, I agree," Charles said. "It was very formal when we approached you in Teatro La Fenice. I do apologize for that. I was so excited to see a familiar face that I didn't anticipate my father approaching you and your friend."

"I regard Mr Elliot more as my mentor than a friend," Angus said. "He is teaching me much."

"I imagine so," said Charles. "What a wonderful profession to be able to learn if you love drawing so much. I expect my sister must be highly envious of you. I am sure if there was such a thing as a woman architect, she would want to be one!" he added, chuckling.

At the further mention of the young woman Angus had stood and watched from the shadows near the Rialto Bridge previously, he felt compelled to change the subject. He'd replayed that view over and over in his mind - the one of the young woman sitting at her easel, highly focused on putting to paper what she could see with her eyes. He loved the image, but equally felt somewhat ashamed that he'd stood and stared at her for as long as he had.

"Are you excited to shortly be travelling to Rome?" Charles asked.

"Aye," Angus replied. "It is a great city, I hear. Have ye been?"

"No, I haven't travelled beyond here, London, and my home," said Charles. "You are very fortunate to have a mentor who wishes to take you to so many places."

On thinking about the countries and cities he was on a journey to with Mr Elliot, Angus couldn't help but think of his mother.

"Aye," he agreed. "But it has been a long time since I was home. I do look forward to returning when this tour is complete."

Sensing the change in mood in the Scotsman, Charles decided to leave him to get on with his work. Watching him was something Charles knew he could do all day, just as he'd never found it boring watching his sister create her paintings, but of course it was different with the man in front of him. He was training to be an architect, and his images were required for him to be able to move forward in that. As much as Charles felt he'd like to stay and simply watch, he knew he had to go.

"I shall not hold you up any longer," he said. "But I have no doubt that one day I shall see your name on structures of great architecture."

Angus scoffed but smiled and nodded. As he watched Charles begin to walk away, he felt disheartened that he'd not done better in his speech. Once charcoal hit paper again, however, he felt it easy to push the interaction far from his mind.

43

After removing himself from the scene, Charles felt more inclined to be around people. Journeying to Piazza San Marco, he felt his mood begin to soar. Merchants lined the square with their wares, while prospective buyers lined up to inspect and purchase them. There was a general hum of busyness that Charles found highly invigorating.

"Mr Chisholm," he heard from behind him as he happily wandered among the crowds. When he turned, he saw Lord Byron standing within close distance, with Gilberto on one side of him and a woman on the other.

"Lord Byron. Gilberto," said Charles. "It is a fine day to be out, is it not?"

He watched the face of the lord, wondering if the previous evening would be addressed. Not sure if he wanted it to be or not, he felt nothing when there was no mention of it.

"It is indeed," Gilberto said, grinning as he snuck a sly look at the other young woman of the party, standing beside but a step behind him. "What brings you out today, young Charles?"

"The need for fresh air," Charles replied before seeing Gilberto throw his head back and laugh.

"That is a very polite response indeed," Gilberto said. "I am sure the reason is more that my great aunt's home is close to bursting with far too many people, and you feel the need to escape."

Charles was surprised by the accuracy of the statement, but couldn't think of any polite reply before Gilberto was speaking again.

"Worry not," he said. "I understand completely. On every occasion I have stayed with our great aunt, it has felt luxurious and grand for the first day, and then felt far too confined for the rest. Hence why I prefer staying with this rogue for the moment. His lodgings are perfectly suited to my simple needs."

"Simple?" Charles saw Lord Byron ask before laughing, as if he'd told a great joke. Charles didn't know what the joke actually was, but the response of laughter from Gilberto told Charles that he obviously did.

"Let us move on, Gilberto," he saw Lord Byron say quietly. "We should not keep these ladies in the sun for too long. It would be a great shame to taint their complexion."

"Indeed you are right," Gilberto replied before turning to face Charles again. "We shall see you this evening, young Charles - although whether we know who each other is, who can tell!"

With another burst of laughter from the two friends, they began to walk off with their two lady friends beside them. For some time, Charles stood and watched the group of four. He had no idea what had inspired their intense laughter, but he watched them continue to laugh among themselves even as they walked into the distance.

"Be wary of those two," he suddenly heard a woman's voice say, breaking his attention on the small group. When he turned around, he saw it was an older woman addressing him. "Lord Byron especially."

"Why do you say such a thing?" Charles asked, surprised but intrigued.

"Overindulgent rogue with too many women to sow his wild oats with, and too many men wanting to be just like him," the woman said. "Has he tried it on with you?"

Despite his increased level of surprise, Charles fully understood the question. Having attended a boys' school, he knew that the traditional way of things - men being attracted to women - was not always the way things went. He'd never felt attracted to any man himself, but he did have friends who'd quietly admitted having such feelings.

"He has not," he replied. "He may

have taken a particular interest in my sister however."

"Then be sure to warn her," the woman said. "If he succeeds in doing to her what he's done to a great many other women, her character will forever be blackened. He enjoys petty conquests, usually with women or men who are silly enough to believe he will love them if they do what he tells them he desires."

"Is this ... that is ... oh, I do not..." Charles started to say in preparation for asking what he wanted to know.

"You wonder if I am one of his discarded?" the woman asked. "Is that what you wish to know?"

"Yes," Charles admitted. "Please forgive me, but I do not know you."

"It is good that you ask," the woman said. "You are not someone to just take the word of a stranger. That is good. Believing all that we hear is often the downfall for any of us. But to answer your question, no, I am not one of his discarded, but my younger sister is."

"Can you share her story with me?" Charles dared to ask, feeling he was being far too intrusive, but it had been the woman herself who'd initiated the conversation. Surely she must have known that if she said what she had, questions would be asked.

"There isn't too much to tell," she said. "He met her, he charmed her for many weeks, and he led her to believe that he wanted to be with her."

"By 'be with her', you mean…"

"My sister took his words to mean that he was interested in marrying her," the woman said. "He … he has a special way, you see, of leading someone to believe that he's interested in them, but it's all an act. He enjoys having associations with fashionable society but I have heard that it's so he can get money. Debts up to his ears, I've heard, although I know nobody who can confirm that."

"Debt?" Charles asked in surprise as

he considered the lavish clothing he'd only seen the lord wearing. "Lord Byron?" he further asked and saw the woman nod.

"You wouldn't believe it, would you, with the way he presents himself as a man about the town," she said. "I have heard there are many who've suffered from knowing Byron. He seems friendly and he seems charming, but believe me - as nice as he seems, he is a man who has the power to ruin you."

Charles took some time to study the woman's face. He didn't know her, and for all he knew she could be making up the story because she'd been shunned by the handsome lord. Charles had heard plenty of stories about such instances from his friends at school who'd shared tales of what their older siblings had endured.

Although he was young, Charles was confident he was good at reading when people were being deceitful. He didn't think the woman facing him was. Her story - that of being the sister of someone hurt by Lord Bryon - appeared true. He knew he couldn't put full faith in it, believing it unconditionally, but she'd certainly said enough for him to consider and keep in mind, especially when it came to his own sisters.

"I see your uncertainty so I shall leave you," the woman said. "If you choose not to believe what I've told you, be it on your own head, but I hope you will at least consider this: you cannot believe a word that Lord Byron says!"

As Charles watched, the woman curtseyed to him, turned, and then disappeared into the crowd. After she'd left, Charles remained still, his mind racing. He'd suspected things might not be very good when he'd seen the lord with Elizabeth, huddled in a corner late at night. He was sure that no respectful gentleman would put a young lady in that position.

Overwhelmed with the way he was feeling, and the way his emotions had been pulled this way and that when all he'd wanted to do was find some peace, Charles made his way back to his great aunt's home. He didn't rush, but he was aware of having a new level of enthusiasm to be around his family.

Ahead for the evening was a masked ball. He knew many people he'd met would be there. He'd been told that many new people would be there. He also knew Gilberto would be attending, along with Lord Byron. Gilberto was distantly related to Elizabeth. If his friend was a rogue, would he seriously do nothing to prevent Lord Byron from possibly damaging Elizabeth's reputation? Charles wanted to believe it couldn't be a possibility, but the fact that Gilberto didn't appear to have said anything about his friend's reputation and debts made Charles wary of trusting his distant cousin.

Before he reached the grand home, he stopped still and took some deep breaths to try and refocus his mind.

Despite what he'd heard, he would walk inside. He would sit with his immediate and extended family and enjoy the hospitality that his great aunt provided. Then he would do as others in the house were going to do - embark upon getting into costume, including the most disbelieving aspect of all – the wig.

Charles scoffed as he thought about that. He'd never worn a wig in his life, but for his great aunt, he would. To him they seemed archaic, but what did he know? He was a young man who hadn't even started to see the world. Elders knew all. Youth knew nothing. He'd been told that by older people for as long as he could remember, and he decided to put faith in the words.

Finally, he took one more deep breath and then entered the grand home. The last thought he had before joining his family was that Lord Byron might have extreme debts, and Charles's great aunt might be extremely wealthy. Was there any chance that

Lord Byron thought Elizabeth might be inheriting some of that wealth? As the thought struck him, Charles halted in his steps. It was a passing thought only and, on reflection, it made no sense. Lord Byron had obviously established a relationship with Caterina long before the Chisholm family went to Venice. If he was after Caterina's wealth, Elizabeth wasn't needed for that, or likely to be any kind of favourite of Caterina.

Sure that wasn't the case, Charles shook his head, plastered on a smile, and entered the large dining room.

44

In their room, Elizabeth, Isabella and Florence all giggled as they each tried to secure the wigs that had been given to them.

"Should it sit like this?" Florence would ask as she placed one of them on her head in an obviously silly manner.

"Florence!" Elizabeth kept saying as she pretended to scold her youngest sister. In truth, the three of them had been in their room for over an hour, helping each other to put on their gowns, powder the edges of their dark hair to make it look lighter, and then try to get the wigs to fit properly. The result had been much laughter, and Elizabeth felt happy because of it.

Day to day she told herself she was content and patient, happily waiting for something to change in her life. Day to day, she didn't laugh much. When she did, she always ended up wondering why she didn't do it more often. After a good amount of laughter, she felt cleansed, like all bad thoughts or happenings had been washed away. It had to be healthy. She was sure of it.

"Come now, Elizabeth," Florence said. "You enjoy my silliness, I am sure."

Elizabeth saw Isabella grin at her before Elizabeth delivered a similar smile to Florence.

"I do, surprisingly," she said. "But if we do not want our parents marching in here, unhappy with us for not being downstairs when they have told us to be, then we must get this right!"

"Yes, you are right - as always," Florence said reluctantly. "I shall sit here now and let the two of you secure this on me."

Elizabeth further smiled. She'd been shown how to secure the wigs, but as yet hadn't managed to actually succeed in doing it.

"Let us try this again, Sister," she said to Isabella.

"Yes," Isabella replied obediently as she picked up Florence's wig and positioned it. "I think if we put hair pins here, Elizabeth…"

The two sisters worked together until they thought they'd made progress.

"Now shake your head, Florence," Elizabeth said, then watched as their youngest sister tried hard to dislodge the wig. "I do believe we might have success!" she declared when she saw Florence's efforts fail to shake it off.

"One down, two go to," Isabella said. "Your turn now, Elizabeth."

As Elizabeth sat down in front of the looking glass, she took in what she looked like. She had on the gown that her great aunt had commissioned for her. Although she rarely wore blue by choice, she could see that the particular pale blue that the gown was primarily made of did agree with her skin colour.

"I like your gown," she heard Florence say. "Down the front of it, you have butterflies."

Looking down, Elizabeth had no idea what Florence was talking about.

"There," Florence said as she pointed to the bodice part of Elizabeth's dress.

"The bows?" Elizabeth asked. "Yes, I suppose they do look a little like butterflies, Florence."

Turning her attention back to the looking glass, she watched Isabella take her time to ready the wig. It took minutes to change what Elizabeth saw. One minute she was staring at herself, with her flowing powder-edged hair and her dark eyes. The next, the woman facing her had no dark hair at all. Replacing her natural hair colour was the very light blonde of the wig, pulled up high in a way that made her look elegant.

"There," she heard Isabella say. "Now do the same test that Florence did, Elizabeth."

Elizabeth obeyed, vigorously shaking her head from side to side, then forwards and backward.

"It seems very secure," she said, again taking in the image in front of her.

"But we do need to…" she heard Florence say before moving away for a moment and then returning. "Add these!"

In the reflection, Elizabeth watched as Florence placed two long white feathers into the side of the blonde wig. Picking up and securing her brown choker, with its small gem, then adding dark earrings, she allowed herself to like what she saw.

"Only gloves and your mask to be added, and you'll be complete, Elizabeth," Isabella said. "I do love your gown - the colour, and the lace of the trim. I believe our great aunt has a sound understanding of fashion."

"Indeed she does," Elizabeth said as she tore herself from her own image and stood. "Your turn now, Isabella."

Repeating the process for a third time, the sisters finally completed their readiness.

"Look at us," Florence said as the three of them approached the doorway. "With these new gowns, these wigs, and these beautiful masks on, will anyone know who we are, do you think?"

Elizabeth laughed. "They will see us as soon as we go downstairs, Florence. As much as our great aunt has enjoyed using the word 'mystique', I am not sure it shall be any surprise at all, who anyone is."

"Well, I shall certainly pretend to not know anyone," Florence said. "And if anyone addresses me by my name, I shall also pretend I do not know who that is."

Elizabeth saw Isabella grin at her as they walked out of their bed chamber. The three of them were masked and ready for whatever lay ahead and the night would bring.

"We were just coming to find the three of you," she heard her mother say from further down the passageway.

When Elizabeth turned, she realized she wouldn't have recognized her parents or her brother if she hadn't just heard her mother's voice.

"We all look so different," she said, smiling from behind her mask.

"We certainly do," Edward said as he moved forward and lightly placed a kiss above each of his daughter's masks. "You all look very beautiful. Take note of what your mother and I look like now. Later, I suspect many men shall be vying for your attention. If anyone makes you feel uncomfortable, come to us at once."

"Yes, Father," the three sisters said in harmony. In the confine of their bed chamber, they'd already discussed escape plans if anyone made anyone feel uncomfortable, including seeking out their parents.

"Florence, you in particular shall stay by my side for much of the evening," Alessandra said before receiving the reply she'd suspected she would.

"But Mother!" Florence cried out.

"Only while you are not dancing with one young man or another, Florence," Edward reassured her. "And no stepping outside with anyone!"

Elizabeth laughed at the expression on Florence's face, even though the subject was a mildly serious one. She expected her parents to deliver a similar set of rules to her and Isabella. Surprisingly, neither she nor her sister received any such guidance.

"It must be time for us to go to the ballroom now," Florence said. "Could we perhaps be a little mysterious, Father?"

"Oh? And how do you intend to do that?" Edward asked, bracing himself for whatever was to come. Nothing his youngest child said ever seemed too farfetched to surprise him.

"If you enter first with … Elizabeth," Florence said. "Then I enter with … Charles. And then Mother enter with Isabella."

"Do you feel that if we do this, we

shall cause confusion about who we are, Florence?" Isabella asked, laughing at her sister's idea.

"Perhaps," Florence replied. "It is not too much to try, is it?"

"Indeed it is not, Florence," Alessandra replied as she moved up to her youngest daughter, placed an arm around her shoulders, and squeezed her close. Although she and Edward could have held balls at Chisholm Manor, they never had, preferring a quiet life over a sociable one. The entire experience was something relatively new for her. Seeing all four of her babies grown enough to be able to attend such an event made her emotional.

Seeing his wife's eyes begin to water from behind her mask, Edward moved up to her and pulled her into an embrace. It wasn't a new thing for them to do in front of their children, even though they did it rarely. As his arms circled Alessandra, he felt her lean against him and rest her head on his shoulder before pulling back and standing tall again.

"Right, then," Alessandra said as she refocused on the evening ahead and glanced around all of her children. "Let us try this grand plan of confusion. Elizabeth, take your place with your father. You shall enter first. Charles, come here and stand with Florence, and Isabella, please join me."

One more look around all of them and Edward moved forward, guiding each pair within their little group to the ballroom door, and then nodding to the doorman to open it.

On seeing the many people inside, Elizabeth felt her heartbeat increase dramatically. She'd seen the ballroom on an initial tour of the large home when they'd first arrived, but had not since given it a thought. To see how it was decorated, with large tapestries lining the walls and candles everywhere that highlighted the many colours the costumes displayed, was magical.

Taking a deep breath, she held her head high as she entered the room with her hand enclosing her father's arm. Glancing around, she realized that perhaps her great aunt and everyone else who'd said nobody would know who anyone was, had actually been accurate. She could see a great many women wearing a great many beautiful gowns. She could see an entire room full of light-coloured wigs styled into a diverse range of looks. On top of all of that, she could see masks that provided the highest level of beauty.

"Ready?" she heard her father ask. Facing him, she smiled and nodded.

The masquerade was underway.

45

Once the music began, Elizabeth felt like she'd escaped into a world of glorious and vivid colour and imagination. Everything she saw could have been something she'd seen in a painting somewhere. Although it was a short time before each member of her family seemed to be guided away by one mysterious person or another, she was happy to walk around the exterior walls of the room, absorbing everything there was to look at.

She couldn't deny that the women all looked very beautiful. The gowns were obviously all of the highest standard, as she believed she should have expected, given the level of wealth her great aunt seemed to have. Did wealthy people attract wealthy friends? Always? She'd never regarded her own family as wealthy, although as she'd gotten older, she'd learned far more about poverty, which had led to a better understanding that the life she lived with her parents was far more fortunate than what life could be like for many others.

Scattered among the women were men in a wide variety of outfits. Mostly they comprised the standard day wear, but of a higher quality of presentation. Some looked more English, some looked more Venetian, and then there were others. She knew that people had travelled from a range of different countries. To see them in their native costume was intriguing. Some types of clothing, Elizabeth had seen before in books. Others, she knew nothing about.

"May I have this dance?" she heard a gentleman ask when he approached her. He didn't do anything to declare who he was or why he'd chosen her but he sounded English, even though his voice didn't sound familiar.

"Yes, thank you," Elizabeth said. She was expected to dance, and she knew her parents were in the room with her, as were her sisters and brother. She might never know who anyone was that she'd end up dancing with, but she felt relaxed about that. After all, that was the entire point of a masked ball.

"Do you enjoy such social events?" the gentleman asked.

"As this is my first, I am not sure I can answer that question," Elizabeth said, looking into his eyes. Had she met him before? Since arriving in Venice, she hadn't conversed with many people who'd also travelled from England. She was sure she didn't know who he was. "However, now that I am here, I certainly am enjoying myself."

In response to her answer, she saw the man's eyes change to show he was smiling. She was relieved. No more was said between them for the rest of the dance. When it ended, she allowed him to walk her to the edge of the room.

"I sincerely thank you, Signorina," Elizabeth heard him say as he bowed to her and then turned to walk away.

For a moment, she tried to assess how she felt about what had just happened. She'd been asked to dance by an English gentleman. He'd shown a little interest in her, but then been quiet for the rest of the dance. After the dance had ended, he'd thanked her and disappeared into the crowd. But who was he? Had he asked her to dance because he knew who she was and had a particular interest in her, or had he asked just because she was one of so many women in the room?

"Who was that?" she heard a familiar voice ask. Turning, she faced Isabella.

"I know not," Elizabeth replied, still amused by the oddness of it. "I am sure that before this evening, I did not fully comprehend just how strange it would be to dance with someone and not know who they are!"

She heard Isabella laugh softly before a man approached, held out his hand, and led Isabella away. From where she remained, Elizabeth watched her sister for a long while. It was rare that she did so, but it proved a joy to see her sister float around the room, perfectly matching the gentleman's moves as the dance progressed.

"Do you wish to dance also?" she heard another voice ask. The question had been voiced from just behind her, as if the lips that had spoken had been very close to her ear.

Remaining perfectly still, Elizabeth processed the fact that she knew that voice well. Lord Byron. He was at the ball, he was standing dangerously close to her yet again, and he was asking her to move onto the dance floor with him. Should she? Feeling a natural, physical reaction to his voice flow through her body, she very much wanted to. She'd wondered what he wanted from her. If she said yes, it could provide the perfect opportunity…

"You hesitate," she heard him say, breaking through her brief but in-depth assessment of the invitation.

"I accept," Elizabeth said, determined to sound more confident than she felt.

As if on cue, she watched as he stepped forward from behind her, held up his arm, and then led her out into the dance that was already underway.

"I wish to talk to you," she heard him say when the dance brought them close together.

"And talk to me you may," Elizabeth responded.

"Alone," he said to her.

"I believe nobody is hearing us now," Elizabeth said. "Tell me what you wish for me to know."

As the dance parted them, she began to feel more and more empowered. He wanted something from her, but would he go so far as to tell her what it was? She suspected that if she didn't play a game the way he might want her to, he was a man who would walk away. Considering that, she tried to summon how she might feel if he did.

"Your suitors," he said when they came together again.

"Yes?"

"You do have some," she heard him say in surprise.

"I do?" Elizabeth asked, purposely coy.

"I see the mask is providing you with a new kind of confidence this evening," Lord Byron said.

Elizabeth couldn't tell by the sound of his voice if he found his observation amusing or upsetting.

"There is safety in not seeing someone's face, I am learning," said Elizabeth. "After all, am I who you think I am? What if you are addressing someone completely different from who you think you are?"

Once again, they separated. It provided Elizabeth with enough time to appreciate she was enjoying such a newfound banter. When they rejoined, she felt ready for anything.

"I once again begin to wonder if

there may be somewhat of a poet in *you*, Miss Elizabeth," she heard him say.

"I believe there is one strict rule tonight, and that is to address nobody by name, Sir," she said.

"Sir?" she heard him say as he laughed. "You have not been so formal with me before."

On hearing the music end, Elizabeth stopped moving, stood back, and looked into his eyes.

"I know not what you want from me," she said quietly.

"What does your heart desire?" he asked her.

To ensure she had time to consider her answer, Elizabeth began to slowly walk away from the dance area. Knowing he was close behind her, she felt satisfied that he was indeed concentrated on her for some reason. That was not in her imagination at all.

"My heart desires…" she finally said as she turned to face him again. "My heart desires to find a heart that desires mine."

She waited for him to reply, or to react in some way. It took some time, with him seeming to have to take his own amount of time to review what had been said.

"I esteem you greatly," she heard him say.

"Perhaps you do, but perhaps that is not quite enough," Elizabeth said. Her heart was racing as she suspected he would turn and walk away from her. Despite the strong attraction she had for him, he was much older than her, and she just couldn't escape the feeling that, despite how attracted she was to him, she was reading everything about him very, very incorrectly.

"May I have this dance?" she heard her brother ask.

Without another glance toward the man who affected her so, Elizabeth gladly accepted Charles's hand and let him lead her to the dance floor.

"Is all well?" he asked when they

began to move.

"All is well," Elizabeth confirmed. Was it true? She thought so, but as she said it, she did experience a small amount of doubt. If she were to never see the handsome older man again, would she be saddened by that? Would she have missed a vital opportunity to be a wife and a mother if she didn't proactively let him know just how attracted to him she was?

The siblings said nothing more as the dance progressed. When it ended, she saw Charles look at her, letting her guide him to either walk with her, or to leave her. She was glad when she saw him accurately interpret her wishes, and walk off in one direction as she turned and walked in the other.

Taking some time to stand back and watch the next two dances, her attention was focused on all of the different types of clothing that the men wore. There were differences in the women's gowns, of course, but they were all that - gowns.

The men demonstrated entirely different appearances.

"Are ye imagining painting such a scene?" she heard a foreign voice ask.

Glancing at the owner of it, she could see he was wearing what looked like a skirt, and some kind of sash over one shoulder. She'd noticed several of the men in the room dressed the same, but had no idea what it represented.

Painting. He'd mentioned that, so he must have been someone who knew her. She looked closely at the eyes. His voice had betrayed that his accent sounded the same as the young man she'd seen drawing several times. Unfortunately, with him having spoken so rarely to her, she had to assume it was someone from his country, but not necessarily him.

"I can certainly imagine capturing this in colour," she replied. "And you? Would you like to draw it also?"

"I am not an artist," he replied, confusing her further. Not an artist? Not the young man she'd previously met then. "This is not a scene I could paint - at least, not well."

"Perhaps not paint," Elizabeth said, wondering if she needed to play on words to ascertain his identity. "Perhaps something more like … charcoal."

On saying that word, she saw his eyes change, as if he was smiling behind his mask.

"Perhaps," he said without any type of commitment. "A new dance is about to begin. Would ye like to dance with me?"

"Yes, I do believe I would," Elizabeth replied as she placed her hand on his.

"I should warn ye, however," the man said, with more happiness in his voice than Elizabeth had heard before. "I dinnae ken how to dance."

Elizabeth laughed and nodded at him, but was pleasantly surprised that once the music begun, there was nothing about his dance ability that was of concern.

When they were close on the dance floor, she seized the moment to ask questions.

"Do you feel your mask allows you to speak more freely than how you feel when you have no mask on?" she began, then watched as he appeared to consider the question.

"I must admit, I do feel safer behind this mask," he said.

"Safer?" Elizabeth asked. "Do you imply that you do not feel safe without your mask on? I hope that is not the case!"

"No," she heard him say as he chuckled. "Not exactly. Safer possibly isn't the right word."

"Then whatever do you mean?" asked Elizabeth.

"Hmm," he started to reply. "Sometimes … often … when I meet new people, I feel … I can feel like I do not know how to talk."

"How odd," said Elizabeth. "But you speak well at the present time."

"Is it I who speaks well, or the mask?" he asked cryptically.

Elizabeth laughed softly. "I believe the mask is not doing the talking, Sir. It is you, and you alone."

"Perhaps," he said. "Perhaps it is the confidence of wearing my kilt that gives me the power to speak then."

"Kilt?" Elizabeth asked.

"Aye, my ... this," he said as he pointed to what he was wearing.

"Oh, I see!" she said. "I know nothing about where you come from, so I do not know your method of dress. Thank you."

"For what?"

"Why, for teaching me something about where you come from, of course," she said, holding back a giggle that was trying to break free. Although there was no forced humour behind words being said, it felt like she'd fully relaxed with the man who periodically was holding her in his arms, then moving away from her. "Scotland?"

"Aye, of course," the young man

said. "The greenest and most beautiful part of our world."

Hearing the music come to a halt, Elizabeth stood still for a moment, looking into his eyes while trying to tell herself she could be certain she was facing the young man she'd seen drawing previously. But was it him? She supposed it had to be. There were too many likenesses to the conversation they'd had for it not to be. Weren't there?

46

As Angus McKay heard the music end, he felt a change flow over him. It had been easy to approach the young woman and ask her to dance with him. It had also been easy to talk normally, as if he was the confident man he generally didn't consider himself to be.

When the dance ended, he was left with choices. He could ask her to dance with him again. He could walk with her to the edge of the room and stand with her to continue their conversation. He could let her walk away from him, with him knowing that once his mask came off, he might not be able to talk to her so easily.

He was still contemplating which option seemed best when another man stepped between Angus and the woman he wanted to dance with again, and asked her to dance with him.

Although Angus thought he saw her

hesitate for a moment, he was resigned to accept what had just happened. He'd had an opportunity to extend their friendly banter and he'd let time gloss over it, perhaps making it seem as if he hadn't cared about talking to her any further.

After he watched her be led to line up for the next dance, Angus walked away. He'd tried to be a different person, at least for a little while. Trying to continue to be that would only prove to be as big a masquerade as the one he was currently in.

Feeling he could no longer endure such a crowd of people, and so many lost opportunities, he walked out.

After exiting the large ballroom, he instantly felt better. That life wasn't him. It wasn't even something he wanted. He'd grown up on a simple piece of land, to a simple heritage of people. That kind of life was where he was happiest. He'd never desired wealth, or fashion, or the glamour of trying to look wealthy or fashionable.

"You are very handsome for a young man," he heard a man say around the very corner that he was about to approach. Whoever was talking to whom, the comment had sounded intimate. For that reason, Angus was tentative about walking around the corner to begin exiting the large building. But what were his other options? He could walk back into the ballroom, or he could walk around the corner with his head respectfully lowered and hope that nobody thought he'd heard anything.

After contemplation, he knew he had no choice. He didn't want to return to the ballroom. At the very least, he wanted to be outside in the fresh air. That left only one thing that he could do - move forward.

As he rounded the corner, he noticed three things. The first was that both men had their masks off. The second was that one of the men was the infamous

Lord Byron that Angus's mentor had told him extensive stories about, having heard much about the lord from all over the continent. The final thing that he noted was that the young man the comment had been made about was the same young man who'd spoken to him several times before - the brother of the woman Angus had just danced with.

He was so stunned that it took him a moment longer than it should have for him to gather himself and resume his walking. Head down, he just wanted to get out of the passageway, and out of the entire building.

"What do you want from my sister?" Charles asked Lord Byron. They'd met up in the passageway by accident - or so he thought. He had to admit that the chances he would come face to face with the lord, out of all the people in the ballroom, had seemed slim. He'd hoped he wouldn't see Lord Byron at all on that evening, not wanting to risk any scene that might prove uncomfortable. Unfortunately, fate had proved to have other ideas.

"Your sister?" he heard Lord Byron ask with a distinctly sly smirk on his face. "You believe I am interested in your *sister*? Perhaps it is not she who I am interested in at all. Perhaps it is *you*."

When the words came out of the lord's mouth, Charles was stunned. He wasn't surprised by a man saying such a thing to another man, but as far as he'd witnessed, Lord Byron most certainly had been paying attention to Elizabeth. That he was going to try and make things look differently made Charles even more wary of the lord than he had been before.

"You are very handsome for a young man," he then heard the lord say.

Charles remained still and quiet, trying to ascertain how he might turn the conversation around so he could ask Lord Byron about all that he'd heard about him so far. That was the moment when he realized someone else was nearby. Although the person was masked, he was sure the man who walked past them had been the young man training to be an architect - Angus.

Charles was horrified. If Angus had just heard Lord Byron's words, would he think there was something going on between the two of them? The thought of someone thinking he liked men wasn't even a consideration. He had friends like that, and he thought nothing of it.

Someone thinking he was somehow involved with a man who appeared, to many, to be chasing his sister, however - *that* was a scenario he would not allow to be mistaken.

"Tell me this, young Charles," Lord Byron said as he took a step closer. "What would worry you most - if I was interested in your sister ... or if I was interested in you?"

Charles automatically took a step backward, not giving the lord a chance to touch his cheek, as the movement of his hand indicated he intended to do.

"You..." Charles started to say. Given his background, having been taught to be respectful of all people older than himself, he couldn't quite bring himself to say or ask what he wanted to.

"Me?" Lord Byron taunted. "Yes?'

Resolved that he just wanted to be away from the older man, Charles gave up his decision to question him.

"Please stay away from my sister,"

he said before beginning to move in the direction he'd seen Angus go. "We are not wealthy. Neither she - nor I - will be able to help you with your debts."

Seeing the lord throw back his head and laugh so loudly startled Charles, but not enough to stop him from continuing with the decision he'd just made.

With no more words, Charles began to walk swiftly toward the main foyer of his great aunt's home.

48

At the main entrance, Angus hesitated. He'd not been keen to go to the ball in the first place, but Mr Elliot had pushed the idea, saying that if Angus truly wanted to be an architect, he was going to have to learn to communicate more confidently with people. The logic had seemed sound at the time, but as he stood so close to the means to leave the home he'd spent so much time drawing from the outside, he felt conflicted.

It was his natural reaction to want to retreat from any form of interaction with people, but he did want to challenge that reaction. That would mean going back into the ballroom. It would also mean walking past the two men again. If it had been any other two men, he might not have hesitated, but it was that older man, and that young man.

He hadn't made any progress in trying to decide what to do when he heard footsteps approaching with a noticeable degree of urgency.

"Good. You are still here," he heard Charles say as he approached, a little breathless. "I am glad."

"Worry not about what I just saw," Angus said, certain he was going to have to listen to some conversation along the lines of 'I do not like men at all' - a conversation he'd long been aware of having taken place in many sectors of society, and which he equally didn't have any care about. What anybody did behind closed doors, he didn't consider was any business of his.

"I do not worry about that at all," Charles said. "The only reason I would ever want to talk to Lord Byron, now that I have heard so many things about him, is to make sure he stays away from my sister, Elizabeth. That is why I was in the passageway with him."

Angus considered what he'd just been told. He knew it could be a ruse - a way for Charles to explain away something that he felt he didn't want to be public knowledge. Mention of protecting his sister, however, prompted Angus to at least consider that perhaps the explanation was a sound one.

"Elizabeth?" he asked.

"Yes," Charles replied. "Since we arrived in Venice, Lord Byron has been paying her particular attention - in my view, anyway. It does worry me so."

"As it should," Angus said quietly. "I, too, have heard things. If what ye say is true, I, too, would not want yer sister to be attached to that gentleman."

"I must confess I am confused about everything to do with him now," said Charles. "I thought debt must be his driving motive…"

"I have heard such things about him, and the scandals about his level of … indiscretion," said Angus.

"Indiscretion?" Charles asked. "Please tell me what you know."

"It is not my business to say…"

"Please, Angus," Charles pleaded.

"The thought of my sister being under the spell of someone who does not love her and is only leading her on is unbearable to me. Perhaps I should not care so much…"

"It is admirable that ye want to protect yer sister," Angus said, for a moment wishing he had any family nearby to protect and keep safe. "All I shall say is that there have been many women, and many men, and I have also heard that he is married, and he does have a child who he does not see."

Charles was shocked. Nowhere in any conversation he'd heard had anyone mentioned Lord Byron being a husband and a father. That the man could *be* a husband and a father was a surprise, given the detail of information Charles had received about him.

"I … Elizabeth…" he muttered, his mind thinking. "I left Lord Byron in the passageway where you saw us. He could have returned to the ballroom by now. I must find Elizabeth at once and do what I can to not let her be ... swayed by him."

Angus's first thought was that he admired Charles for wanting to protect his sister. Further thought made Angus aware that he didn't want Elizabeth swayed by Lord Byron either - or any other man.

"I shall come with ye," he said. "Come. Between us, we shall find her and stop anything that may be happening."

"Yes," said Charles, appreciative of the support. "This may all be for nothing. I could simply be a brother who has read too much into a situation."

"If that is so, no harm will have come, and nobody else will know anything about this," Angus said. "But if not - if ye are right - we shall find her."

49

As one dance ended and the latest dance partner had delivered her safely to the side of the room, Elizabeth felt weary. Unused to such socializing, she was tired from dance, but just as tired from making conversation. She was only glad that not too many of the men she'd danced with during the evening had actually had much to say - or expect her to say.

"May I?" she heard that familiar voice ask yet again. It was the third time in the evening Lord Byron had approached her. With each successive interaction with him, she felt the same confusing array of feelings. Was she feeling closer to him? Or was each conversation she had with him actually beginning to help her feelings to fade? At times, she felt like both were happening, which of course made no sense at all.

"Or may *I*?" she heard a second voice ask before she had a chance to accept Lord Byron's invitation.

Glancing at the man who seemed rather insolent to be asking for a dance when his words indicated he knew full well that another had just done the same, Elizabeth couldn't help but smile. It was that other familiar voice. He'd earlier run away without showing much enthusiasm for talking to her anymore, and yet now he was back. Although the scenario she seemed to be in made little sense, she was able to note to herself that she felt much lighter at the second voice asking her to dance, than she had from the first.

Without sneaking another look at Lord Byron, Elizabeth confidently placed her hand on the arm of the man she was certain was the young Scottish trainee architect who kept crossing her path. The two of them said nothing as they moved into position. Once the dance had begun, Elizabeth took her time to get some conversation underway.

"Twice in one evening," she said.

"I hope that does not disappoint," Angus replied.

"If it did, I would not have accepted your hand," Elizabeth teased him. "But do you know who I am? I am not sure that you do, and the thought of you thinking you are dancing with someone you are not is worrisome indeed."

"Who do I think ye are, ye ask?" Angus asked. "I believe that under that mask is a young lass who might enjoy painting. A young lass not of pale hair, but of dark hair, to match her dark eyes. Dark hair, dark eyes, but skin as fair as the snow on the Scottish Highlands."

On hearing his description, Elizabeth felt her heart soar. It wasn't the same feeling she'd had with Lord Byron's attention. Lord Byron was handsome. The man she was dancing with was different. There was a large aspect of her life that Lord Byron would never understand, but the man she danced with understood perfectly.

"I ... I do not know what to say to that," she admitted. "I have never seen the Scottish Highlands," she added as an afterthought. "But I have seen the work of a young architect in training, and I believe he has a kind of talent that I admit I am envious of."

Angus smiled before he felt his shyness start to encroach. He didn't want that, partly because he wanted to change anyway, but also because he wanted to help keep the notorious flirt away from Elizabeth. Even though that was part of the reason that had driven him to ask her to dance, he was very happy to be with her again.

"Aye, I know that ye know who I am," he said. "It is no secret to ye."

Elizabeth laughed softly.

"I was not sure," she admitted.

"And now that ye are?"

"Now that I am ... I am very relieved that I am not dancing with a stranger," she said. "But I am also very happy, because I would like to know you."

She knew it was a bold thing to say, and perhaps not how ladies should act, but as she danced with him, now and then meeting and touching him and then moving away as the dance dictated, she knew it was true. She wanted to ask him why he'd appeared to shun her on previous occasions, but she knew she could never ask that.

"Would ye like to draw together?" Angus dared to ask. The thought of doing so frightened him, but he pushed forward with the idea regardless. "Perhaps we could draw each other."

"I have no talent for drawing people," Elizabeth said.

"Nor I," said Angus. "However, if we are both not good at drawing people, might we both not get better at it from trying?"

Elizabeth, considering she was hearing the most she'd ever heard him say to her, felt enraptured with the idea.

"You would not laugh at my

attempt?" she asked, and was rewarded by him laughing.

"Would ye laugh at mine?"

"Of course not," she replied.

"Then I shall promise not to laugh at yers," Angus said, feeling light-hearted. "So, ye see, what could we have to lose? Ye are not good at portraiture, and I am not either. We can paint, and we can try not to laugh."

As the dance pulled them apart, Elizabeth considered his idea further. She liked it. It would take her outside the comfort of what she usually did, without any threat of feeling horrid if what she produced was not of any notable quality.

"Very well," she said when they joined up together again. "When and where shall this event take place?"

Thinking about the practicality of that, Angus realized his error. He was going to have to travel with his mentor in coming days. He knew he would rather seize the opportunity and spend some time with her, but he had a commitment that he couldn't walk away from.

"I am to go with Mr Elliot to Rome," he said, trying to think of a way to make their planned idea happen.

"When?" asked Elizabeth.

"Three days, but I must finish my work here before I go," Angus explained. "I do believe I could finish the remaining sketches with one day to spare, but it is important my work is completed first."

"Yes, of course," Elizabeth reassured him. She didn't know if he was being truthful and sincere, or making an excuse to get out of something he didn't really want to do. Given that he'd been the one to suggest it, she felt drawn to believe he was being honest. "You must complete your work."

"Aye," Angus agreed when the music stopped. "May I ... that is, perhaps I could ask yer father if I may visit once I have completed my projects?"

Elizabeth felt her face blush at the

suggestion. Thankful to have her mask to cover the redness, she nodded.

"If you are certain, we can go and speak to my mother and father now, or my great aunt, who owns this home," she said.

"Lead the way," Angus said. He was nervous, but he knew what was right.

"Father, do you remember Mr McKay?" Elizabeth asked when they reached where her mother and father stood.

"Yes, of course," Edward said. "How do you do, Mr McKay?"

"I was not aware that you knew my aunt, Mr McKay," Alessandra said as she recognized who they were speaking to.

"I do not, Mrs Chisholm," Angus said. "My mentor, Mr Elliot, received an invitation for him and one other to attend, from an acquaintance who, in turn, was invited this evening."

"Father, Mr McKay wishes to ask..." Elizabeth started to say before seeing the young Scotsman turn his head to face her, his eyes visibly showing surprise at her eagerness.

"Yes?" Edward asked, curious about what was to come.

"If I may be so bold to ask, Sir, I have suggested to Miss Elizabeth that she and I do some drawing and painting together," Angus explained. "I hope I am not seeming impertinent but would … would ye agree to this?"

He waited for a long while as he saw Elizabeth's father look at her mother and receive a small nod.

"I would, but where will this take place?" Edward asked. "You know that this home belongs to my wife's aunt, so we cannot invite you here."

"Of course," Angus replied. "Perhaps … perhaps Miss Elizabeth and I could sit outside, where I sat when I was drawing yer aunt's home. That would not be too intrusive, I trust?"

As he waited for a reply to be given, he felt his nervousness increase. He was a nobody, with no grand family that he was a part of, and no grand income for at least the immediate future. He understood that part of Elizabeth's parents bringing her to Venice might be to find a wealthy husband for her.

"That is very acceptable to us, Mr McKay," Edward said upon seeing Alessandra give another nod. "When shall this happen?"

"As I have explained to yer daughter, Sir, I must complete a further two projects for Mr Elliot before he and I head to Rome next week," Angus said. "I feel it most important that I complete these first, but I am sure I shall have a little time after they are done, before we leave. May I call here once my time is my own?"

"Yes," Alessandra said, very much appreciating the manners of the man who seemed interested in her oldest daughter. "Please do, Mr McKay."

Edward was surprised by his wife's quick reply, and amused, but didn't say anything.

"Thank ye," Angus said before bowing to all, glancing at Elizabeth to try and assess if she'd want him to remain with her or not, and quietly withdrawing himself when he could see she was happy where she was.

As he walked away, he glanced around the room and caught the eye of Charles, who nodded at him. If nothing else came of the evening, Angus had at least helped Elizabeth's brother to keep her safe, and her reputation intact. He'd kept her from dancing with Lord Byron, and he'd delivered her to stand with her parents. He wouldn't be able to stop all efforts the handsome lord might attempt, but Angus felt happy in knowing that he'd at least stopped one.

The masquerade was over. As Elizabeth replayed the evening in her mind, she considered it had been a good first ball to attend. She'd danced with many, and two men in particular. She didn't know who the rest of the men were that she'd danced with, but she knew those two. Did that bring her joy? She'd thought so as each of the dances were taking place. As she thought back over the night, one seemed far more favourable than the other.

"I enjoyed my first ball," she heard Florence say sleepily from her bed.

"As did I!" Isabella agreed before turning to face Elizabeth. "Am I right in thinking you did also, Elizabeth?"

Elizabeth could see the look of cheeky suggestiveness on her sister's face but didn't want to reply with full honesty while Florence was in the room.

"I did," she said. "It has left me rather

tired, however. I believe I may sleep till noon!"

She saw Isabella give her a look of amusement before she lay down and closed her eyes. Once Elizabeth felt she was able to be alone in her thoughts, she forced herself to remember every detail of what had happened, what she'd seen, and what had been said in her presence. It was a lot. She particularly wanted to focus on what her eyes had absorbed, so she could recreate the scene in paints in following days.

Painting. It was something she loved to do but had always done alone. Now someone had proposed she sit with them and they paint together. The suggestion seemed even more daunting than the idea of Elizabeth showing her artwork to other people. She'd agreed to the idea while in the midst of dance, not thinking entirely clearly. Thinking more about it as she lay in her bed, however, she knew she was growing to like the idea more and more. As Mr McKay had said, they didn't have to take their efforts seriously, or to judge one another. They could paint together purely for the sake of it. It would be a new experience for both of them.

As sleep began to take hold, Elizabeth felt at peace. She didn't know why Lord Byron had been paying her attention. She didn't know why the Scotsman training to be an architect had asked to see her again. What she did know was that she'd just enjoyed an evening of much dancing, and many glorious sights that she would enjoy recreating on paper. That was enough. For now, that was more than enough.

51

The following morning, as was to be expected, conversation around the large dining table centred completely on the night before. As Elizabeth listened, she felt happy. Some people were talking about the dancing and the joy it brought. Some people were complaining that nobody had seemed interested in dancing with them (the scoundrels!). Others were talking about what they'd seen and heard.

While she didn't exactly expect to hear anything about Lord Byron in the chatter that was happening around her, she did find herself focusing on the various conversations, ready to hear anything she might. On hearing nothing at all, she felt relieved but also intrigued. The lord was as handsome a man as she'd ever seen, and he had vast charm and grace. How could nobody have noticed him, or have anything to say about him? Granted, he'd had a mask on all evening, as had everyone, but the people at the table had all met him at least in passing. The lack of mention of him was curious indeed.

After the dining had finished, she was pulled aside by Isabella.

"Will you paint outdoors this morning, Elizabeth?"

Elizabeth stopped walking, surprised by the question. Her sister knew when she would be painting, and never showed any interest in it.

"I am going to retrieve my tools now, and then go outdoors to work on my painting for our great aunt, Isabella," she said as the two began to walk again. "What is it that you truly wish to know?"

"How well you know me, Sister," Isabella said, laughing. "In truth, there is nothing I wish to know, but certainly something I wish to speak to you about."

Elizabeth, highly intrigued by the words of her sister, quickened her steps. It wasn't entirely out of the ordinary for

Isabella to share things with her, but making such a broadcast about the fact in advance of it happening was new.

Minutes later, both sisters were walking out into the morning sunshine. After taking her time to assess where was the perfect place to set up her easel and seat, Elizabeth felt satisfied that her preparations were complete.

"Do you wish to share your news now that we are completely alone, Isabella?" she asked. "I must admit, I am eager to hear what you wish to tell me."

"I met someone," Isabella said in almost a whisper, while looking around as if to be sure nobody else was within listening distance.

Elizabeth grinned at the tone of her sister's voice. She'd always thought that Isabella had no interest in getting married or having children, so she'd assumed she also had no interest in meeting anyone either. To hear such enthusiasm was surprising but also satisfying.

"Do tell me about him," Elizabeth said. "Is this someone I have met?"

"That is difficult to tell, Sister, since we do not truly know who was there last night," Isabella said.

"But … you did *see* who the gentleman was, that you are talking about…"

As Elizabeth studied the face of her sister, she saw a red blush appear. It was the first time she'd ever seen such a reaction on Isabella.

"Oh dear, Isabella," she said. "I do not understand. Perhaps you could tell me everything, from the first moment you met this person."

As she waited for Isabella to begin talking, Elizabeth picked up a pencil and began to draw, thinking it best to wait to work on the painting. There was no conscious image in her mind, or anything in particular that she wanted to draw, but she suspected that her not looking directly at Isabella might help the conversation to begin.

"I danced with several men at the ball," Isabella finally started to say.

"Yes, you did appear rather popular every time I saw you," Elizabeth agreed, teasing.

"They were all genial enough," Isabella continued. "There was nothing unpleasant about dancing with any of them, but it was the fourth person that I danced with who I ... I found myself drawn to."

"I see, and what was it about him that drew you to him, do you think?" Elizabeth asked as her pencil continued to make its mark on the page before her.

"He was ... oh, I am not entirely sure, exactly," said Isabella. "When he held me in his arms during those few moments in the dance, I felt very ... oh, I do not even know how to describe it, Elizabeth. When I was close to him, I thought that everything felt right, that is all."

"And you spoke?" asked Elizabeth.

"Oh, yes. He asked me where I was from. When I told him, he said he lived north of Bath, and that he knew our land well. It was rather a surprise, I must say. I could tell from his voice that he was an Englishman, but to hear him say he was from so close to our home ... surely that was a sign."

"A sign of what, Isabella?" Elizabeth asked.

"Why, that ... that I am to see him again, of course!" Isabella replied.

"And he has asked to see you again."

"Yes, he asked where Father was, and I am sure he would have gone to speak to him, even though I did not see him do so," Isabella said. "Does that not speak greatly of how much of a true gentleman he is, Elizabeth?"

"It does indeed but, Isabella, have you seen this gentleman ... without the mask that he wore last night ... or have you not?" Elizabeth asked, beginning to feel uneasy. She wanted happiness for her sister, just as she was sure Isabella wanted happiness for her. The thought of either of them desiring a man they'd never actually seen, however, didn't seem entirely wise.

"Well, no, but I shall see him when he comes to call on me," said Isabella. "Are you not happy for me, Sister?"

"Yes, of course I am," said Elizabeth as she stopped drawing and faced Isabella. "I want nothing more than for you and I both to find love."

"Love?" Isabella asked. "Yes, I agree that is a fine idea, and something we should want to find, however I am beginning to fear you and I have been somewhat spoiled in wanting to find that."

"Why do you say such a thing, Isabella?" Elizabeth asked.

"Why? Do you not know?" Isabella asked as she scoffed. "For all of our lives, we have witnessed daily the love of our mother and father. They are a married couple who enjoy time together, and it is my understanding that this is not common at all. They have always shown affection to one another, even in front of us. They talk as though they speak a language that only they know, but both understand." She paused for a long while before continuing. "Yes, I would like to find love, but I fear there is no possibility that you or I could ever find a man who could demonstrate love to us like we have seen our father show to our mother."

Even though she'd had similar thoughts herself in the past, Elizabeth felt saddened by her sister's words. Surely it should have been a great thing to witness proof that love was a solid thing that could indeed exist. Why, then, did it feel to both Elizabeth and Isabella that their having witnessed it for all of their lives, ensured they could never find it themselves?

"I think that the love shared between our parents is only one example of love," she said. "There must be many types, in all shapes and sizes. Perhaps it is better for you and I to not compare anything we find with what our parents have shown to us. The love that you and I find in our own lives, Isabella, will be just ours - the love we share with our husbands. It might not be the same, but that does not mean it shall not be just as wonderful."

"Yes, perhaps you are right," Isabella said.

"Does this gentleman have a name?" Elizabeth asked.

"Oh, yes, I am quite sure he does," she heard Isabella reply, prompting both of them to laugh out loud.

"Oh dear, it would seem that the mystique and intrigue of our great aunt's masquerade is not complete just yet!" said Elizabeth before turning back to her drawing, and moving her pencil once again.

52

"Father, may I speak with you alone?" Charles asked when he saw his mother and father leaving the large dining room.

"What is it that you would not wish your mother to hear, Charles?" Edward asked, uncertain about what the strange request could mean.

"I … that is … no, I do not mean that you cannot hear what I wish to say, Mother," Charles said. "It is just that … I would not wish to say anything…"

"That I am too delicate to hear?" Alessandra asked, amused even though she suspected the subject about to be broached was not going to be humorous. "Whatever you wish to tell your father, I am sure I shall be comfortable hearing also, however if you feel more at ease only speaking to your father…"

"No," Charles said. "No, it is not something private about me. Could we speak somewhere else, however?"

"Yes, let us walk out to the herb garden," Edward said, having already begun to appreciate the peace he'd discovered there since he'd arrived in Venice. "I have not seen anyone else grace that part of this vast property so far. I am sure we shall be quite private."

As the three of them walked, they said nothing to one another. In the minds of Edward and Alessandra were questions about what their son could possibly ask them about, since he rarely did ask them for anything. In Charles's mind was concern about whether he should dare to discuss with his parents the concerns he had for his sister.

"What is it, Charles?" Edward asked when they reached their destination and could see nobody else in the immediate area. "You have me quite worried. Has something happened?"

"To me? No. That is..." Charles replied cryptically. "It is not I that I wish to talk about. It ... it is Elizabeth."

"Elizabeth?" Alessandra asked, not having anticipated that subject at all. "What is it? What has happened that we do not already know about?"

"It is this … thing … with Lord Byron," Charles started to say. "I am sure you will have noticed that he has been paying particular attention to her."

"We have noticed his attention to her, but had not assumed it was especially particular," Edward said. "What has you so concerned?"

"I have heard things … things about him that have stemmed from all over the continent, it seems," Charles replied.

"Perhaps you best tell us all that you know, Charles," Alessandra said as she guided him to a long stone bench.

"In truth, I do not know what is accurate and what is not," said Charles. "How could I know, since I have not been with the lord during his travels."

"Of course, but share with us all that you have heard," said Edward.

"I have heard several things from

different people, but mostly that he has very large debts throughout England, in particular, and he ... he is also a married man who has a child he does not see," Charles said. "On top of that, I have heard several people mention particularly scandalous behaviour of ... of a very ... intimate nature."

"I see," Edward said. "That is very worrisome indeed, and I thank you for bringing this to our attention. You seem to have seen more happening than we have, although your great aunt did mention to us early in our stay here that Lord Byron was a man to keep an eye on."

"She did?" Charles asked, surprised. If his great aunt knew enough about Lord Byron to suggest his behaviour be monitored, how had he managed to spend so much time with Elizabeth unchaperoned at all? "But ... nobody has been watching the two of them!"

"Charles, you are a very good brother to feel and share concern for your sister," Alessandra said as she moved her arm around his shoulders. "We are aware that any of your sisters will attract suitors - possibly *many* suitors - and that some of those will not be what your father and I would deem acceptable. Most of all, we hope that each of you, in time, will find someone who you love and who treats you as well as you should be treated. Before then, each of you may meet people who encourage feelings that are not reciprocated."

"What your mother may be trying to say is that Lord Byron's attention to Elizabeth is something that we have been watching and monitoring from afar, while allowing her the freedom to find her footing, so to speak, in the world of social interaction," said Edward. "You have been at school, meeting many people and gaining skills in this, but your sisters remain at Chisholm Manor consistently. They do not have the opportunities that you have, and they must develop them."

"Father, I do not disagree with your sentiment, however I ... as impertinent as I know it is for me to say ... I do not think that permitting these interactions between Elizabeth and Lord Byron is a suitable way to help her ... practice her social skills!" Charles said. His mother and father had lived much longer than he had, but he couldn't help but wonder if even they weren't aware of the kinds of people there were in the world, and the many significant ways someone could inflict damage to someone else's reputation. "I would not like the scandals following him around to indirectly result in my sister's ruin."

"We know that you are closer to the ground here than we are," Alessandra reassured him. "Your concerns, we shall take to Aunt. Worry not - she will not know they have come from you. Please be easy now. We will find out as much as we can about Lord Byron, and if we need to take action to stop him from seeing Elizabeth, we shall."

"Thank you," Charles said, feeling somewhat exhausted from having invested so much time into thinking about whether he should say anything or not.

"Now, while we are on the particular subject of your sister," Edward said. "Mr Angus McKay - the young man from Scotland - came and asked me if he could visit Elizabeth here. You seem to have had a strong feeling about her spending time with Lord Byron. What is your thoughts on this other young man?"

"Angus?" said Charles. "No, Angus is someone I have felt is genuine. In truth, it was he who shared some of what I learned about Lord Byron, claiming that he had been told such things by Mr Elliot, his mentor."

"And you feel he can be trusted?" Edward asked. "This particular situation could stem from him wanting to try and put a wedge between Elizabeth and Lord Byron, for his own purpose and to increase his own chances with her."

"I concede that is a possibility, Father, however the many things I've heard about Lord Byron have come from a wide range of different sources, including some people who I only overheard talking about him in the street," said Charles. "Those people had no advantage to my hearing what they were saying, nor even would have known that I did. Therefore I do believe at least some of what I've heard must be true. With regard to Angus, he seems authentic enough. I have not heard anything untoward about him, but I confess I do not know who knows him, so how could we judge what he is truly like?"

"Very well. Leave all of this news with us, Charles," said Alessandra. "I believe it would be wise to not say anything to Elizabeth about this conversation. I know you are protective over all of your sisters, and we are proud of you for that, but let this sit on your shoulders no more."

"Yes, Mother," Charles replied, sure that he wanted to follow his mother's advice, and equally sure that he might not be able to.

53

After Charles left his parents, Edward and Alessandra remained sitting on the stone bench, enjoying the quiet that the spot provided to them. At their home in England, there were many places around the estate that were perfect for solitude and peace. Where they currently were, there were fewer places available to them to be truly alone.

"We did hear of some things about Lord Byron shortly after we came here, Edward," Alessandra said. "Should we have told our children about them?"

"It was not our place to," said Edward. "While it does seem certain that Lord Byron has a scandalous background, I am still not convinced that he sees Elizabeth as someone to seriously pursue. Why would he? What could she possibly offer him?"

"Money?" Alessandra suggested.

"She has none!" Edward said.

"No, but does he know that?" asked Alessandra. "He could well see her as our oldest child, and somehow associate all of this, which does belong to someone I am related to, as something that might one day go to Elizabeth."

"But that's preposterous! We are not even from Venice," said Edward. "I do understand your logic, but I cannot see that he - an older man who we know has already married a woman, had a child, and then stopped contact with both - could be enticed by our daughter. We know he's been seen around the town with various women on his arm. If he had any serious design on Elizabeth, surely he would not risk being seen with someone else."

"Yes," Alessandra said. "I know not why he would have been giving her his attention, but we cannot pretend that he has not been."

"Agreed, however let us see if he continues to try," Edward said, pulling her close. "We have not heard anything bad to make Mr McKay unworthy of our daughter's attention…"

"Yes, but does not hearing anything bad equate to goodness, Edward?" Alessandra challenged. "Just because we have heard nothing, does not mean he is any different from Lord Byron. At least with Lord Byron, we know what kind of character he has and we can keep watching to see how that evolves in our daughter's company. With Mr McKay, I understand that Charles likes him, and he certainly seemed a fine young man, but…"

"Perhaps we are just over protective," Edward said, trying to turn the conversation to being a little more light-hearted, or at least a little more positive. "Perhaps I shall never see any man as good enough for our daughter."

"Yes, now that we are here, I do wonder how any parent ever fully lets go of their child, to let them live and learn from their own mistakes," Alessandra said.

"Your parents never had to worry," Edward said, grinning. "As soon as they met me, they knew how wholesome and good I was."

Alessandra laughed but nodded. She knew he'd said what he had to make her smile, but what he'd said was also the truth. Leaning toward him, she happily placed her lips on his. As far as she was concerned, there never had been before, and there never would be again, a man quite like the one she'd married.

54

Two days later, Elizabeth noticed the general mood of Isabella had changed significantly. Elizabeth initially held back from asking any questions, knowing that her sister usually spoke up whenever she had anything she felt was worth saying. The silence was confusing and worrying. After exerting as much patience as she could, Elizabeth finally sought her sister out and asked her to take a turn of the garden with her.

"What is bothering you, Isabella?" she asked once they were walking out in the fresh air. "You do not seem your usual self at all. Will you not share with me what is the matter?"

"Oh, Elizabeth, I fear that the man I spoke of to you - the man I particularly enjoyed dancing with the night of the ball - did not mean anything that he said," Isabella replied.

"I see, but what is making you think

this?" Elizabeth asked.

"It has been two days, and he has not come," said Isabella. "Why has he not come?"

"With as little as we know about him, it is not possible to even guess why he has not come, Sister," Elizabeth replied. "Perhaps he is busy with his work, or perhaps he has commitments that have taken him out of Venice…"

"Then why would he have said that he would visit me here, if he was leaving?" asked Isabella. "No, I have been fooled. It was only a passing fancy for him that evening, making me believe he had enjoyed our dance so much that he would like to see me again."

"It is possible this is the truth, but it is also possible that it is *not* the truth," said Elizabeth as she linked her arm with Isabella's. "Perhaps the masquerade was such for more reasons than just that everyone wore a mask on their face. I have not seen or heard from Mr McKay, even though he said he would come here to paint with me. Perhaps that is our fate, Isabella. We shall be the spinsters who once thought they were going to be courted, but never were."

"I have no desire to be a spinster!" Isabella exclaimed as she stopped walking and faced Elizabeth.

The dramatic pose that she struck in her body and her facial expression made Elizabeth laugh at the sight.

"Oh, I see you are teasing me," Isabella said, smiling ruefully. "Forgive me. The thought of neither of us finding anyone to love us for an entire lifetime does not sound pleasant at all."

"Until now, I believed that marriage was not something you wished for at all, I must admit," Elizabeth said. "I thought only I dreamed of finding someone to love."

"I am not sure we are in agreement about the concept of love, Elizabeth, however I am open to meeting someone who could be my friend, my confidant, and a great companion," said Isabella.

"You do not mention motherhood at all," said Elizabeth. "You do not seek that?"

"I believe motherhood is something that is decided beyond any of us," Isabella replied. "I have heard that some women never do get with child, while, for others, children come easily. It is something I would rather not focus on, knowing that something far greater than me - or whoever I marry - will make that decision for me."

Elizabeth pondered her sister's statement and nodded in response. As they continued their companionable walk around the garden area, they both remained deep in thought. Something had to change at some point. It had to!

55

"Aye, this is a very fine piece of work, Angus," Mr Elliot, the architect, said as he perused the final two drawings Angus had submitted to him. "You have done well indeed. I am proud to be yer mentor, and to have ye as my architect in training."

"Thank ye, Mr Elliot," Angus said, warmed by the kind words. "Do ye require any more to be done before we leave for Rome?"

"No, not at all," Mr Elliot replied. "Ye have done plenty, and ye have done very well. Go and take the time off now that ye deserve. All I ask is that you please ensure ye and yer cases are ready early tomorrow morning, and then we shall be off."

"And we are later to return to Venice?" Angus asked, hopeful.

"Venice?" Mr Elliot said. "No, we shall not be returning to Venice, lad.

From Rome we shall travel on to Florence, and then begin our journey back to Scotland."

"Of course," Angus said, saddened by the news but determined to not be ungrateful for the ongoing opportunity being provided to him by the older man. "Thank ye. I shall leave ye now."

Walking out of the highly glamorous accommodation he and Mr Elliot had been staying in, he felt a plethora of emotions. He was glad he'd worked hard enough to complete his assigned projects, and to have received such high approval for them from his mentor. He was also glad he had time to go and visit Miss Chisholm before he would leave Venice, in the hope that she might still want to paint with him.

As his thoughts turned to him only having the opportunity to see her once more, and then possibly never again after that, he felt uncertainty grow. Was it fair to visit and spend time with a lady, letting her believe he might wish to court her, when he knew there was never going to be any opportunity for him to do so? Would it be kinder to not visit her at all, to ensure he was forgotten by her as quickly as possible, so that she did not have any lingering sadness over what might have been?

His mind shifted to and fro, wanting to seize the limited time he had to see the young woman who'd captured his interest, but then not wanting to promise her anything he felt he could not.

Even as his thoughts continued to argue inside the silence of his mind, his feet began a journey of their own. It wasn't long before he found himself in the very spot he'd been when he'd first met her.

"Hmm," he mumbled to himself as he finally grew aware that even though he'd been trying to figure out what to do, he had travelled right to where he'd said he'd meet her, his sub consciousness having made the decision for him.

For a long time he stood and looked

at the grand palatial home. Even though he'd drawn it for the purpose of submission to his mentor, he did enjoy how it looked, just as he'd enjoyed looking at each of the properties he'd drawn in recent times.

Knowing he was trying to procrastinate to avoid any possible upcoming discomfort, he shook off his thoughts and began to walk forward. He'd made the suggestion of him and Elizabeth painting together. Perhaps she might not want to do that anymore but even if that was the case, he had asked her, and he would do the right thing and follow through on the plan.

56

Elizabeth watched as her great aunt played the perfectly amusing hostess to the family members still in her home. All of Elizabeth's immediate family were in the morning parlour with her, and while many of their other relations had left the day before, once the masquerade was over with, there were still many people in the large building.

As she sat quietly and listened to the chatter of voices all around her, she felt startled when the door opened and in walked Gilberto and Lord Byron. She'd seen neither since the evening of the ball.

"Mio pronipote!" Caterina exclaimed when the gentlemen walked in and approached her. "Where have you been keeping my great nephew, Lord Byron? The very reason I invite Gilberto here is because I wish to see him!"

Elizabeth watched Gilberto as he

approached Caterina, the smile on his face as smooth and charming as she imagined any man could deliver.

"Prozia, you know I prefer to stay elsewhere, rather than encroach upon your hospitality," Gilberto said before kissing her cheek. "It is not the influence of our friend here who makes that so. It is simply because I do not wish to inconvenience you."

As Elizabeth continued to watch, she saw her great aunt throw her head back and laugh heartily. It was such a sight that Elizabeth couldn't help but giggle herself. As she did, she grew aware of the other newcomer turning and looking straight at her.

With a slight nod of her head to acknowledge him, she hoped no more would come of them being in the same room together, and she hoped even more that he would not try and talk to her alone again in the manner he had the last time she'd seen him. She liked things to be as they were in that exact moment - him close enough for her to be able to look at him and acknowledge just how handsome he was, but him also far enough away that he didn't affect her and play with her emotions as much as he had done when he'd been a little too close.

Feeling other eyes on her, she glanced around and saw her mother looking pointedly at her. Elizabeth wasn't sure why that was, but she smiled and looked down to be sure that her mother didn't see the admiration Elizabeth had for what Lord Byron looked like.

When the room resumed the relaxed state it had been in before the two men had walked in, Elizabeth heard the distinctive voice approach her.

"May I escort you on a turn about the room, Miss Elizabeth?" Lord Byron asked her.

For a moment, Elizabeth felt conflicted. Did she want to? Yes, she was certain she did. Was it wise to? The answer to that question, she was less sure about. Even so, he had asked and was standing before her, waiting for an answer, and she had been raised to always treat people with respect and friendliness.

"Of course," she finally said, smiling nervously before standing and allowing him to take her hand and place it on his arm.

"I have not seen you since the ball," he said in a hushed voice as they walked along the outer wall of the room.

"No, indeed," Elizabeth said, trying hard to not focus too much on the warm feelings flowing through her fingertips from touching him. "You have been noticeably absent from visiting my great aunt this past day."

"Noticeably absent, you say?" the lord replied with a smirk evident on his face. "I must say I feel rather pleased that you noticed I was not here, Miss Elizabeth. Might I be so bold as to wonder if you might have missed me?"

Elizabeth's natural inclination was to scoff. She fought to not let that particular inclination follow through, knowing it would look impolite to whoever might have been watching them. Holding it inside, she tried hard to speak only with words and not with body language.

"You might be bold indeed to wonder that, Lord Byron," she said, feeling empowered as she saw him laugh at her lack of a true answer.

When the door opened again, her heart was beating too loudly for her to notice. It was only when she heard another voice that sounded familiar that she stopped her walking and turned to see who had just entered.

Walking in, Angus had no idea how many people would be there, or if he would know anyone. The sight that greeted him would have made him turn and run away if he hadn't wished to be far more of a gentleman than that.

Looking around, he caught the eye of Alessandra who, thankfully, used a hand movement to subtly point at her aunt.

"Mr McKay, at yer service," Angus said as he bowed to the elderly woman that had been pointed out to him. "I am here in the hope that I may speak to Miss Elizabeth."

On hearing him say her name, Elizabeth felt herself blush but didn't hesitate to step away from the handsome lord who'd continued to create so much confusion in her.

"Please excuse me, Lord Byron," she said before walking over to where her great aunt sat.

"Mr McKay, I am very pleased to see you again," Elizabeth said. "Great Aunt, Mr McKay recently sketched your home."

"And did a wonderful job of it too, Great Aunt," Charles added when he saw Angus had entered.

"Did he now?" Caterina asked as she looked over the young man in front of her. "You sound Scottish, young man.

Are you an acquaintance of Mr Elliot?"

"Aye, Mr Elliot is my mentor," Angus replied, desperately trying to not shift his focus to where it truly wanted to be, on Elizabeth.

"He is a great architect indeed," Caterina said. "And what business do you have with my great niece, may I ask?"

"Mr McKay proposed an idea to me, Great Aunt," Elizabeth answered. "As he enjoys drawing so much, and I enjoy painting just as much, he did suggest we might indulge in drawing together. We need not do it here in your home. I thought that outside, where he drew your home from..."

"You shall not go outside, in front of my home, to sit and draw with this young man, Elizabeth!" she heard her great aunt say, momentarily making her panicked that the opportunity was going to fall through. "Where you normally draw, out in the garden - that is where you and this young man may set up your easels to draw and paint what you wish, so long as your madre and padre approve, of course."

"We have no objection, Aunt," Alessandra called out. "Mr McKay already asked for our permission and we have given it."

"Very well," said Caterina. "You are excused for now, but when we dine mid-afternoon, you shall both come in and join us."

Elizabeth curtseyed then saw Angus bow to her parents and Caterina before the two young people left the room.

"That … was not comfortable," Angus said as he exhaled deeply in relief that it was over with. When he heard Elizabeth giggle in response, he relaxed further. "Should I ask if ye do wish to still draw together?"

"You need not ask that at all, Mr McKay," Elizabeth said. "Of course I wish to still draw and paint with you. If you wait here, I shall run up and get my things, and be down again shortly."

Angus nodded and prepared for a lengthy wait. When he saw her returning, walking down the grand staircase with her easel under one arm, and a basket of art supplies in the other, he felt his breath deepen. He hadn't considered her beauty to be anything to focus on, with his attraction to her primarily being that she loved art as much as he did. He could not deny, however, that when she walked toward him with her arms laden with her pencils, paints, paper and easel, he was indeed overwhelmed by her beauty.

"I wonder if you forgot what my hair and face are truly like, with the way that you stare at me, Mr McKay," Elizabeth dared to tease him. She didn't often feel confident enough to act in such a way. The stark difference between how tense she'd felt moments earlier as she'd walked around the room with Lord Byron, and how at ease she felt with Angus, was refreshing. "Perhaps you preferred the fair wig I wore at the masquerade, and the mask that hid my face."

"Oh, no!" Angus said, awestruck. "No, I do not think that at all, Miss Elizabeth! No, ye … ye must always embrace exactly who ye are, and never try to hide or change that."

Elizabeth grinned at him. He'd been so dismissive of her when she'd first tried to speak to him and she didn't know why that was. Acknowledging that she was about to be seated close to him, and he was less likely to ignore her, she smiled further with the discovery that she was possibly going to be able to ask him as many questions as she liked.

57

Once set up in the garden setting with easels erected and seats facing one another, Elizabeth felt a moment of panic. What was she doing, sitting and doing something that felt so intimate with a man she didn't even know?

"I am nervous," she heard Angus say, surprising her. His voice revealed his words to be true, helping to relax her and make her not worry so much about her own nervousness.

"Oh but why would that be, Mr McKay?" Elizabeth asked him. "Do I scare you?"

Angus couldn't help but smile.

"I fear I have no great confidence in conversing with people, Miss Chisholm," he explained.

"But from what I have heard of you speaking, you appear to talk well," Elizabeth said.

"Aye, perhaps I seem to talk well, at

least for a short time," said Angus. "In truth, I find being around people very difficult at times."

Elizabeth stopped in her progress to finish setting out her drawing tools, and looked at him.

"May I ask … is that why you did not speak to me…" she began to ask. She suspected by the look on his face that he knew what she was asking.

"Miss Chisholm, I hope ye will forgive me for the first times we saw each other," he said. "It was not that I had no desire to speak to ye. It is only that I … I do find it so very hard. It has always been the way. I feel I want to talk to someone, so I embark on doing so, but then … after a few minutes … I get this feeling, as if I cannot do it anymore."

"That is … very odd," Elizabeth said, not sugar-coating what she thought. "But as I am not sociable either, I can understand and, yes, I do forgive you."

"Thank ye," Angus said, smiling at her. "Coming here today has certainly taken all of my strong, manly, Scottish bravery."

"Because I am very scary?" Elizabeth asked, teasing him again.

Angus laughed. "Ye are very good at helping to relax me. Thank ye again."

"I wonder if we both love drawing so much because it is our way of escaping being around people," Elizabeth said, pondering his situation. "My sister, Isabella, recently used the word 'cocoon'. She used it in a different context but, when she did, I considered that word sometimes describes how I feel - like I've spun myself tightly into a protective shell, not in the least ready to break free of it."

On hearing such words, Angus stared at her for a long time. He'd not guessed from their previous short encounters that she was quite so conversational.

"Ye speak very well, Miss Chisholm!" he said. "What a wonderful picture ye just painted for me - being in a cocoon and waiting to emerge from it."

"Was it a picture I just painted, Mr McKay?" Elizabeth asked. "I have not even started mine yet."

"Aye, that is indeed what we are to do today," Angus said, feeling more happy than he had in a long time as he felt all previous stress and nervousness fall away. "I suggested we draw or paint each other, even though we both insist we have no skills in portraiture. Should we begin?"

"We should," Elizabeth said. Knowing there were no expectations of skill or quality, and believing Angus was someone who most likely would laugh at his own errors if there were any made, was refreshing. "Will you tell me about yourself as we draw?"

"What would ye like to know?" Angus asked.

"Tell me about your home - where you grew up, your family, and why you wish to become an architect," said Elizabeth. "I confess I did not understand much of what you said when you first spoke to me, although I am finding it easier with each conversation we have."

"Aye, it is difficult for many people to understand us Scottish," Angus said. "Have ye been to Scotland?"

"Never," Elizabeth said. "I have been nowhere except my home in England, and here."

"To be in England and in Venice is certainly not 'nowhere', Miss Chisholm," Angus said. "Many people in yer home country - as in mine - will never travel this far. We are both very blessed to be able to see such pleasing sights."

As Elizabeth looked at him over the top of her easel, she felt exactly the same way. On further observation, she took a moment to study his features. She wasn't sure he would be described by many as handsome, but she liked the way his face changed and grew almost joyful when he smiled. With dark hair, dark eyes, and a complexion that was golden but already worn, there were aspects of his look that she liked. She didn't know why, since he wasn't traditionally-looking, but she did.

"And your family?" she asked as she finally put pencil to paper and started to draw the outline of his head and shoulders.

"I have only my mother," Angus replied, feeling a sliver of sadness flow over him at the thought of her and how long it had been since he'd last seen her.

"And she ... only has you?" Elizabeth asked.

"Aye."

"But then, you are here," Elizabeth said.

"Aye, and I miss her every day," Angus admitted. "She is alone at our home, and she is far away. When I have finished my tour with Mr Elliot, he has encouraged me to return to my home and to spend some weeks there before rejoining him again in Edinburgh."

"That is not where you live then - Edinburgh?" Elizabeth asked.

"No, not quite," said Angus. "Our land is far from any city or town. When I am studying or working with Mr Elliot, I take lodging with him in Edinburgh. It is too far for me to travel each day."

"I cannot imagine not seeing my mother every day," Elizabeth admitted. "That must be very difficult for both of you."

"For me, it certainly is," said Angus. "But that is the way of life, is it not? We are born, we pass through childhood as a bairn, and then we must grow up and go live our own life."

"Yes," Elizabeth agreed. "I am not sure where my future lies, but I believe I shall stay at our family home in England for many years yet."

"Oh, but, if I may be so bold as to ask, what if ye wed and the man lives away from where ye live?" he asked.

"That is not something I am yet to ponder," Elizabeth replied, beginning to wonder if the conversation might be approaching an area that could venture into uncomfortable territory. "But tell me, Mr McKay, what do you draw with today?" she asked to change the subject.

"Charcoal," Angus replied, equally relieved they'd stopped talking in the direction they had been. "It is always my preferred choice, over pencil or paint. Have ye tried using it?"

"I have not," Elizabeth said. "May I watch how you use it?"

"Aye, of course," Angus said. In response, he saw her stand and walk over to him, then lean over him.

"How wonderful," Elizabeth said as she looked at what he'd already drawn. "I do not understand at all how you can create such lines of all kinds, and this shading, with this," she said as she pointed to the charcoal he held.

"Perhaps ye would like to sit here, and I can guide ye in how to use it," Angus said before standing and encouraging her to take his seat. As he leaned down, taking care to not get too close, he felt enthusiastic about teaching her in what he knew so well. "Hold it like this, see. Aye. If ye apply it this way, you can use the edge of yer finger to slightly smudge it to get this effect, and when ye shift the charcoal like this…"

Elizabeth moved the charcoal this way and that, changing the angles just as he suggested. In the centre of the page she could see what he'd started to draw of her. She kept her focus off that, instead using the edges and corner areas of the page to experiment on.

While he stood behind her, leaning over her, she assessed her feelings about him doing that. She'd experienced Lord Byron doing a similar movement, but when he'd sat or stood so close, he'd affected her in a way that she didn't feel affected by Angus. Was she happy about that, or saddened by it? All she could definitively know was that it was quite confusing for her.

"The way ye move the charcoal is quite enlightening to watch," Angus said, his voice so soft that it startled Elizabeth.

"Do you not move it the same way?" Elizabeth asked when she checked herself.

"I do. However ... I do not know," Angus replied. "I must confess I have always been fascinated by watching others work on drawings or paintings. There is something quite..."

"Magical about it," Elizabeth answered for him.

"Aye!" Angus said, surprised by how easily she'd understood what he'd wanted to express.

Suddenly aware that her heart might have been reacting to him being so close, Elizabeth felt the need to move away. She'd been too close to another so soon before. The confusion it caused seemed too much to bear.

"Thank you, Mr McKay," Elizabeth

said. "You have given me much to think about when it comes to what I use to draw. I do feel now, however, that I should return to my seat so that we can resume this exercise we have set for ourselves. Your picture is already looking far too good…"

As she stood, she heard Angus laugh out loud.

"I have only started to draw the top of yer head, Miss Chisholm," he said. "I do not think it can be classed as a masterpiece quite yet!"

Despite how serious she'd felt moments earlier, Elizabeth laughed as she sat down in front of her own easel. She'd felt tense, and he'd easily relaxed her. That was a skill that she could only appreciate and very much like.

"I do believe your conversational skill may be improving even as you sit here," she said to him.

"Aye, I feel ye may be right, but I am not sure if it might be…" Angus started to say before he stopped, wondering if he should continue with what he was about to say.

"Might be?" Elizabeth asked, trying to nudge him to continue.

Angus stopped the movement of his charcoal and studied her face for a long while. What was happening between them? He was going to be leaving, and didn't expect to see her again after that day. Should he say anything that might indicate they could see each other again in the future? He worried about what was the right thing to do, but finally decided he should be honest with her. She deserved that, at the very least.

"I do feel more at ease when I am talking to ye," he finally admitted. "Indeed, in this moment I feel more at ease with ye than I sometimes feel with someone I have spent much time with."

On hearing his words, Elizabeth felt her heartbeat quicken. She felt fortunate she had a valid excuse to look at him as closely as she wanted to - and for as long as she wanted to. Because, at that moment in time, she realized just how much she did indeed like looking at the man facing her - far more so than any other man who might have claimed her acquaintance.

58

After a great deal of back and forth unimportant conversation, intermingled with joyous moments of friendly banter and laughter, Elizabeth heard her sister, Isabella, call out from the doorway.

"Elizabeth! Mr McKay! It is time to come in and dine!"

The sound of Isabella yelling so loudly made Elizabeth laugh softly. Her sister was usually far more discrete when around people other than their immediate family, but Elizabeth didn't mind. The expression of amusement she could see on Angus's face told her he didn't mind either.

"I cannot stay very long," Angus said when he saw Elizabeth stand to move. "I must allow time to return to my lodgings and prepare to leave tomorrow."

"Yes," Elizabeth said as she felt the full heaviness of that realization hit her. "You shall be leaving. I hope you do not mind me saying that I wish I could converse with you for longer than just today."

As Angus walked up to her he was driven almost by a need to reach out and touch her arms with his fingertips. He held back, certain that acting in such a forward manner would not be welcome.

"I certainly wish I could stay," he said. "Ye are refreshing to spend time with, Miss Chisholm…"

"Will you just call me Elizabeth, since we are alone?" she dared to ask.

"Elizabeth," Angus said, taking one step closer. "Aye, but if I do, then ye must call me Angus."

"Yes," Elizabeth said, moving closer still. "Angus."

Angus smiled at her. There was only a short space between them, that he knew could easily be filled, but it wouldn't have been right.

"We should not keep yer great aunt waiting," he said. "It is an honour that she has invited me to dine with ye. I do not wish to disappoint or offend her by being late to her table."

Elizabeth nodded and returned the smile before turning so the two of them could make their way inside.

"How goes the portraits?" they heard Alessandra ask when they entered the room.

"As you know, Mother, I have no skill at all in portraiture," Elizabeth said as she sat down and watched Angus take the only available seat, directly across from her. "I fear my drawing will not be anywhere near as magnificent as Mr McKay's will be."

Alessandra watched the young man grin at her daughter. It was a sight to see. She'd been watching the way Lord Byron acted toward Elizabeth but, based on all that she'd heard about that gentleman, she had no idea how much of it was real.

Looking at the young Scotsman, and the way he looked at Elizabeth,

Alessandra was far more inclined to acknowledge he did appear to hold a genuine fondness for her.

"Do not believe what yer daughter says, Mrs Chisholm," Angus said. "Whatever she draws will be fine indeed."

"Will you finish them today?" Isabella asked.

"No, Mr McKay must leave shortly after we dine," Elizabeth said.

"Aye, I must prepare for travel to Rome in the morning," Angus said.

"When will you and Mr Elliot return, Mr McKay?" he heard Caterina ask. "I still maintain hope that I may see your drawing of my home."

"I am afraid we shall not be returning to Venice," Angus reported. "Mr Elliot has said that we will go to Florence after Rome, and thereafter return a different way to go home to Scotland."

"Oh," Alessandra said, surprised. "But perhaps you may have reason to visit England after you return to your home," she added in an effort to plant a seed in his mind.

Angus smiled at her before doing the same to Elizabeth. He wasn't ready to say goodbye yet, even though he couldn't foresee any reason not to.

"Aye, perhaps," he agreed, reluctance strong in his voice.

"I must say I find this news very sad, but what can be done," Caterina said. "For now, let us eat, drink, and be merry!"

Elizabeth smiled at her great aunt as best she could before casting her eyes around the table. When her eyes met Lord Byron's, she saw a look she hadn't seen on him before. The look inspired her to focus on the fact that something - someone - may have surpassed the lord's importance to her.

As she accepted her great aunt's cue to begin eating, her eyes glanced over Angus again. Seeing him look at her at that same moment, the combined happiness and sadness that Elizabeth felt was intense. She supposed he was just one man who might cross her path before she found someone to love her, just as Lord Byron had been. Two men who had met her and paid attention to her, but nothing substantial would ever come from.

Even though she expected that would be the case, she smiled at Angus. If nothing else, it had been a great pleasure to meet someone who loved drawing as much as she did.

"I shall leave ye all now," Angus said when the meal was finished and everyone stood to move, following the lead of Caterina. "I thank ye for granting me this privilege…"

"Not at all, young man," Caterina retorted, cutting short his attempt to deliver the most gracious speech he'd have ever made. "It has been a pleasure having you here, and I can tell my great niece is fond of you. It is only regretful that you shall not remain in Venice for any longer, but of course I understand commitment. With Mr Elliot as your mentor, your future is very bright. Although you might not come back to visit us again here in Venice, perhaps Mr Elliot will be commissioned to complete some work in England - specifically, close to Bath."

On hearing the forward suggestion of her aunt, Alessandra grinned at Edward before they both saw their oldest daughter blush. The insinuation had been vastly more obvious than anyone in the room would have expected to hear, but nobody seemed to mind in the least.

Angus smiled at the elderly woman, overwhelmed with not knowing how to handle the suggestion she'd just made, but determined to leave the discomfort as elegantly as he could. After turning to bid farewell to Alessandra and Edward, he turned to Elizabeth.

"I shall see Mr McKay out," she said. With no more words, she encouraged him to follow her out of the great doors enclosing the dining room.

As the two walked through the passageway they said nothing, each deep in thought.

"I wish there was some way..." Angus started to say when they reached the door separating him from the outside world. He wanted to tell her how highly he'd come to regard her in the short time he'd had the courage to open up and truly talk to her. His fear of his words not being welcome were too great. Instead of speaking, he shut down again.

"As do I," Elizabeth said as she walked right up to him. "Meeting you has been a great joy. I do hope that if you are in England at all - if you are close to where my family live - you will consider finding a way to inform me. I should very much like for us to have the opportunity to draw together again."

"I would like that very much," Angus said. Would he call on her family if he was in England, even if he was close to where she'd said they lived? He suspected that long before that happened, she would meet a man who would sweep her off her feet and she would no longer be so eager to see him. "Guidbye, Elizabeth."

"Goodbye, Angus," Elizabeth replied as she opened the large door and watched him walk out.

After he'd disappeared from her

sight, she stood where she was for a long while.

"The heart will break, but broken live on," she heard Lord Byron's voice say. "You seem very thoughtful today, Miss Elizabeth."

When she looked up and saw him approaching, she realized just how little she'd begun to regard him. He'd made such a strong impression on her at the start, with his beautiful face, his outgoing nature and his confident words. Had he changed since then, or had she been the one who'd changed and stopped looking at him the same way? Was that the way things went? That when a woman met a man, she was inspired to greatly esteem him, but that esteem was easily lost when she met another man? If that was the case, how was she to know who she could love? It all seemed so fickle, not to mention so unbearably confusing!

"I believe I have been mistaken in thinking your affection lay with me, Miss

Elizabeth," he continued.

Elizabeth took as much time as she needed to assess how she felt about him, about Angus, and about anyone. She hadn't known what to expect when her parents had told her she would be visiting Venice again, but she did feel as if she'd grown a little in the time she'd been there.

"That, Lord Byron, is difficult even for me to know for certain," she said. "However, as I am to return to England with my family shortly, I do believe it does not matter."

"There is still time before you go," Lord Byron said as he moved close to her. "We can spend some time together … if you wish. For you to not have someone help you feel as beautiful as you are, seems utterly unfair."

Before she could reply, Elizabeth watched him move a step closer and reach out to lightly stroke the bare skin of her arm.

"Let me make you feel like the

beautiful woman you are. Nobody ever need know," she heard him reply in the barest of whispers.

Hearing the tone of his voice as he spoke, Elizabeth was instantly wary. She knew nothing about relationships between men and women but she did feel like she was becoming more in tune with what she felt was acceptable for her, and what was not. His suggestion most definitely was not.

"I thank you," she said. "But I do not think we can spend time together, Lord Byron. You have been ... you *are* ... a very handsome man, as you are quite aware. I would not let you think that I do not find you so, but what meeting you has helped me to understand is that handsomeness, even as great as yours, is not enough ... not for me."

Watching his face, she saw him smile sadly and nod, for the first time looking defeated in something he'd very much wanted to win at.

"You are a very beautiful and a very

talented young woman," Lord Byron said as he stepped closer to the door. "You are quite right to not be swayed by a handsome face or a charming word. Follow your heart, Miss Elizabeth, and love will most certainly find you. I am sure of it."

Elizabeth remained still as she felt him move even closer to her. As he leaned in and gently placed his lips on the side of her cheek, she allowed him to. They were saying their farewell. She'd already overheard he was no longer welcome to return to England due to some bad behaviour. When she looked at him, she could hardly align the things she'd been told, with the man in front of her, but the details were of no importance to her. He was the first man she'd felt attracted to. She suspected he wouldn't be the last.

"There is no instinct like that of the heart," she heard him whisper before he pulled away, smiled at her, and then walked out. "Remember, Miss Elizabeth, the artist - the great art of life is sensation - to feel that we exist, even in pain. Farewell!" he called back before Elizabeth finally closed the door.

"Are you well, Sister?" she heard Isabella ask as she re-entered the passageway. "Two men you have enjoyed the attention of while we have been here. Two! Where does it lead now?"

Elizabeth took her sister's arm in her own and smiled.

"The only place I am to be led now, Isabella, is home," she said. "No man I have met while here is who I shall be with for the future to come."

"You cannot know that..."

"Oh, I think I do," Elizabeth said. "How could anything come from getting to know either of these men?"

"I know not, but I do not regret having come here and met all who we have," said Isabella.

"Nor I, Sister," Elizabeth agreed. "Nor I indeed!"

60

As the Chisholm family secured their trunks into the transport that would take them far from the palace-like building they'd enjoyed staying in, Elizabeth walked to where her great aunt stood, and handed her the painting she'd been working on.

"Oh!" Caterina said on receiving the painting and taking some time to study it. "Oh, but this is very fine work indeed, Signorina Elizabeth! You have captured the beauty of the Rialto Bridge perfectly!"

"Thank you, Great Aunt," she said before extending her arms and eagerly embracing the elderly woman she'd loved getting to know.

"Hai fatto bene! You have done well," Caterina said as they pulled apart. "I hope you shall return again before my days are complete. You are very welcome here and there is much society that I know could benefit you."

"Do you mean to find me a husband, Great Aunt?" Elizabeth asked, grinning.

"Sì," Caterina said. "I fear that your madre and padre seem to have forgotten that you should be meeting suitors for that very reason!"

"You wish to find us husbands, Great Aunt?" Isabella asked as she joined them. "How very generous of you!"

"You are a cheeky girl, Signorina Isabella," Caterina replied. "But here is your madre. You must try harder to find suitable husbands for these beautiful signorine, Alessandra!"

"Yes, Aunt," Alessandra replied before embracing the elderly woman who'd helped her to better know who her mother had been when she'd been a girl. "It has taken Edward quite some time to accept our daughters are not little girls anymore."

"Did someone mention me?" Edward asked, joining the crowd.

"It is your duty as a padre to wed

your daughters off, Edward!" Caterina said, pretending to scold him. "Before you know it, they shall be as old as me…"

All laughed at the attempted wit.

"If I wed, Great Aunt, I shall send you an invitation to my wedding," Elizabeth said.

"I always wanted to see England," Caterina said. "I thought my sister would invite me one day, but alas … let us not dwell on that, however. I fear I am far too old for such a journey now, young Elizabeth, but do send me an invitation all the same, along with some more of your paintings. I do very much love this one that you have completed for me. All work that I receive from you will have pride of place in my home."

Elizabeth hugged her great aunt one more time and then stood back and watched all of her family do the same. Once farewells were complete, there was no more to be said or done.

Her time in Venice was complete.

61

After their lengthy journey back to England, a stop was made in London. As the family all travelled to deliver Charles safely back to his school, he teased them about not possibly needing an escort since he was so used to travelling by himself.

"Nonsense, Charles," Edward said as they made their way through the city by carriage. "We had to travel through London on our way home, and it is good to see where you spend almost all of your time."

"You saw it before I was enrolled here, Father!" Charles exclaimed, not finding his father's arguments to have much of a solid or logical grounding. In truth, he didn't mind his family visiting the school, although what his friends might think of it, he wasn't sure. For the most part, Charles had never seen anyone's parents in the area at all, with all of his friends appearing to be sent to school without any particular family escort.

Elizabeth laughed at her brother. Usually he was jovial and not bothered by anything. Hearing him sound like he didn't particularly want his parents close by when he got back to his school was amusing, to say the least.

"I believe you do not like us being here in London, Charles," she heard her mother tease him. "However, it is a busy city. It seems highly improbable that you shall even know we are here for this one night."

"Yes, Mother," Charles said as he glanced at Elizabeth and, seeing her grin, couldn't help but smile back.

Instead of trying to argue his point with either of his parents any further, he sat back and resumed watching the view outside. One thing he did love about London was the overabundance of people that he could watch. Rich, poor, happy, sad - there was always a healthy plethora of people to see on the rare occasion when he saw beyond the school gates.

"Stop!" he called out when something captured his attention.

"Charles?" Edward asked, concerned. "What is it?"

"Stop the carriage!" Charles called out again. As soon as the carriage stopped, he opened the door and jumped out. "Wait for me," he threw back.

"Whatever is he doing?" Alessandra asked, concerned. A few minutes later her question was answered.

"What are the chances that we would go past this fellow on our way to my school?" Charles asked rhetorically when he returned.

"How do you do, Mr and Mrs Chisholm," Elizabeth heard the familiar Scottish voice say before the head further leaned around and looked straight at her. "Miss Chisholm."

"Angus…" Elizabeth started to say in

a low, hushed voice, almost forgetting convention just as Isabella spoke over the top of her in a way that made her mishap not heard by their parents.

"Mr McKay!" Isabella said, grinning as she discretely took Elizabeth's hand in hers. "What a lovely surprise! But how have you happened to be here on this day? We thought you were travelling to Rome!"

"Aye. Mr Elliot and I did travel to Rome, however once we arrived there, Mr Elliot received news that he had to get back to Edinburgh at once," Angus said. "As I was going to primarily assist him when in Rome, he suggested I enjoy a relaxed journey back to Scotland. London was in my path, so I thought I would take a day or two to look around. Mr Elliot had hoped to see a new bridge that recently opened here - Waterloo Bridge. He referred to it as a feat of engineering brilliance, so I hope to draw the detail of it and show it to him when I return."

"That is very admirable of you," said Alessandra. "He will appreciate you taking the time to do that for him, I am sure."

"We cannot continue to stop here," Charles said as he saw the carriage driver indicate to him to either get in or get out of the way. "Will you come with us, Angus? My parents feel the need to see me right to the door of my school."

As Elizabeth watched, she saw Angus look directly at her, with what appeared to be a slight blush appear over his cheeks. That a man could look so endearing, she'd had no idea about before that moment.

"Yes, do come with us, Mr McKay," Alessandra said to nudge him along in making a decision. "We have plenty of room, as you see."

Angus, not wanting to dither about and delay them any longer, climbed into the carriage and settled into the available seat. Being seated across from Elizabeth made him nervous, but thankfully her parents took the matter of conversation into their own hands, leaving him no time to wonder what the woman across from him was thinking about him invading her family yet again.

"I hope it was not bad news that Mr Elliot received, to take him home so urgently," Edward said.

"I am not sure," Angus admitted. "It was all very rushed, from the moment he received the news to when he left. I did not want to ask any questions."

"I am sure all shall be well by the time you reach Edinburgh," Alessandra said. "Where do you stay here in London?"

"For this one night, I was fortunate to secure lodgings in the west," said Angus. "Early in the morning I shall make my way to the new bridge, draw as much as I can, and then continue on my journey north tomorrow evening."

"Then you shall dine with us this evening," Edward said. "We are in the west also, and the lodgings we have are well known for their evening meals."

"I would not like to intrude…"

"It would be no intrusion at all, Mr McKay," Alessandra reassured him. "Remain with us while we escort Charles here back to his school and then you can continue with us and we can deliver you right to your door."

"Thank ye," Angus said, feeling certain that 'no' might not be a suitable reply to give.

Looking across the carriage once more, he saw Elizabeth watching him and smiling. He didn't want to appear forward in front of her parents, but he couldn't stop himself - he had to smile too.

62

Sitting in his room of the inn that would be his home for the night, Angus felt very alone. Although he'd stopped in London for the night, he'd only done so out of a desire to do something for Mr Elliot. In truth, Angus was eager to get back to his mother, but the level of interest his mentor had shown in the new London bridge, combined with the appreciation Angus felt toward Mr Elliot, told him it was right to share what he could with the man he admired.

Being approached by the Chisholm family as he'd been walking through the streets of London had been a surprise, but a pleasant one. Seeing the young woman who'd caught his attention in Venice had been particularly pleasant, and he was appreciative that her parents had asked him to join them for their evening meal.

Having established he was staying

only a short distance from where they would be overnight, he had no valid excuse not to attend, even though he felt his heart heavy at the thought of spending more time with Elizabeth, but still seeing no further interaction with her thereafter. It was bittersweet, but he'd accepted their invitation and wouldn't pretend like he hadn't.

After washing his face and checking his reflection in his looking glass, he inhaled deeply and readied himself. It would be another opportunity for him to further practice his conversational and social skills. That alone was reason aplenty to seize the moment.

Finally he was on his way. Spending time with anyone that evening hadn't been something he'd desired to do, but the closer he got to the inn where he would be dining, the happier he felt.

63

After initial greetings were exchanged as her family saw Angus approaching, Elizabeth guided him to sit with her in a small seating area away from her parents and sisters.

"Did you go to view the new bridge after we left you earlier?" she asked, excited on his behalf at the prospect of drawing something completely new that few would have drawn previously.

"Aye, I did," Angus replied. "And what a sight it is! I have not seen one quite like it before. What men can build! Sometimes it astounds me."

Elizabeth smiled at his enthusiasm. He was passionate about things that he saw with his eyes. She understood that completely.

"Will it help Mr Elliot in his work in Edinburgh?" she asked. "Do you have bridges in Edinburgh?"

"We have waterways enough to

need bridges," Angus said, grinning at her. "Would ye not like to travel to visit Scotland?"

"I would very much like to travel and see more things," Elizabeth admitted. "I am not sure that it is very likely. My parents would require me to have a reason to go anywhere."

As soon as she'd said the words, she felt her face blush. She hadn't meant for what she'd said to sound quite so forward.

Seeing her blush, Angus chuckled quietly. It had certainly sounded like a bold thing that she'd said, but he suspected she hadn't meant for it to.

"As is quite right," he said to help her relax again.

The door opening and two inn workers bringing in a large platter each prompted Elizabeth to stand and move toward the table her family already sat at. As she felt Angus sit down beside her, she turned to look at him. The way he looked when he glanced at her was enough to make her heart pound.

"Thank you," she heard her father say before the two inn workers removed themselves and left, closing the door behind them. "This all looks very tempting. Let us not hold back."

As everyone filled their plates and sat back to enjoy the meal, Edward turned to Angus.

"Did you indulge in any drawing time today, Mr McKay?" he asked.

"Aye, I visited the new bridge, and it was very fulfilling, Mr Chisholm," Angus replied. "At times it was difficult to maintain a clear view as there were many people around, admiring it, but it is, indeed, a truly beautiful bridge to behold."

"And have you had any word from Mr Elliott since we saw you earlier today?"

"I have not," Angus said. "Whatever it was that took him so hurriedly from Rome, it appeared to be very important. Once I am back in Edinburgh, I shall try and see him."

As Angus talked to her parents, Elizabeth discretely watched him, not wanting to seem too bold but enjoying the view greatly. A nudge in her side, followed by the smile she saw on Isabella's face, told her she might not have been quite as discrete as she'd hoped.

"I understand the land of Scotland is very beautiful, Mr McKay," she heard Isabella say when there was a break in the conversation.

"Aye, it is that, Miss Chisholm!" Angus agreed. "Rolling hills of green, and rivers of blue."

"It sounds very beautiful," Alessandra said. "I admit, I have never been there at all. Have you, Edward?"

"I do remember visiting Glasgow when I was very young," Edward replied. "It seemed a very long journey up there."

"You have been to Scotland, Father?" Isabella asked. "You have never mentioned it to us."

As Elizabeth watched, she saw her father smile at her sister. It was very easy to see where Isabella's questions were going to lead. Elizabeth suspected her father knew that just as well as she did.

"Did I not?" Edward asked. "As I say, it was when I was a child. I cannot remember why we went there."

"For a holiday, perhaps?" Alessandra asked.

"I think not," said Edward. "Can you imagine my parents going somewhere for a holiday? I cannot. No, I expect it would have been due to something to do with the estate. There is much trade up that way, Mr McKay?"

"Aye, there is much centred around the tobacco and cotton that comes from the colonies," Angus replied. "The Clyde was expanded not too long ago. It helps much trade to be possible, but especially linen such as muslins and the Paisley silks."

"You seem to know quite a lot about

linens, Mr McKay," Isabella said, grinning at him.

"Aye, it is strange, is it not!" Angus replied, smiling sheepishly. "That is due to my mother. She has always worked hard on our land, keeping everything running. Whenever I go home, I like to take her something nice. Then, whenever I go to leave, she tells me what she wants me to bring back next time. It is because of her that I even know what a Paisley silk is!"

"You must miss her very much," Elizabeth said quietly as she studied his face. Although his voice sounded jovial enough, she could see a hint of tears forming in his eyes as he talked about his mother. "I trust you will go home and see her once you reach Scotland?"

"Aye, I certainly would like to," said Angus. "Upon arrival, I shall go and see if Mr Elliot wishes to see me. After that, I will be able to go and see my mother."

As all enjoyed the rest of their meals, conversation relaxed, allowing Elizabeth to see, before her very eyes, Angus open up and talk. He'd been so closed down when she'd first attempted to talk to him, and then he'd explained that was how he was, and not any reflection on how he felt about getting to know her. As she watched him enjoy the evening meal with her and her family, she could see how much he'd changed just in the short time she'd known him. With his dark hair and his unique looks, she considered not many would find him attractive.

At that moment, she knew she was not one of those many. In contrast, she found him very attractive indeed.

64

When it was time for Angus to leave the Chisholm family and return to the inn he was staying in for the night, he felt the same kind of sadness he'd experienced when he'd left Venice.

"Thank you for coming," Elizabeth said to him as the two of them stood outside the door to the suite her family had dined in. "It has been a great pleasure getting to see you again ... Angus."

On hearing her use his first name, Angus felt his sadness intensify. She was one of very few people who used his first name when addressing him and, from her, his name slid off her tongue beautifully.

"It has," he agreed as he stepped toward her. He didn't want to promise her anything, knowing he couldn't. Even so, without conscious thought, it was natural for him to move closer to her and take her hands in his. "It has been a great pleasure seeing you also, Elizabeth. If only there was a way…" he began to say before then feeling he shouldn't. "I must leave and get to bed. I will rise early in the morning to go work on my drawing again before I begin my journey north."

"Would you … would you like to write to me?" Elizabeth dared to ask. She'd never indulged in writing to anyone, but she knew it was common practice.

"I am not much of a writer," Angus admitted. When he saw her face change, as if he'd rejected her, he proposed a compromise. "But perhaps instead of written words, I could send you a drawing, and you could send me one back."

Elizabeth smiled. Perhaps it wouldn't be a conventional way to stay in touch with someone, but drawing and painting was certainly a language that they shared brilliantly.

"Yes, I would like that," she said. "If

you address it to me at Chisholm Manor near Bath it will find its way to me, I am sure."

Angus nodded before pulling his hands back and beginning to turn away. In truth, as he looked at her and stood close to her, he'd felt a longing to kiss her. If the situation had been any different, perhaps he would have.

"Guidbye, Elizabeth," he said before walking out into the darkness.

When Elizabeth returned to the room where her family still sat, she saw her mother hold out her arms to her. It made Elizabeth feel like a child to walk into them, but it also felt as comforting as she remembered it always had in her earlier years.

"You like him a great deal," she heard her mother say quietly.

"I do," said Elizabeth. "But, for now, I feel tired so shall retire."

After all said their goodnights, she took herself off to the room that was hers for the night. Before she got into bed, she felt exhausted. Once she lay down, her mind woke up. She was lying in an inn in London. The following morning, she would return to Chisholm Manor estate. Later that same day, Angus would be leaving London to travel far north to his homeland. Their paths had crossed twice, but were unlikely to again.

It should have been easy to forget the artistic Scotsman, Angus McKay. She suspected it never would be.

65

Walking into Chisholm Manor, Elizabeth felt exhausted, relieved, happy and sad. The journey had been long and it was good to be home, but she knew she would always have fond memories of the unique city that held a little piece of her heart, and just as fond memories of the two men she'd met, including the one man she'd grown to highly regard.

Before she'd left England, she'd wondered if she'd find love in Venice. Had she? She'd gained the attention of two men - one very handsome but with questionable repute, and one she wasn't sure would ever be regarded as handsome but seemed to understand so much about her, so very well.

"Go and unpack, Daughters," she heard her mother tell her and her sisters. "Rest for now and we shall see you at the evening meal."

Although surprised by her mother's

serious tone, Elizabeth didn't question what had inspired it. Gladly, she walked up to her bed chamber, sat on her bed, and then lay back. Even changing out of the clothes she wore didn't seem as important as taking some time to simply concentrate on the feeling of being home.

Out in the hallway she could hear her sisters noisily entering their own rooms. The back and forth banter between them made her smile even though exhaustion tried to fight through her happiness.

From where she lay on her bed, she could see the greenery of the estate, and the one large hill that graced the property. Angus had described his homeland as green as well. If he were to visit Chisholm Manor, would the greenery look different? If Elizabeth were to go to his homeland, would she think the greenery looked different?

Her mind wanted to keep thinking about the man she'd met and seen as recently as the night before. She knew it was pointless. What kind of future could they have if they lived in different countries?

Scoffing quietly, she had to remind herself that Angus hadn't offered her anything. In that regard, he was no different from Lord Byron - friendly, giving her attention, and suggesting he might regard her highly enough to want something from her, but never actually saying that he did. An enthusiasm for love that might have been implied but never declared. Was that how ladies found themselves without husbands? They invested their time and attention onto men who they believed were going to propose to them, but the proposal never eventuated?

Dwelling on such thoughts was getting her nowhere. With a renewed determination to get on with what she had to do, and put the subject of men out of her mind, Elizabeth jumped up and began to unpack her large travel case.

As she pulled items out of it, one by one, she smiled at her paints and pencils. They were her comfort. They were something secure that could never hurt her or make her feel wanted then disregarded.

Taking her time, she placed each item where it lived in her room. Returning to the chest, she pulled out the new gown that her great aunt had commissioned to be made for her. Looking at it, Elizabeth couldn't help but wonder where she would ever be able to wear it again. It was too beautiful to wear at home and it didn't seem her family would be travelling again soon or holding any social event that would demand the wearing of such a beautiful item.

With reluctance, she took the gown to the closet. Next to all of her usual dresses, it looked even more magnificent. It made it seem such a waste, having had it made at all.

Next from the chest, Elizabeth pulled out the wig that she'd worn that night. She'd tried to leave it behind in Venice, but her great aunt had insisted it was to travel back to England with Elizabeth. Holding it up, she laughed softly to herself. Her natural colouring was brown eyes and dark hair. The wig forced her to look like she had blonde hair, but it was just a disguise - something to help her pretend to be someone else for that one evening.

Not sure what she was ever going to do with that again, she placed it down on her dresser and then reached in to pull out the mask that had been made for her.

"Elizabeth!" she heard Isabella say as the door opened. "Oh, you are far ahead of me in your unpacking, but I thought I should return your gowns to you."

"Thank you, Isabella," Elizabeth said as she watched her sister place her dresses on the bed.

"It is so beautiful," Isabella said as she moved close to where Elizabeth stood, holding the mask in her hands. "They all are. It is dull to be home after such a time away, is it not?" she asked as she sat on the bed and sighed.

"We have only just arrived home!" Elizabeth exclaimed affectionately. "How could you say it is dull? You have not been here more than an hour yet!"

She watched her sister smile sadly, before then seeing her begin to weep.

"Oh, Elizabeth, how can you bear it?" Isabella asked, passion deep in her voice.

Seeing Isabella look and sound so out of character, Elizabeth rushed to her side and pulled her into her arms.

"Isabella!" she exclaimed. "What has happened that affects you so?"

"He has not come!" Isabella said.

"Isabella, we have returned to our home less than an hour ago," Elizabeth said. "It is unfair to expect that your gentleman would be here, waiting for us!

Come now, Sister, this is not a fair assessment of his character, or his intentions..."

"He has no intentions!" Isabella said. "If he did, he would have spoken to Father! No, this has all been some silly mistake on my part. My head was turned by a man who danced well and said all the right things. I see now that I was silly."

"No, Isabella," said Elizabeth in an attempt to soothe her sister. "We have just finished a great journey, and we are all tired - yes, even you! What you say you expect of your young man..."

"He is not my young man," said Isabella.

"He said enough to you to make you believe he would come and see you, and you are not wrong to maintain belief that he may," Elizabeth said. "But, Sister, you must be fair and give him a chance to come. He will not know when we returned from our journey, and even when he does, he may not be able to come right away. Do not be so sad. Your young man will come. I refuse to believe he won't."

Isabella pulled away far enough to be able to look Elizabeth in the eye.

"And yours?" she asked. "Do you believe Mr McKay will come?"

"That is a very different situation…"

"Is it?" Isabella asked. "How so?"

"Mr McKay has not made any declaration or promises to me, Isabella," Elizabeth said. "He is a gentleman who I enjoy the company of greatly, but he has not said anything to infer that he will come to … to court me."

"I saw the way he looks at you…"

"Perhaps you did, but that does not mean he has any intention," said Elizabeth.

"You ask me to maintain hope, but you do not seem so inclined to maintain it yourself, Elizabeth," said Isabella. "The way that he looks at you surely must be how many women wish their gentleman to look at them. I have seen his face change from being serious and shut down, to revealing the greatest joy. No, I cannot listen to your uncertainty about whether he will come. He will."

"Then it is settled," said Elizabeth. "You shall not give up hope, and neither shall I. They may not come today, or tomorrow, or next week, or next month, but that does not mean they will not come at all."

"Yes," Isabella said before leaning in and pulling Elizabeth close. "My only regret is that whenever either of us does wed, we shall no longer be able to live in the same location together."

"Why ever not?" Elizabeth asked. "I … you know that my place is here, on the estate, and in this manor. I shan't be going anywhere."

"No, not you," said Isabella. "But I… it will not be my place to be here."

"We need not speak of this now, but I promise you, Isabella - if you wish to continue to live here, even after you wed, then you shall, if your husband wishes for it also. You will not be asked to leave, just as Florence will not be asked to leave, and Charles too, if he wishes to stay here."

"I doubt he'll need to live here," Isabella said, laughing softly. "He continues to meet far more people every week than you and I will ever meet. No, when our brother falls in love, I expect he will be driven to be anywhere except here. It is too quiet for him now."

"For now, perhaps," said Elizabeth. "As he grows, however, he may come to appreciate the peace of home more."

"Perhaps," said Isabella as she pulled away and stood up, wiping away any small beginnings of a new tear that threatened. "It is all too far in the future for us to ponder. I apologize, Elizabeth. I know not what came over me, to barge into your room and present myself so."

Elizabeth forced herself to laugh softly.

"You and I are allowed to be silly on occasion, Isabella," she said. "Our hearts … what do either of us truly know about our hearts yet? Perhaps that is why Mother and Father have not yet spoken of finding us a match - they know we are not yet ready."

"I am not sure that is true at all, Sister," Isabella said as she opened the bed chamber door. "But I feel better after our talk so I thank you."

Elizabeth saw her sister smile before closing the door, leaving Elizabeth alone again. Picking up the mask once more, she ran her fingers over it before moving to sit on the bed, holding it close to her chest. The night it had been worn had been out of the ordinary, and it had seemed to be important, but had it been? It had been her first ball. Perhaps all young women felt the same way after their first ball, but the first ball was just that - the *first* ball. Perhaps it held no importance at all.

66

"Isabella does not seem herself," Alessandra said to her husband two weeks later as they sat together on top of the summit near their home. "I worry about her."

Edward took his time to study her face and consider her words before he replied.

"I do not know what could have made her so forlorn," he said.

"Do you not?" Alessandra asked, wondering how a father couldn't read his daughters when it came to affairs of the heart.

"What is it, Alessandra?" Edward asked, growing concerned.

Alessandra smiled sadly at him before she reached out and took his hand in hers. He was a loving man, a wonderful husband, and an attentive father, but in tune with his daughters and their desires, he was not.

"I believe Isabella waits for a young man to visit," she said.

"What young man?!" Edward demanded to know. When he realized how he'd sounded, he smiled ruefully. "Forgive me for speaking with such a tone, but you have surprised me. Who is it that you speak of?"

"I know not," Alessandra admitted. "She has not spoken to me about this."

"But you believe you are right?" Edward asked. "How could you possibly know, if she has not shared such a detail with you?"

"Oh, Edward, sometimes … I believe that sometimes a mother just knows," Alessandra said. "I cannot be certain I am correct, however. I will take some time with her this evening to ask what is making her so unhappy."

"You are a wonderful mother," said Edward as he squeezed her hand. "When our parents matched us, I wonder if even they knew how happy our future together would be."

"Yes," Alessandra agreed. "We have been very blessed indeed, Edward. There is not a day that goes by when I am not thankful to my mother and my father for their suggestion that we travel here to meet you and your family."

"It was always meant to be," Edward said. "That is what I believe."

Before Alessandra could reply, her lips were claimed, and passionately so.

67

As Isabella sat on a stone bench with her mother in what Alessandra had always called the 'glass jungle room', she waited to see what the subject of their talk was going to be. While she'd always considered her mother would be approachable about any subject at all, it was the first time Isabella felt there was a true reason for whatever was to come.

"What is it, Mother?" she asked when it seemed her mother wasn't going to begin the conversation. "Have I … done something I should not have?"

"No, not at all, Isabella," Alessandra said. "I … your father and I … have noticed that you do not seem like your regular self. I have requested to sit with you only so I can ask if you are well."

"Yes, of course, Mother," Isabella said. "I am not sure why you ask…"

"I ask because I have seen your face every day of your seventeen years of life," said Alessandra. "I know your facial expressions. I know when you are not well … and when you are not as happy as you have been. Please share with me what has happened to leave you less happy than what is usual for you. Whatever it is, you can share it with me."

"I do know that I can talk to you about anything, Mother," Isabella said. "I am not sure if I have anything to tell you, however…"

"Is there a young man?" Alessandra asked, seeing the only way she might get an honest answer would be to be far more direct.

"I … I … I am not sure," Isabella admitted. "I did … wonder…"

Alessandra, seeing her second daughter blush and appear more timid than she'd ever seemed before, was intrigued. She'd always known Elizabeth had inherited the unfortunate state of 'beetroot face' from her. Isabella had never before looked as she did in that moment.

"Please share your thoughts and concerns with me," Alessandra said, encouraging her daughter to continue. "You have never before mentioned any young man. Is he someone you met in Venice?"

"I did meet someone in Venice," Isabella said.

"And? Isabella, I cannot help but be direct, even though it may make you feel uncomfortable," said Alessandra.

"No, it … I understand," said Isabella as she turned to face her mother. "The night of the ball, I danced with several men."

"Yes, you and Elizabeth both were very popular indeed that night!"

"Yes, but there was one man in particular who … I am not sure what exactly he did, but I enjoyed dancing with him so very much," Isabella said.

"I see," said Alessandra. "And … you saw this man afterward?"

"No," Isabella admitted as she felt

tears threaten yet again. "While we danced, he spoke to me in such a way that I thought … I thought he was being sincere. I believe now that I was completely mistaken. The words that he spoke, he only said in jest. It was very silly of me to take heed of them."

Alessandra watched as her second daughter's eyes filled with tears. It was such a rare thing for her to see that she was momentarily stunned before she pulled Isabella close against her.

"I do not think it is ever silly to open our hearts, Isabella," she said. "Any man who is fortunate enough to secure yours can only be a very silly one if he does not act on such knowledge."

"But how do I move forward, Mother?" Isabella asked as she pulled away. "The only example I have of love is what I see of you and Father. I am sure you were in love as soon as you saw one another. You were not silly enough to give your heart away to someone you barely knew."

"We are all able to give our hearts away to someone who may not reciprocate our feelings," Alessandra said. "Even I."

"You?" Isabella asked as she wiped her eyes. "But you met Father, and you married him…"

"He was not the first man that I … admired," said Alessandra. "There was another before him - someone who I believed was going to make me an offer of marriage."

"What happened?" asked Isabella.

"He wed someone else," Alessandra replied.

"Were you … heartbroken?"

"At first, yes - very much so," said Alessandra. "But, Isabella, if I had wed him, then I would never have met your father, and you and your brother and sisters would not be here. That could never have been my destiny. No, he may have been the first man who turned my head but I do not believe he was ever meant to be the man that I married.

Only one man is for me - your father."

"Did you ever see the other man again?" Isabella asked.

"Yes, several times after I married your father," Alessandra said.

"Does Father know about him?"

"Yes, he met this gentleman," said Alessandra. "I shan't speak any more about that but what I do want to stress to you, Isabella, is that sometimes we meet someone and our hearts are affected, even if that person isn't to become our husband."

"I know I have been silly…"

"No, not silly at all," Alessandra said. "You are a wonderful young woman, and of course you are going to attract young men."

"But I believed the words of a man who I only danced with!"

"Do you know anything about him? Was he from Venice?"

"No, he said he was from close to Bath also - not far away from us at all," said Isabella. "Perhaps he may have not been honest about that, but I am confident he was from England."

"He sounded English?" Alessandra asked, curious. Casting her memory back over the evening, she could remember having heard an English accent only a few times that night.

"Yes, very much so," Isabella said. "But I understand I have mistaken the few words he said to me. I shall put him out of my mind now."

"It is much easier for us to say we'll put someone out of our mind, than it is for us to do so," said Alessandra. "Do not worry about this, but do not say you have been silly. We have all felt things for people. Giving your heart away - it is nothing to be embarrassed about, or regretful about. If this man did not see what a wonderful young woman you are, he does not deserve your love."

Isabella nodded. Inside, she felt her heart breaking. Even though she knew she'd continue to regard herself as silly for feeling the way she did, she resolved to at least try harder to forget about him. She suspected it wouldn't be easy, but she had to at least try.

"There will be others for me to meet, I am sure," she said, hoping her mother would hear the suggestion.

Alessandra smiled. Her not-so-subtle daughter was very good at suggesting something without overtly suggesting it, and always had been.

"I agree that it is time for you and Elizabeth to be meeting young men, with a view to finding a match for you both," she said.

"I do not think Elizabeth will need to meet anyone else," Isabella said. "She … that is, Mr McKay seems very good for her."

"Mr McKay does seem to be a very nice man," Alessandra agreed. "But do you not feel that your sister is in the same situation as you? That she has met a lovely young man, but has no contact with him?"

"No, I cannot believe that he will not

find a way to see her!" Isabella exclaimed. "I saw the way he looked at her..."

"Perhaps but, Isabella, Mr McKay lives in Scotland," Alessandra said. "It is very far away, and you heard him say that he has commitments with Mr Elliot, and to his mother."

"You think Elizabeth and I should both give no further thought to the men we met during our time in Venice?" Isabella asked, dismayed about the entire prospect of finding love.

"I think … I think that I need to encourage your father to make available to both of you far more opportunities to meet new people," said Alessandra. "He has been too protective of you and Elizabeth, and you are both young women, ready to meet someone and fall in love."

"I am only seventeen, Mother," said Isabella. "You do not think me still a child?"

"You are young, I agree, however I

was not much older than you when I was introduced to your father," said Alessandra as she remembered the first moments of her acquaintance with Edward. "I was timid and shy, but he was wonderful. It took some time - and quite some effort on his part - for us to learn much about each other."

"But you always knew he was the right man," said Isabella. "Even over the first man that you thought you loved?"

"Yes," said Alessandra. "There will always be men who are handsome, so will turn your head, but handsomeness is not enough - not for a future lifetime together. Over the many years you will spend with someone, you will surely experience many things happening, Isabella - good and bad. You must have a strong enough grounding to be able to support each other through it all."

Isabella took some time to think about the conversation she'd embarked upon with her mother. While she knew her mother was open to talking about anything, it was rare for her to seek Isabella out for such talks.

"Thank you for coming to find me," she said. "I know that I must let him go. It was a passing fancy of an idea, driven by the excitement of the evening, I am sure. Do not worry about me any more, Mother."

Alessandra pulled her daughter close and kissed her forehead.

"That is my job."

68

As a new season set in at Chisholm Manor, Elizabeth continued to push from her mind any thoughts about her time in Venice. While she hoped she would one day be able to return to the unique place, and preferably while her great aunt was still alive, she knew it was wise to forget everything else about it.

Since being home, her father and mother had already held one small ball in the large gallery of their home. Although they had no ballroom, and the manor house wasn't anywhere near as large or grand as where they'd stayed in Venice, the room had proved sufficient for their needs. Almost forty people had been able to fit into the gallery that was transformed into a dance location for the evening. It may not have been considered a large number to other people, but it was plenty for a family who hardly ever socialized at all.

On that evening, Elizabeth had danced with five or six young men, some of whom she'd met at different times through her brother, or through her parents. There was nothing wrong or unattractive about any of the partners who'd claimed her hand for a dance. They'd moved well, they'd spoken well, and they'd smiled at her as they'd talked. After that first ball, she'd received several cards from one man or another who she'd enjoyed some time with, asking to call on her. It had started a new routine in her life - fitting her minor duties on the estate, around when people were welcome to call and say hello to her.

"It is getting rather busy around here," Isabella teased her as they prepared for the second ball to be held. "I do not remember it being quite like this before we went to see our great aunt!"

"You say that as if you are teasing me, Isabella," said Elizabeth, grinning.

"But I do believe you may be receiving far more callers than I have been!"

"That is not true!" Isabella exclaimed before giggling. "Perhaps we are both doing very well in this newfound chapter of our parents' lives."

"Perhaps," Elizabeth agreed. "It is not getting us any closer to being wed, however."

"Yes, I fear that you and I had been spoiled before Venice, with the love that our mother and father share," said Isabella. "And now, after going there and meeting…"

Elizabeth heard her sister's voice tail off. Day to day, she knew Isabella tried to give the impression she'd moved on from hoping something would happen with the gentleman who'd made an impression on her. Day to day, it was clear to Elizabeth that Isabella hadn't yet let go of that particular hope.

"Come, Isabella," Elizabeth said. "We must get ready for tonight's ball."

"Yes and, at this one, we can wear

our masquerade costumes, with Mother having had the forethought to make it a masked ball," said Isabella, already sounding happier. "Although I do wonder what everyone else will be wearing, Elizabeth! They have not been to Venice and had beautiful masks made!"

Elizabeth laughed softly before moving to embrace her sister.

"I believe they shall wear any mask they can find," she said. "While we are all very fortunate to have had these masks made for us, I do believe masks are not solely found in Venice, Sister! Whoever comes tonight will be prepared, I am sure."

"And then there are our favourite parts of the costumes ... the wigs!" Isabella said, sending both young women into laughter before resuming their efforts to get ready for the night to come.

69

While Elizabeth could appreciate her parents' efforts to help her and Isabella meet other young people, there was a part of her that still felt discontent. She didn't want to feel that way, and she didn't feel that she *should* feel that way, but she did.

As people began to flow into her home once more, she put on a smile that she hoped would help. With her mask on, she knew her smile wasn't necessarily visible, depending on the angle someone looked at her from. Even so, she thought it was worth smiling all the same. It might not make her feel blissfully happy about some aspects of her life, but it certainly wouldn't make her any more sad!

Glancing around the room that had been once again transformed, she took note of each of her family's costumes. They were the same ones they'd all worn in Venice, of course, since there was hardly any reason to get new gowns for such an occasion.

As her eyes settled on those of Charles, she saw his usual smile appear through his eyes. He had returned home for the previous dance, bringing with him a select few young men who were of his acquaintance. Although the thought of her brother's friends courting her was not a thought that Elizabeth liked, she was still grateful to him for bringing some new faces to at least make up the numbers of dance partners. She didn't know who he'd brought with him this time, but their body shapes and sizes told her he'd brought some friends who hadn't been at the previous ball.

More people. New people. She supposed she should have felt elated that more opportunities were being presented to her for romance or even just for friendship - something she did feel she'd missed out on due to her isolated upbringing. As faces began to appear in front of her, asking her to dance, she smiled as she knew she should. All of them had their individual strengths in conversation, and there was nothing she took offence to or did not like to hear. Just as she'd felt about life in general before she'd gone to Venice, it felt as if every day was the same as the last - and every ball was the same as the last.

When she heard a deep English voice ask her to dance, for a moment she was startled.

"May I have this dance, Miss Chisholm?" the voice loudly asked, momentarily flustering her as it sounded - but it couldn't be of course - and yet, it did sound like it belonged to Lord Byron.

"You may," she eventually said, confused. She knew it couldn't be him. Since returning to England, her family had heard even more about Lord Byron, and his repute that had left him most unwelcome to return to England at all.

Once the dance began, she felt more

reassured by the minute. Whoever the man was that had asked her to dance, he moved in a completely different way to the handsome lord who'd caused so much confusion in Elizabeth's heart in Venice. Elizabeth breathed easily as she realized she'd been silly to have been moved by the voice, no matter whose it sounded like.

"I trust that your sister is well," she heard the man say when they came together in the dance.

"Both of my sisters are well, Sir," Elizabeth replied, surprised and intrigued. Did she know the gentleman guiding her in their dance?

"Yes, of course, but I ask specifically about Miss Isabella," the deep voice said. "She is … well?"

Elizabeth smiled to herself. It was an odd beginning to a conversation, but refreshingly so.

"She is," she replied. "She is also here at the ball, should you wish to…"

"Oh, no!" the man said. "I … I …

your sister is someone of superior nature. I fear I am not worthy..."

Elizabeth felt even more surprised by his words before they had to part again in their dance. When they were brought closer once more, she felt invigorated. Something was happening. She didn't know what it was, but finally something felt different!

"I am not sure my sister is of a superior nature, Sir, nor is she someone who would ever regard another person as unworthy of her knowing them," she said. "Tell me, are you and I acquainted?"

"No, not at all," the man replied.

"Intriguing," Elizabeth muttered. "Then perhaps answer this, Sir: have you ever been to Venice?"

With the dance separating them once again, Elizabeth had to wait for the reply. When she received it, she felt her own despondency raise out of her, replaced by joyfulness.

"I was in Venice recently, Miss

Chisholm," the man said.

"And did you enjoy it there?" Elizabeth asked, beginning to hope she was talking to someone she'd heard spoken of greatly since their time away.

"I enjoyed it very much," came the reply.

"And the masquerade?" Elizabeth probed in an attempt to be sure she was talking to the person she suspected she was. "Did you enjoy that equally so?"

"Yes!" the man said. "What a night! The ballroom, the costumes, the masks … and … Miss Isabella."

Elizabeth laughed softly, hearing in the music that the dance was about to end.

"You danced with my sister that night," she said and saw him nod in reply. "Then I believe you must seek her out and ask her to dance again. She will not regard you as unworthy. In fact, if I am right, I suspect she will very much be pleased with you asking her."

As the music ended, she watched

the man bow to her and then turn, looking as if trying to find who he sought. Elizabeth watched his movements, wondrous about how he'd happened to be in their home on the night of the second ball but not the first. As she maintained her focus on him, she finally saw him approach Isabella, appear to ask her to dance, and lead her out to the floor.

"Ye are very popular this evening," she heard a voice say from behind her. The sound of it made her heart beat faster. It wasn't English. It was Scottish. "I have been hoping that ye may wish to accept my invitation to dance."

Turning around, Elizabeth was confronted once again with the sight of a man wearing a kilt and matching sash. He was also wearing the same mask he'd worn to the masked ball in Venice.

"Mr McKay," she said in barely a whisper.

"I believe we agreed that ye would call me Angus," he said as he held up his hand in invitation for her to join him for the dance.

"That might not be regarded as appropriate for the environment we are currently in, Mr McKay, as I am sure you are aware," Elizabeth said as she felt her body relax.

"Aye, I believe ye are quite right," Angus replied. "If we wish to speak to one another with such familiarity, we must be alone to do so."

Although Elizabeth didn't think he'd said such a thing as a way of being suggestive, she still felt her face blush deeply at the thought of being alone with him. She was thankful that the mask she wore would hide most of the redness she so desperately disliked.

For the duration of the dance, they didn't speak, only studying each other's eyes as they came together in places, before the dance would separate them again. When the music ended, Elizabeth felt conflicted. She felt a strong desire to take him away from the crowd so they could sit and talk alone. She equally didn't want to seem so forward. Fortunately, Angus took her dilemma completely from her.

"I must say, I feel very thirsty, Miss Elizabeth," he said. "Would ye be so kind as to direct me to where there are refreshments?"

Elizabeth grinned as she nodded, then began to walk to the corner of the room set up with large bowls of various concoctions the cook had created for the evening.

"So many to choose from," Angus said as he glanced over the table. When he looked back at her, he saw she'd removed her mask. The sight took his breath away before he managed to stutter out further words while removing his own mask. "Which is yer favourite?"

As Elizabeth watched his eyes flickering over her face, she felt her face darken in colour again. Even though she disliked that part of herself, she had no wish for him to stop looking at her like he was. When another man had looked at her in such a way, she'd felt flustered and uncomfortable about it. When the kilt-wearing Scotsman looked at her as he was, she felt an entirely different sensation flow through her body.

"They are all delicious, I am sure," she said quietly, forcing herself to glance over the bowls. "To know which one is your favourite, you must try a little of each of them."

She watched him smile at her before turning toward the table and preparing to embark upon a journey of taste discovery. It gave Elizabeth time to study him, watching as he filled a cup with a little of one beverage and drink it, then repeat the process with each of the bowls.

"Aye, I like this one most of all," Angus said as he pointed to one of them. "Have ye tried it?" On seeing her shake her head, he grinned and pointed. "Yer turn then."

Elizabeth felt self-conscious as she

moved forward and tasted the beverage. Raising the cup to her mouth, she could feel his eyes on her. It was unbearable but, at the same time, highly effective on her sensibilities.

"Yes, I like this one," she said as she faced him again.

Looking at one another, she couldn't stop feeling that she wanted to be closer to him, and to truly talk to him without the worry of anyone else hearing.

"It would not be seemly for ye and I to leave and go somewhere alone, Elizabeth," Angus said as he leaned in close to her ear.

Thinking back to her few alone moments with Lord Byron, she knew he was right. Nothing had happened between her and the lord, but she'd certainly been affected by his handsomeness so much that she'd wondered since if something might have, had her brother not appeared when he had.

"No, it would not," she agreed, even

though her heart was pounding at the thought. "How long are you here for?"

"When the invitation arrived from yer parents, Mr Elliot insisted I take a week to come down here to ... to see ye," Angus replied. "I haven't stopped thinking about ye."

"My parents invited you?" Elizabeth asked and saw him nod in reply. "How remarkably sneaky of them!"

"Aye, they are sneaky indeed, that mother and father of yers," Angus said, laughing softly. "I cannot be angry at them, however, since I am here with ye. Are ye angry at them?"

Elizabeth knew she couldn't be, and never would be.

"Angus," she whispered as someone else approaching for a refreshment reminded her they were far from alone. "Would you dance with me again?"

"Aye," Angus said, grinning before he put on his mask once more. "Gladly."

As Isabella moved through the motions demanded by the particular dance they were undertaking, she felt nervous … and excited … and happy. She had no idea what the face under the mask looked like, but she was sure she was dancing with the same man who'd danced with her in Venice - the man who'd made an impression on her even though she knew so little about him.

Each time they came together and his arms encased her, she felt more certain she was in the arms of the same man. His voice was the same, his movement in dance was the same, and the way she felt in his arms was the same. It was difficult for her to even consider she was dancing with someone different.

"Were you in Venice long?" she asked when she could. He hadn't said he knew her, or that he'd ever danced with her before. Somehow, she needed to find out if it was him.

"No, not very long at all," he replied before they separated again. "But it was very pleasant being there."

"And the masked ball?" Isabella asked. "How did you enjoy that?"

"Dancing with you made it one of the most enjoyable nights of my life."

On hearing those words, Isabella was so surprised that she momentarily stopped moving, before people around her quietly nudged her to resume the dance.

"That is a rather remarkable thing to say," she said. "Particularly when I do not even know your name."

"Forgive me," she heard him say before they parted again. When she then heard the music slow down and end, she was left none the wiser about who she was dancing with.

As couples left the dance floor, she could sense his hesitation, but being certain she'd just danced with the man she'd been thinking about for quite some time, Isabella remained by his side.

"Would you like to walk about the room with me?" she asked, knowing some would consider it forward, but not caring in the least about that.

In response, she saw his arm come up for her to place her hand onto, but he said nothing in reply.

After several minutes of walking in silence, she stopped, turned to face him, and removed her mask.

"Do you know me?" she asked, wondering if it had all been a simple misunderstanding. Had he thought he was dancing with someone different altogether?

"Yes, of course, Miss Isabella," the man said.

"But I do not know if I know you," Isabella said. "Will you please remove your mask and reveal yourself to me?"

After waiting patiently for what seemed unbearably too long, Isabella watched as he brought his hands to his face and removed the mask he'd been hiding behind. Even after its removal, Isabella stood still, studying the face she didn't remember having ever seen before, before she finally spoke.

"How do you know who I am?" she asked.

"I ... we ... we met a very long time ago," the man said, his voice revealing a distinct lack of confidence, and perhaps concern that having shown himself, she might turn away. "I am ... Victor ... Victor Jones."

As Isabella heard him speak, she sensed he thought she'd know who he was. Dismayed, she had to admit to herself that neither his face nor his name was familiar to her. The only thing connecting them, in her mind, was their short time of becoming acquainted in Venice.

"But ... that is, I fear ... please forgive me but I cannot remember having met you," she finally admitted.

"It is understandable," Victor said,

dropping his head. "We were only children. There was a fine day, and I was with my mother and father, near the waterfall…"

On hearing the description, Isabella had her moment of recognition.

"You and your parents were all splashing in the water!" she exclaimed and saw him look embarrassed but nod.

"Yes," Victor replied. "You and your mother, father and sister walked past, but stopped to say hello to us."

"I remember!" Isabella said. "You all looked to be enjoying it so much that I wanted to go into the water and join you. I pleaded with my mother and father…"

"But your father said he wouldn't allow it," Victor said. "He said…"

"It wasn't something a young lady should wish to do," both of them said at the same time, making both laugh softly.

"Oh, but how remarkable that you are here," Isabella said. "But … Venice?"

"It was a rare stroke of luck on my

part," Victor said. "My father's brother lives in Venice, and had become acquainted with your ... great aunt? She had invited him to the ball at the same time that I had travelled there to visit with him."

"You were at the ball with your uncle?" Isabella asked and saw him nod. "I did not hear many voices that were English."

"My uncle is much more Italian than English," Victor said. "He was born here, but has lived there for many years. To someone from England, he may sound a little foreign."

"I see," said Isabella as she indulged in absorbing what he looked like. "That night, I enjoyed dancing with you very much."

"As did I," Victor said. "I had not known your great aunt was a relation of yours. When I asked you to dance, I had no idea who you were, but when you spoke, and when I looked into your eyes ... I knew it was you."

"But you must live close to here then," Isabella said.

"My parents still live here - on the Chisholm Manor estate," Victor replied.

"And you?" asked Isabella.

"I moved away," said Victor. "I live north of here, on my own land. At times, I have asked my mother and father to come and live on my land, but they do so love it here. Your father has always been kind to all of my family."

"This is much to take in, Mr Jones," Isabella said. "I thought … I did not know who you were when you danced with me. Why did you not say anything? Why did you not go and speak to my father in the days afterward?"

"I am a mere farmer, Miss Isabella," Victor replied. "I am not sure that it is acceptable…"

His voice tailing off intrigued Isabella.

"Acceptable … that I should know someone who loves and works the land?" she asked and saw him nod. "Someone who speaks fondly not only of his mother and father, but also of my father?"

"Yes," Victor said. "I was not sure if I should dare to ever speak to you, but when I realized the opportunity had arisen for us to be in the same room, with masks on, dancing together, I knew I had to at least try to seize that opportunity."

"It all seems rather mysterious, I must say, Mr Jones," Isabella said, feeling a calm ease flow over her. "There must have been some years when our paths could have crossed. They did not again after that day near the waterfall?"

"As I was growing up, I did see your father many times," Victor said. "He would ride out and check on us every few weeks at least. He has always been very kind."

Isabella took some time to process what she'd learned. In Venice, she'd thought she'd met a man of English society who seemed taken with her.

While she suspected that some women would have felt let down to learn that such a man was only a farmer, she felt her heart pump even harder. He was a man who loved the land, and his family was of her family's land. Her father must have known his father very well indeed.

Grinning at the realization, she stopped walking and turned to face him.

"Will you dance with me again, Mr Jones?" she asked as she slipped her mask on again and held out her hand. She had no idea why seeing her as a child would have remained in his memory at all, but when he'd spoken of that day, she could remember it too. Above all else, she'd seen that day just how close a family could be, and if he had a sound understanding of that, she could only imagine him to be a loving husband, and an even more loving father.

"Gladly," Victor replied. Prior to a few minutes earlier, he'd been afraid to show himself, sure she could never want to get to know someone of his background and heritage. The way she'd reacted had been remarkable, to say the least. It gave him the confidence to indulge in another dance with her, hoping there might be even more after that.

71

As Alessandra and Edward stood back and watched the young people dance, now and then they would turn and look at each other, not trying to hide the smiles of satisfaction that graced their faces.

"Who is that?" Alessandra asked when she saw the countenance of her second daughter. "Whoever it is, Isabella looks somewhat enamored by him. I did think she held feelings for a man she met in Venice. If she has found another to focus on, I must admit I shall be rather pleased. She has pined over the young man in Venice for quite long enough."

As she watched, she saw Edward deliver her the most incredible smile, momentarily holding back from speaking to her. She couldn't help but grin at his effort to obviously create some form of mystery about something he knew and she didn't.

"What do you know?" she asked when she could wait no longer, making him laugh. "Edward!"

"That is Victor Jones," Edward finally informed her.

"Jones," Alessandra repeated, trying to find memory of who she knew with the name. "Tenants?" she asked and saw him nod. "But he would be old … and married!"

"I fear, my love, that you are thinking about Mr Jones Senior, who is indeed older, and married to the very dear Mrs Jones," Edward said. "Victor is their son. He is twenty three years of age."

"But how … how has he come to be here?" Alessandra asked. "Have you invited all of our tenants to this ball?"

"No," Edward replied, turning to her and gently kissing her. "Victor has been away for some years, establishing his own land north of here. His father and mother both speak very highly of him, which of course is to be expected of any parent, but I have sensed they wish for him to find a wife and begin a family of his own."

"So you and his parents have conspired..."

Edward laughed out loud. It wasn't a word he would have used, but supposed it was relatively accurate.

"But if he is twenty three, he is closer in age to Elizabeth," said Alessandra. "Why would you hope that he and Isabella could grow a fondness for one another?"

"Because, my love, the man that Isabella met in Venice - I suspect - is Victor. His father told me Victor was there when we were, staying with his uncle, and that he'd attended a great masked ball," Edward said. "I was not sure it was the same person - and indeed it may turn out that it isn't - but if there was any chance..."

As he turned and looked out toward the dancing couples, he once again saw how Isabella was looking at the man who held her at that moment.

"Yes, if it is not him, then I do believe the man in Venice may have finally been forgotten," Alessandra said. "She looks…"

"Like a young woman who has met someone very special indeed," Edward said, summing up his wife's assessment very nicely.

72

"It is time for me to say goodnight," Elizabeth heard Angus say quietly as the musicians began to prepare to leave. The glamour of the coordinated dancing had ended and people were drifting out of the manor home at various rates. Hearing Angus say his farewell, Elizabeth felt the beginnings of a sense of loss.

"You are nearby for a week, you said?" she asked and saw him nod.

"Aye," Angus confirmed. "I am staying at an inn in Bath, so not very far away. Could ... would ye like ... may I call on ye while I am this far south?"

"Yes," Elizabeth replied, not even trying to hold back the grin that wanted to burst forth at the thought. "I would like that very much."

"I look forward to it," said Angus before looking around. "I shall say my goodnight to yer mother and father before I leave."

As Elizabeth guided him to where her parents stood, saying their farewells to guests as they prepared to depart, she saw each of them focus on her and the man at her side.

"It has been an honour to be able to see all of ye again, Mr and Mrs Chisholm," Angus said, feeling far more at ease around people than he had when he'd first arrived in Venice. He knew who he had to thank for that.

Elizabeth saw him turn and smile at her before she heard her mother speak.

"It has been our honour, Mr McKay, to have you travel all this way to attend our ball," Alessandra said, trying not to look as pleased with her plan as she felt. "I trust Mr Elliot is ... well?"

"Aye, it was a family emergency that called for him to return, however all appears to be well for him now," Angus replied. "I am grateful to him for allowing me to step away from my work and training to come down this way."

"How long will you be in our part of the land?" Edward asked, equally pleased with the expression on his oldest daughter's face, and hoping that her re-acquaintance with the young Scotsman wouldn't end in heartbreak.

"As Mr Elliot has asked that I return a week from when I left, I am staying in Bath for several nights yet before I shall begin my journey north once more," said Angus. "I should like ... with yer permission ... to visit and see Miss Elizabeth again."

Edward looked at his oldest daughter, then turned to look at his wife. At that moment, he wasn't sure who had the biggest smile on their face. Regardless, he couldn't deny that he still felt a calm strength in the young man his daughter seemed to have formed a strong regard for.

"You are very welcome here, Mr McKay," he finally said. "Whenever you are able to travel here, we shall be happy to receive you."

"Or perhaps, if you are unable to easily travel here, we might ... travel to Bath for a day or two," Alessandra suggested, enjoying the look on her husband's face as soon as she'd said it. There were many fond memories they shared from time they'd spent in Bath when they'd been younger. "I am sure we could take a short time from our duties, could we not, Edward? You enjoyed the Roman Baths when we visited once before, and there are always many sights to be seen in the Grand Pump Room."

"Oh, yes, what a wonderful idea!" Elizabeth exclaimed. While she had enjoyed the thought of Angus spending some time at her family home, the thought of the sights her mother had suggested she might see in Bath made her feel excited. They lived so close to the small-but-growing town, but rarely had ever ventured into it. "May we, Father? I have not spent any true time there, and Mr McKay has travelled all this way from Scotland. Would it not be preferable that he see more of that?"

Edward grinned at the excitement he could hear in his daughter's voice. He'd been protective over her for all of her life, wondering if any man would ever prove good enough for her. Seeing and hearing how animated she was over the idea, he couldn't say no.

"I believe this may be a grand idea," he said, grinning at the young couple and then at his wife. He and Alessandra had particular memories associated with Bath. He had to work to keep them from flooding over him as he stood in front of his daughter and her potential suitor. "Go now to your inn, Mr McKay, and tomorrow we shall send word to you confirming when we shall follow, if you agree with this."

"Of course," Angus said before bowing to Edward and Alessandra then starting to walk out, happy as Elizabeth naturally began walking with him.

Once at the front door of the manor,

he turned to her.

"I am very pleased to see ye again, Elizabeth," he said quietly, seeing nobody too close by.

"And I you," Elizabeth replied, her heart pounding again. "I hope my mother and father will agree to us travelling to Bath tomorrow."

Angus smiled at her, bowed, then removed himself completely. As he embarked on his journey to the town where he was staying, he realized just how much harder it was to walk away from her every time he had to do so. He also realized that walking away from her was something he very much did not want to keep doing.

"Are we being too relaxed about all that is happening with our two oldest daughters, Alessandra?" Edward asked his wife as he held her close after they'd finally said their goodbyes to all guests and gone to bed. "They are still so young."

"They are, but Elizabeth and Isabella are both wise young women…"

"Wise?" Edward asked. "They are eighteen and seventeen!"

Alessandra chuckled.

"I believe you may be worrying about nothing, Edward," she said. "Neither of our daughters has said they have been proposed to. There is nothing but friendship and admiration as yet."

"Yes, but how well do we know these young men?" asked Edward.

"It is true that we do not know anything about Mr McKay, other than what he has told us himself," said

Alessandra. "Mr Jones, however, you have seen grow up before your own eyes, Edward. You know his mother and father, and you knew him when he was a boy. If there was anything of concern about his nature, would you not already be aware of it?"

"Yes," Edward agreed reluctantly. "Why do I worry so?"

"Because you are a good, loving father," Alessandra said before leaning in and kissing him. "I am sure my parents felt the same way when I came to meet you, but such is the duty of a parent. At some point, we must say goodbye."

"I confess I find it very difficult to think about," Edward said. "I have never been as protective over Charles, but our girls..."

"I know," said Alessandra. "And, if you like, we can explore further what there is to know about these young men. The land Mr Jones owns is north of here, but close enough that I am sure you will be able to ask around - perhaps even in Bath when we go - to find out if there is anything about his nature or current circumstance that is concerning. And, as for Mr McKay, I am sure that with him being the apprentice of Mr Elliot - such a well known architect - it will not be difficult to find out if there is anything we should know about him either."

"Yes," said Edward. "And you are right in saying I am getting ahead of myself. Neither of these young men has asked for our daughter's hand in marriage. Perhaps this shall all turn out to be only a passing flirtation, or the beginning of a friendship."

"Would you truly wish for that, Edward?" Alessandra asked. "Elizabeth and Isabella both seem to enjoy the company of these two gentlemen. If they are happy getting to know them…"

"I shall try harder to accept what is happening in our daughters' lives, and not worry so," Edward promised as he nudged his wife onto her back. "Perhaps it is time for us to remember other times that you and I had in Bath, a very long time ago."

"I remember those times very well indeed, Husband," Alessandra said, grinning before she found her lips quite engaged.

No more was said.

"Is this not exciting, Elizabeth?" Isabella asked as they sat close together in the carriage on their way to Bath. "I have hardly been to Bath at all, even though we live so close to it. I must admit I am rather excited to be going into society!"

Elizabeth grinned at her sister. That Isabella was outwardly expressing enthusiasm for seeing the town and people of society, rather than her obvious excitement for seeing the man she'd gotten to know further at the ball, amused Elizabeth greatly.

Sitting so close to their parents and younger sister, she didn't tease Isabella about her pretence. That could wait. They'd shared their individual news and feelings that morning, talking at length about Angus and Victor, and their dancing and conversations of the night before. To Elizabeth, it felt like she was embarking on a new kind of relationship with her sister. Although different in natures, the common subject of men seemed to finally be providing them with something they could both chat about easily enough. It made for a refreshing change in their life of what otherwise had seemed unchanging day to day.

"I have not seen Bath at all!" Florence exclaimed, helping to put Elizabeth at ease as the focus shifted from her and Isabella. "I believe I shall be the most excited of all of us!"

Elizabeth chuckled but didn't say anything. Her thoughts kept shifting to the prospect of seeing Angus again. She wondered if she was being too forward, making herself so accessible to him, but she knew that her father and mother had found a romance recipe that worked. She put faith in them telling her if she was being too enthusiastic about wanting to see him again.

"Did you bring your paints, Elizabeth?" she heard her mother ask.

"I did," Elizabeth replied.

"You shall be able to paint with Mr McKay again then," Isabella said with a wry smile on her face.

Elizabeth blushed but didn't reply. The idea had been prevalent in her thoughts when she'd packed. Uncertain how long they were going to stay in Bath for, she wasn't sure she'd have time to paint anything, but the thought of the opportunity arising and her not having her paints with her had prompted her to pack them just in case.

"We are only here for one night," Edward said after listening to the banter between his daughters. "We shall go to our accommodation and then we have requested Mr McKay meet us at the Pump Room for refreshment. We will have several hours left in the day before our evening meal."

The thought of seeing Angus again excited Elizabeth more, the closer they got to the town. Beside her, she could feel Isabella almost squirming in her seat. Elizabeth smiled at her, knowing

Isabella had also put into Victor Jones's mind the idea of meeting again in Bath after she'd realized her parents had suggested the trip. There had been no confirmation that Victor was going to be in Bath, but Elizabeth could tell from the way her sister's body moved about in anticipation that Isabella was hopeful he would turn up and she would see him.

"Not long now," she heard her father say, prompting her heart to beat even harder.

"I see Mr McKay, Mother," Elizabeth said as she saw Angus enter the Pump Room. Having walked around the interior of the large room as a family, she'd enjoyed watching the diverse range of people socializing. It had proven to be a temporary distraction from focusing on what her heart wanted her to.

Alessandra followed her daughter's line of sight before delivering a smile and replying.

"There is nothing wrong with being enthusiastic, Elizabeth, however I do believe it will be far better for us to remain here and allow him to join us, rather than for you to approach him," she said. "I can sense your eagerness."

"Is it so very wrong of me to feel close to him without having known him for very long?" Elizabeth asked, trying to shift her focus from the man who'd started to make her heart yearn even more for love.

"No," Alessandra said. "For me, as your mother, I am happy that someone has come along who you seem to regard so highly. But worry not, I believe Mr McKay is as eager to spend time with you as you are to spend time with him."

"Mr McKay," both heard Edward say out loud. "It is good to see you again."

Turning back toward the direction she knew Angus had been walking from, Elizabeth held her breath. Nothing had happened between them since the night before, but she grew very aware that something was changing inside of her every time that she saw him.

"Guid mornin," Angus said when he approached the family who all seemed to be looking at him. "Mr Chisholm, Mrs Chisholm … Miss Elizabeth."

Elizabeth nodded to him, wishing desperately that her heartbeat would slow, while also hoping desperately that her face wasn't transforming into the dark red she'd always disliked.

"May I invite Miss Elizabeth to walk with me?" Angus asked. He suspected there wouldn't be any objection, but he understood English manners. They weren't quite the same as the ones he used in the north, but since becoming Mr Elliot's apprentice, he'd learned a lot more about how the English liked to act in polite society.

"Of course," Alessandra replied on seeing a nod from her husband. "We shall remain here, Elizabeth."

"Thank you, Mother," Elizabeth replied before placing her hand on the expectant arm that Angus had raised.

For some time, they walked in silence, neither saying anything. Eventually, it was Angus who broke it.

"I am enjoying this time in Bath," he said, forcing himself to be more friendly and assertive than was natural for him. "After my morning meal, I walked about the town. It is very pretty."

"Yes, it looks so," Elizabeth said, feeling a little awkward due to her nervousness.

"Oh, but ye must know Bath very well indeed, living so close to it!" Angus said.

"No, not at all," said Elizabeth. "I have certainly been here several times before, when I was younger, but never for any true length of time."

"Do ye spend much of yer time at your home?" Angus asked.

"I do," Elizabeth replied. "I would like to see more beyond my home, but my life does seem to continue to be focused on Chisholm Manor and the estate."

"Ye must see Scotland," Angus said, thinking about his home. "Oh, the green hills and the people - so much to love!"

"I would like that very much," Elizabeth said. "I imagine there would be much to paint."

"Aye!"

"Did you see your mother when you returned?" Elizabeth asked, thinking about him on his home land.

"I did," Angus replied. "It was good to see her, and sad to leave her again."

"Oh, but Edinburgh is not far from your home, is it?"

"Far enough," said Angus. "To work with Mr Elliot each day, it is too far to travel from my home land. It is easiest to remain in Edinburgh mostly, and go home when I can."

"But your mother is well?" asked Elizabeth. "She must miss you deeply."

Angus laughed softly and delivered her a grin before answering.

"Aye, she is well," he said. "When I am away from her, I worry about her. She is not getting any younger, and our land needs to be tended. But when I see her, she always seems much stronger than I remembered."

"But she lives alone?" Elizabeth asked and saw him nod. "Does she not get lonely?"

"If she does, she would not admit it to me," said Angus. "I have always worried about her being a woman living alone, but as yet, she is happy enough."

Elizabeth took some time to imagine that existence - living completely alone, on a land that wasn't near a town. In Chisholm Manor, there were plenty of staff working every day so she knew that even if she lived 'alone', she wouldn't be alone at all.

"She must be a very strong woman indeed," she said.

"Aye, she is that," said Angus as he stopped walking and turned to face her, then took her hands in his. "I wish ye could meet her. She would like ye."

"I am sure I would like her also," said Elizabeth, feeling nervous fluttering throughout her body as she tried hard to not focus on his hands holding hers. "Alas, we are too far apart. It cannot happen."

"No, not at present, but it is something that *could* happen," Angus said, his mind trying to think clearly while his heart kept interrupting the process.

Elizabeth smiled at him. It seemed he enjoyed her company as much as she enjoyed his, but distance would always be in their way, even if he had been considering offering her his heart. He had duties in the north, just as she had duties in the south. It was her destiny to always remain at Chisholm Manor, taking over the management of it when her parents grew too old, or left her completely.

"Are you well, Elizabeth?" Angus asked when he saw her smile fade.

"Yes," Elizabeth replied, smiling once again. "I … it is … that is … I enjoy your company greatly, Angus. I do … I do wish … I wish that we did not live so far apart."

"I also wish that," Angus said. The desire to move closer to her and place his lips on hers was strong, but the ability to do so was impossible. "If only there was something that Mr Elliot needed drawn here…"

Elizabeth smiled to herself as they began walking again. It all seemed hopeless, but she knew that she at least had that afternoon with him. It wasn't all that she desired, but it would have to be enough.

76

As the family sat down together for their evening meal, Elizabeth felt a diverse range of emotions flow over her. She'd enjoyed walking and talking with Angus at the Pump Room, and she knew she was fortunate to have parents who'd allowed her to have that time alone with him even though there was no understanding of a future between them.

For a short time after their walk, they'd had to separate. As the meal began, she felt blessed to be able to look at him across the table, her father having invited Angus to join them. She equally felt more sad than she had previously.

Also across from her, she saw Isabella grinning. After much anticipation, Victor Jones had shown himself at the Pump Room, and similarly been invited to dine with the family. Although Elizabeth hadn't had any time to talk to her sister since Mr Jones had appeared, it was clear to anyone just how happy Isabella was in his presence.

Looking at the two of them, Elizabeth found herself wondering where they could go in any kind of romance. Mr Jones was already twenty three years of age, and living on his own land. Isabella was seventeen and not quite yet old enough to be regarded as ready for marriage. Elizabeth wondered if their parents would agree to such a match. She was only a year older than Isabella, but nobody had ever talked to her about the possibility of marriage when she'd been seventeen.

Refocusing, she saw Isabella looking at her with a curious look on her face. Knowing they couldn't speak, Elizabeth smiled at her sister and tried harder to engage in the conversations going on around her.

When the meal was over, she walked Angus out of the dining room, closing the door behind them.

"I thank ye for this evening, Elizabeth," Angus said as he moved closer to her and once again took both of her hands in his. "Yer family are returning to yer home in the morning?"

"Yes," said Elizabeth. "My father does not believe we can stay any longer. But you are here for several days more?"

"Aye. While I am here I shall do some sketches of the architecture," said Angus, trying to push aside his now-familiar concern that he was never going to see her again. "Perhaps there might be something that Mr Elliot can use in his upcoming work in Edinburgh."

Elizabeth studied his face as he spoke. Thinking back to her first encounters with him in Venice, she could remember not understanding much at all of what he'd said to her. It was a pleasant realization that she now perfectly understood his strange way of speaking.

"What are you thinking about?"

Angus asked her, seeing a small smirk appear on her face. In response to his question, he saw her laugh quietly.

"I did not understand anything you said when I first heard you speak," Elizabeth replied.

"And now?"

"Now, you sound much less Scottish," Elizabeth said. Seeing him throw his head back and laugh heartily, she couldn't help but giggle.

"Less Scottish?!" Angus asked, teasing her before moving close enough for their chests to touch. "I believe it is more likely that we have grown comfortable with each other, and are getting to know each other."

"Yes," Elizabeth agreed as she looked up into his eyes. "When will I see you again?"

"I dinnae ken," Angus replied. "I know not."

Elizabeth felt like everything was impossible, even though in her mind she could see a future with the man holding her hands and inspiring such feelings inside of her. All she could do was nod, smile sadly, and then let the connection of their hands break.

Feeling overwhelmed, Angus bid her goodnight and walked out. It wasn't an easy thing to do but he wouldn't make any promises to her that he might not be able to keep.

"Elizabeth," Alessandra called out from behind her daughter. Having unintentionally heard the end of their conversation, she felt an intense sadness over how she expected her daughter was feeling. Given how Alessandra had felt when she'd learned the man she'd thought was going to make her an offer hadn't done so, she understood the concept of heartbreak very well.

As Elizabeth turned around, she felt tears in her eyes. Seeing her mother open her arms, Elizabeth gladly walked into them. She knew she was young, and she understood that she might meet many more men in coming days, weeks, months, and years. Even thinking about that, she still believed that Angus McKay - a man who loved drawing as much as she did - would always be in her heart.

77

"May I come in, Elizabeth?" she heard Isabella's voice call out from outside her bed chamber door after they returned home the following morning. Throughout their stay in Bath, the sisters hadn't embarked on any talks of the heart, never being very far from their mother, father and younger sister.

"Yes," Elizabeth called out as she wiped her eyes.

"Oh!" Isabella exclaimed when she saw that her sister appeared to have been crying. "What is it? What has happened?"

"It is all so … pointless," Elizabeth said.

"What is?" asked Isabella. "I know you cannot mean your time with Mr McKay because anyone seeing the two of you can see how much you equally admire each other. What is making you so sad, Elizabeth?"

"But it cannot go anywhere, Isabella," Elizabeth said. "His life is in Scotland, and my life is here … forever!"

"You must maintain hope that love will find a way," Isabella said in an attempt to make her sister feel better.

Elizabeth smiled. It was a useless attempt of Isabella's to try and explain that everything could work out and result in happiness, but she appreciated her sister's effort all the same.

"Let us not talk of me, Sister," she said. "I would much prefer to hear about you and Mr Jones. How did you feel at our meal last night? You do look very much at ease with one another."

"Yes," Isabella replied, grinning. "He is a very kind man."

"I thought, when I first met him, that he was very quiet and shy," said Elizabeth. "But last night he was very engaging indeed."

"Do you think Mother and Father regard him that way also?" asked Isabella. "They have said nothing to me about him – nothing at all."

"I do not believe they could not see how highly you and Mr Jones regard each other," Elizabeth replied. "And if he grew up here on the estate, Father, at least, must know him."

"He said he was going to talk to Father," Isabella said quietly. "I do not know if I should wish or hope…"

"He intends to make an offer to take you as his wife," Elizabeth whispered. Whether it was a statement or a question, she wasn't sure. "That must be why he wishes to speak to Father."

"I know not, Elizabeth," Isabella said, in a rare moment of looking uncertain. "He is older than I am. Perhaps I am just being a silly little girl…"

"No, I do not believe that, Isabella!" Elizabeth said. "I have seen how he looks at you and, on the night of the ball, I heard in his voice how he feels about you. Yes, you are young - we both are - but I refuse to believe this is a silly misunderstanding, or that his feelings are not as great as yours are."

"Thank you," Isabella said. "We can only wait and see, I suppose, but what can we do about you and Mr McKay? He is in love with you, Elizabeth. I am sure of it!"

"Love?" Elizabeth asked, smiling sadly. "Wasn't love something that you said I was silly to talk about so much?"

"Perhaps," Isabella replied. "But perhaps when I said that, I hadn't yet felt it … and now I do believe I have."

78

"Two men possibly coming to our home in coming days, to ask for the hands of two of our daughters," Edward said to his wife as they walked in the garden that afternoon. "Mr McKay asking to come and see me was one thing, but Mr Jones coming to see me also? What is this madness that has descended upon our usually quiet home, Alessandra?"

Alessandra laughed at his tone. She'd also been processing the news that two young men seemed intent on courting Elizabeth and Isabella. It was all new territory for her and Edward as parents, but she knew it was how things were meant to go.

"Our two oldest daughters are being pursued by good men," she said. "How can that be a bad thing, Edward?"

"Yes, but will it turn out to be a *happy* thing?" Edward asked. There were aspects of the possible matches that worried him immensely.

"Why would it not?" asked Alessandra.

"I have no concerns about Mr Jones," Edward said. "Although he is older than Isabella, I trust he is old enough to know his own mind very well. I cannot assume he is acting rashly if he believes he is in love with her."

"And Mr McKay?" Alessandra asked. "Surely you do not have concerns about his feelings toward Elizabeth!"

"No," Edward said as he stopped walking, turned to face her, and let out a deep sigh. "But he is from Scotland, Alessandra, and Elizabeth's place is here. How can that possibly work?"

"I know not, but that is something for them to work out between themselves," said Alessandra, moving into his arms. "Let us see what happens when the young men come and talk to you - *if* they come and talk to you."

"You do not think they will?" Edward asked.

"I think we are getting ahead of ourselves in worrying about this," Alessandra replied. "They have both asked to see and speak to you. Let us see if they do come, and what they have to say. Only after that, let us think about what it will all mean for all of us."

As Edward held his wife close, he maintained hope that all would be well. In his youth, he'd never wondered what it would be like to be a father. Since Elizabeth had been born, he'd loved her and all three of the children that had followed. Even considering any of his children being hurt by anyone was enough to make him sure he wasn't going to let that happen.

79

"Elizabeth," Alessandra said when she entered the plant-filled glass jungle room the following morning. "There is someone here to see you."

Looking up, Elizabeth was surprised to see Angus standing by her mother's side. She'd resolved to herself that she was unlikely to ever see him again.

"When you have spoken, you are both welcome to join us in the morning parlour," Alessandra added before removing herself. She remembered many conversations taking place in the very same spot that her oldest daughter currently sat in, when Alessandra had first arrived at Chisholm Manor. So many fond memories. She hoped her daughter would go on to have as many of those as Alessandra had about her years with Edward.

"Elizabeth," Angus said as he began to walk forward. Any concerns about propriety when it came to being alone with Elizabeth for an extended talk, he supposed he didn't need to worry about since her mother had positioned him in exactly that situation.

"Angus," Elizabeth said as she stood. "I ... I did not know you were coming."

Angus smiled at her as he walked to where she stood. Being so close to her enforced his belief that they were meant to be together as husband and wife. He just had to find a way to make it possible.

"Yer father did not tell ye I had asked to see him?" he asked.

"He did not!" Elizabeth said.

The words were spoken with such a stern sound of surprise that Angus laughed.

"Yet again, he is very sneaky then, is he not?" he said in an attempt to lighten the tenseness that he felt inside.

"It would certainly seem so," said Elizabeth. "Will you sit with me?"

Once settled on the stone bench, Angus turned to face her.

"I come to speak to yer father, but of course I feel strongly that I must speak to ye first," he said. He'd thought about and practiced what he wanted to say - and to ask - long into the night. His heart was full. It had to be sorted out, once and for all.

Reaching out, he took her hand in his and held it. It felt so frail in his own, but it was a nice focal point for him to look at as he found his words.

"I..." he started to say before finding he did, in fact, need to look at her while he said what he wanted to say. "Ye and I have only known each other for a short time, but ... but I feel very strongly about ye, and I am happy when I am with ye. After I left Venice, I believed then that I regarded ye highly, but then when I saw ye in London ... and then in Bath ... I truly feel ... that is, my heart feels full when I am with ye, Elizabeth."

Elizabeth sat still, feeling her own

heart soar as he spoke. She didn't want to interrupt his speech, seeing how determined he looked to get out whatever he ultimately wanted to say.

"I live very far away from here, and my mother is important to me," Angus continued. "I understand there are many reasons why I should not ask what I wish to ask, but I cannot keep quiet. I do love ye, and if there is any way for us to be together, I want us to be."

For a long while, Elizabeth processed what he'd said. When she was sure he'd finished speaking, she resolved to ignore the redness she was sure must have been spread over her face, and started to talk.

"I feel the same way, Angus," she said quietly. "Being with you … even just thinking about you … I feel things that I want to keep feeling. I, too, have been wondering if there might be any way for you and I to continue to know one another. I fear that it does seem impossible, but I cannot just walk away.

I love you also, Angus."

"Ye do?" Angus asked, sure he must be dreaming.

"I do," said Elizabeth, laughing softly as his tone of disbelief. "My heart tells me every time I am with you that I want to be with you."

"As my wife," Angus suggested.

"Yes," Elizabeth confirmed.

"As the mother of my children."

"Yes," Elizabeth repeated, grinning.

"As the only woman I will ever kiss and hold."

"Yes," said Elizabeth once again before she saw him lean in slowly then softly place his lips on hers.

It was her first kiss, and it felt as wonderful as she'd thought it might. It was quite some time before she felt him pull away from her, displaying to her the most magnificent smile.

"Ye make me very happy," Angus said. "But how ... how can we be together, Elizabeth? Will ye come to Scotland with me? While working with

Mr Elliot, I have a small apartment in Edinburgh..."

"I cannot leave here, Angus," Elizabeth replied as reality set in. When she looked at him and saw the obvious question on his face, she explained her situation. "My father has always told me that, as his firstborn, it will be my responsibility to take over the management of this estate when he passes. To do that, I must remain here."

It took a few minutes for Angus to understand what she'd said.

"Ye must always live here, in this house?" he asked and saw her nod. "But if ye are to wed..."

"If I were to wed, I have always supposed that my husband ... would have to live here," she said.

"I see," Angus said, feeling a unique combination of wanting to give up on his desire, but wanting to fight to never give up. "But I love ye. I cannot believe that ye and I are destined to live so far apart. We feel too much for each other..."

"I agree," said Elizabeth. "But what can be done? You must stay in Scotland, where your mother and your work is, and I must remain here."

"Aye," said Angus. "We must find a way, but before I speak to yer father, please tell me again, with full honesty, my sweet Elizabeth. If there was no distance preventing us from marrying, would ye like to marry me?"

"Yes. Very much so," Elizabeth said, smiling even though she felt like she was never again going to feel as much happiness as she felt when she was around him.

"I shall go and speak with yer father," Angus said, standing abruptly in determination to find a resolution. "I cannot promise what will come to be, but please do know and remember that I love ye with all of my heart."

Elizabeth stood, moved close to him, and, feeling bold, reached up and placed her lips on his.

"As I love you, Angus."

"Please take a seat, Mr McKay," Edward said to the young man when the two of them had walked to the steward's room.

"Thank ye, Mr Chisholm," Angus said. "Thank ye for agreeing to my coming here to speak to ye."

"I am open to hearing whatever you wish to share with me," Edward replied. He and Alessandra had talked much the night before, speaking about different scenarios that might come from the two young men coming to speak to Edward. He still felt conflicted about whatever might be about to be proposed, but he knew the happiness of his daughters was the most important thing he was going to have to consider.

"Aye," Angus said, feeling far more nervous than he had minutes earlier when he'd spoken to Elizabeth. "I have come from speaking with yer daughter..."

"Elizabeth."

"Yes, Eliza ... Miss Elizabeth," Angus confirmed. "I ... I must share with ye that I have grown to love her deeply, and I would like to marry her."

"And Elizabeth?" Edward asked, even though he was certain he already knew her feelings. "You have told her how you feel?"

"Aye, I would not wish to ask ye for her hand in marriage if I was not sure she wished for it," Angus said. "I love her, and I believe she loves me. I would very much like to wed her."

"I see," Edward said. "Are you aware that Elizabeth is my heir to Chisholm Manor estate?"

"Aye, she has told me," said Angus. "We know there is difficulty with this situation. I do not like to be too far from my mother in Scotland, but I understand that Elizabeth's place is here."

"It is true that Elizabeth has always been expected to live out her days here, with or without a husband by her side,"

Edward said.

"I understand. However, if I may be so bold as to say, Mr Chisholm…"

"By all means," Edward said, keen to see where the young man was going to take the conversation.

"We love one another," said Angus. "You and Mrs Chisholm are still young. It may be quite some time before Elizabeth is expected to take over…"

Edward heard the doubt in the young man's voice. He believed Angus was making a valid point but appeared very uncertain about whether he should actually say it out loud.

"It is a delicate subject that you raise," Edward said. "However, I agree with you. If you wish to wed my daughter, when would you wish to?"

"As soon as she feels she is ready, and we can know how we can be together," Angus replied. "I only have this week before I must return to Mr Elliot. I do take my position with him very seriously. I would not like to let him down."

"As is quite right," said Edward. "Your work, however, seems to take you far and wide. Would marrying you mean that Elizabeth would be left alone for long periods of time?"

"No," said Angus. "I would not agree to my travelling once I am wed. I have felt enough concern about leaving my mother alone. I will not do that to the woman that I love - my wife."

"And if Mr Elliot wishes for you to travel?" Edward asked.

"When Mr Elliot encouraged me to come south to see yer daughter, he spoke to me about the importance of marriage, and how little he enjoys being away from his wife," Angus replied. "He told me that he did not want to go away again himself, and he would not ask me to."

"Mr Elliot knows that you have come here to ask for Elizabeth's hand in marriage?"

"He knows my asking for her hand in

marriage was a possibility if I learned it was what she wanted," said Angus. "Please believe me, Mr Chisholm. I do love yer daughter, and I will do whatever it takes to make her happy."

"Except move here," Edward challenged him. In his heart, he wasn't against the marriage at all, but the words slipped out anyway, perhaps as a way to gauge the young man's declaration of love.

"I … my mother is not young," Angus said. "For now, it is important that I am within reach for her. I do not live with her, and I no longer spend as much time on our land, but I know that while I am in Edinburgh, it is a travel time that is acceptable to me, as I can be with her in a short time if she truly needs me. When I was in Venice, Rome and London, I felt the heaviness of knowing that if something happened to her, I would not be able to get there quickly. I would not be able to be there for her. I do not wish to be in that situation again."

"Yes, of course," said Edward. "Very well, I have heard what you have to say, and I believe that you and Elizabeth are both in favour of being together, so I give my blessing for you to ask her to marry you. How your marriage can work with this problem of location, I am not yet sure, however I can give you my word that if the two of you do wed, Elizabeth's mother and I shall do what we can to find a way to make it work."

Angus felt breath flow out of him as the tenseness he'd felt was released.

"Thank ye," he said as he stood. "I may approach Elizabeth now? To propose to her?" he asked, just to be sure he'd heard right.

"I believe that would be the right thing to do if you do wish to marry my daughter, yes," Edward said, amused at the young man's evident nervousness.

With no more words said, he watched Angus leave the room and close the door behind him. Alone again, Edward sat down at his desk and thought about how things were going to change. The consideration produced in him a strong desire to see his own mother. She'd handed control of the estate over to him when his father had died. She'd then walked away and set up a new life with Alessandra's father on other land that Alessandra owned. She'd done it, and as far as Edward knew, she'd had no regrets about that decision.

Desiring to travel to Missinger Estate and talk to his mother to receive her thoughts on Elizabeth's marriage options, Edward stood. Before he got anywhere, the door opened.

"My love," Alessandra said, smiling at him. "Mr Jones is here to see you."

Edward sighed. He'd only just gotten his head around one wedding likely to be taking place in the near future. Moving back behind his desk, he braced himself for a second meeting that might just go exactly the same way.

"Send him in."

81

Later that night, Isabella sat on Elizabeth's bed, obviously excited.

"How has it come to happen, Elizabeth?" she asked. "You and I both meeting young men at the same time, and them both asking Father for our hands in marriage - on the same day! We are very blessed indeed!"

"We are," Elizabeth replied, laughing softly at her sister's youthful exuberance. "I fear your marriage will be far easier to approach than mine, however."

"Why should it be?"

"Because you can move to be with Mr Jones, Isabella!" Elizabeth exclaimed. "I am … stuck … here. And I could not ask Mr McKay to move here when he so cares for his mother in Scotland. It feels hopeless."

"Well, it is *not* hopeless," said Isabella. "You heard Father. He is going to go to Missinger Estate tomorrow and talk to our grandmother about you and Mr McKay. When he returns, he will have listened to the wisdom of Grandmother, and all will be well."

"I hope so," Elizabeth replied. She'd had a magical day, hearing the many wonderful things Angus had said to her, and experiencing her first kisses. She agreed with his sentiment - they were meant to be together. Distance and location couldn't be a reason for them not to be. It couldn't!

82

One month later, two sisters helped each other into simple but pretty white dresses and covered their faces with veils. It had taken conversations aplenty between relations and the couples themselves, but all had been settled.

"It is happening," Isabella said as she took Elizabeth's hands in her own. "Very soon I shall be Mrs Jones, and you shall be Mrs McKay. I shall move a little north from here, but still be able to come home often."

"And I shall be far away, in Scotland," Elizabeth said. At the thought, she felt a little afraid, but also excited. She still hadn't seen anything of the north, and soon it would be her home.

"Yes, but all is well," said Isabella. "Charles has said he shall be happy to take over the estate in the future if you did not wish to return, and Mr McKay has said that he will gladly move here with you, should anything happen to his dear mother. Truly, has it not all worked out exactly as it should?"

"It has," Elizabeth replied, grinning. She felt happy in the situation that had been agreed. While she would miss her own family, she felt for Angus's mother, all alone on their land in the north. Given the choice of living there or in her own family home, Elizabeth felt happy to be going to reside in Scotland, for however long that would be. "Come, Sister, it is time for us to wed."

Seeing Isabella jump up and down in excitement made her laugh. The future was a long way off, and anything might lay ahead, but it was good to be around her own family while she was able to be.

83

"I am sorry that ye are leaving them behind," Angus said after the vows were exchanged and a long evening of celebration had passed. He and Elizabeth were in an inn in Bath, lying together as the first-time lovers they both were.

Elizabeth leaned in and kissed him. It seemed so recently that she'd had her first kiss. The physical affection had now moved to an entirely different level, but she was glad. Lying naked while wrapped in his arms in the quiet of the inn room felt heavenly.

"It is difficult, but I shall visit them often, as my father has said he will be happy to arrange," she said. "Now is my time to explore new places and meet new people."

"My mother will love ye," Angus said as he pushed aside a stray hair that had worked its way over her cheek. "She was regretful that she is now too old to travel for our happy occasion, but she will welcome ye with open arms. Ye shall be a true Scotswoman in no time!"

Elizabeth giggled. She had no idea what being a true Scotswoman would entail, but she loved the idea of learning and growing with the man who held her tightly.

"I did some learning about Scotland," she said as she moved over him.

"Oh?"

"Yes, particularly about the great Highlanders," Elizabeth added, grinning as she straddled him. "What was it that I learned again?"

Feeling her lower herself onto him, Angus lost any chain of thought he'd just had. Looking at her face as she moved, he suspected she had as well.

Looking down on him, Elizabeth felt like she was in heaven. She'd known nothing about physical pleasure but they'd found their way. All in all, there was a future of exploration ahead of her, in so many ways. The dissatisfaction she'd felt about her life was gone. Ahead of her only lay new things … exciting things … and plenty of change.

That was what she'd been seeking for a very long time.

~~~~~~~~~~~~~~~~~

The End
~~~~~~~~~~~~~~~~~

NOTE FROM AUTHOR

On completing research into England, Scotland and Venice in the year that this story is set, I was excited to find out so many interesting things about what was happening in the United Kingdom and in Venice. Of course, most of all was learning about the gentleman making quite a name for himself on the mainland and around the continent at that time.

There is much to learn online about Lord Byron, and a great many books written about him, his life, and his prose. While he was a real person, and did live in Venice for the duration of this novel, some snippets of his real life have been incorporated into this story, but I hope it will be remembered that this has been a fictional story, written only for entertainment.

I am grateful to my local public library for having so many amazing books on the subjects of 1700s/1800s Venice and Lord Byron. These proved wonderful in helping me to identify the exact time and events that might have surrounded Elizabeth and all of the Chisholm family, had they not been just a figment of my imagination.

Thank you for taking time to read this novel, and hopefully its predecessor, Alessandra. You, as a reader of this story, are greatly appreciated!

OTHER BOOKS
BY
ANN M PRATLEY

TOTAL FREEDOM SERIES
Coming of Age / Romance
Second Chances

TOTAL
FREEDOM
ANN M. PRATLEY

TOTAL FREEDOM

For Debbie King, life began feeling like it was all too difficult. She would never achieve, she would never have friends, and she would simply never fit in. But when she meets someone new who seems just like her, with low self-esteem and no belief in themselves and what they have to offer, Debbie finds strength to focus more on them and less on herself.

So begins an incredible journey of friendship and love that will be tested by other people entering their world, and the shared passion they have for their musical talents and career together. It is a deep friendship that will be tested over and over again by events and an ongoing uncertainty over what their relationship really should really be like.

TOTAL NEW
BEGINNINGS
ANN M. PRATLEY

TOTAL NEW BEGINNINGS

In her early adulthood Debbie had two men who loved her. She wed one. She lost the friendship of the other. Twenty years on, horrific tragedy strikes. Mother to three grown children, she has to find the strength to be there for them, while pushing her own grief aside. Dealing with the loss of the man who's been by her side for two decades pushes her into depression. Every day seems harder to deal with than the last. The feeling of loss is heightened by finding her husband's journals. Hesitant at first to look inside them, she eventually does. Almost instantly she regrets that decision. In the years of her husband's writing she reads things that lead her to question whether she ever really knew him at all, or if they had actually been strangers for two decades.

The combination of the loss of her husband, and the uncertainty about who he really was, pushes her to retire into a dark room. with no desire to leave. She wants to shut out the world and not believe what she knows in her heart is reality. With her youngest daughter, Poppy, still living at home, Debbie's eventually pulled from the darkness by her daughter's pleas. Finally the dark days start to fade and Debbie can start to see the sun shining once more, giving her the strength to keep going and start to move into a period of recovery and growth, knowing that it's okay to accept help and lean on others.

As she starts rediscovering her ability to embrace life again, results appear from her daughter's determination to help. Someone from her past is brought back into her life and a friendship is re-established.

Did you ever hear the words in your head … 'what if'? What if you chose one path earlier in life but later had the chance to walk down the path previously unchosen? Would you?

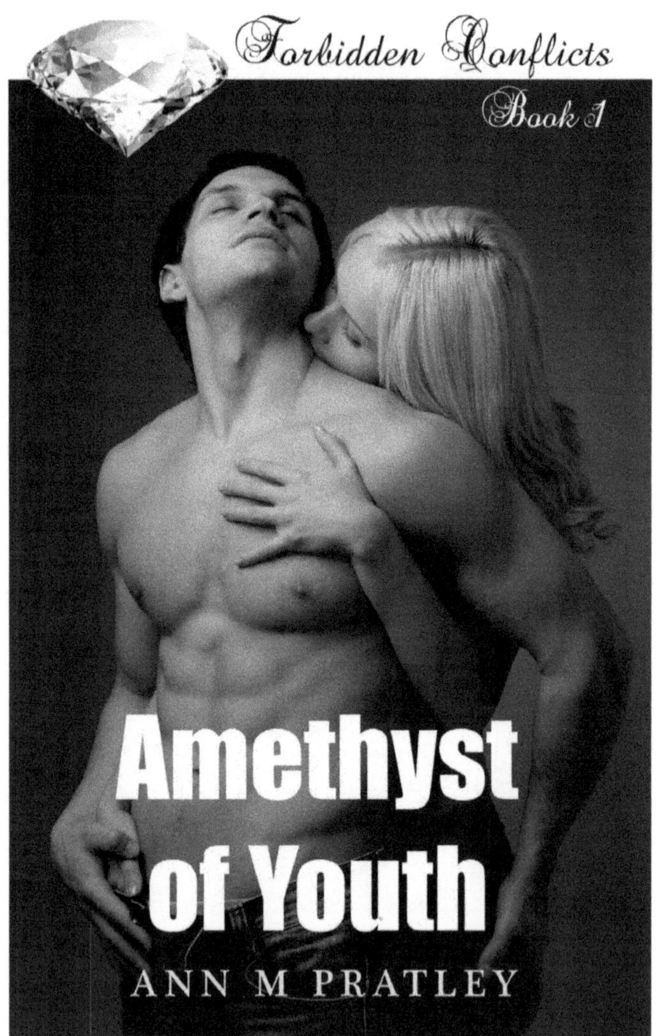

Forbidden Conflicts
Book 1
Amethyst
of Youth
ANN M PRATLEY

AMETHYST OF YOUTH

The youngest member of the Stonewarden family, Charlotte (Charlie), is 18 years old. As with everyone in her family when they reach that age, she's been told that when she turns 19, she'll be recruited into the family business. She has her warning that she has one year to do anything else she wishes to do - travel, study, work. Whatever she wants to do, she has 365 days to do it. On her next birthday, her life will effectively stop being her own, but Charlie wants nothing to do with the business.

How will she chose what's right for her? And what would she have to do to break free from the chains that she can see her father wants to place around her for the rest of her life?

Forbidden Conflicts
Book 2
Ruby
of Law
ANN M PRATLEY

RUBY OF LAW

For generations the Leadbetters have lived off crime. For as long as any of them know, fathers and mothers have taught sons and daughters how to succeed in the criminal world, primarily through theft. Phillip Leadbetter is 29 and still lives at home. One night a potential tragedy brings him into the path of Daisy, an up and coming professional in the legal sector. Seeing Phillip as her knight in shining armor, she can't stop thinking about the rugged guy who saved her. She's also very pleased when fate brings their paths to cross again. Getting to know one another, both leave out major details about who they are. She doesn't want him to know she's a lawyer. He doesn't want to tell her about his family and their long history of criminal activity. How then will things turn when they meet up in a courthouse, each learning in that moment who the other really is? How will they deal with the fact that she is on one side of the law, and he is very definitely on the other?

Forbidden Conflicts
Book 3
Diamond
of War
ANN M PRATLEY

DIAMOND OF WAR

James Stonewarden is a playboy. He has been since the moment he first started to notice girls. He loves them all, and they all love him. Why would he want to get himself into a relationship? Sasha Leadbetter's a hot-headed young woman, known to the law for her quick temper and harsh ways. She isn't one to mess with - especially with the way she keeps a blade in her pocket.

Unaware of who each other are, or how their families are distantly interconnected through crime, the chance of James Stonewarden meeting Sasha Leadbetter is slim. But it happens. A playboy and a young woman who has the mentality to kill. What kind of recipe could that result in? And what will happen when James identifies a car at Sasha's family home, that matches the description his sister Charlie gave after the supermarket shooting months earlier?

Forbidden Conflicts
Book 4
Sapphire
of Prejudice
ANN M PRATLEY

SAPPHIRE OF PREJUDICE

Greg and Rhett. They've grown up together since they were teenagers. They've fought together. They've stolen together. They've even loved women together.

But something deeper has existed in one of them for years. He's hidden it well. Being part of the great Leadbetter gang and family, the prejudice of certain situations has always been loudly expressed by many of its members - too many, and certainly enough to make anyone fearful of what would happen if feelings were revealed and brought out into the open..

Forbidden Conflicts
Book 5
Emerald
of Wisdom
ATLEY

EMERALD OF WISDOM

Mitchell Stonewarden begins to feel like it might be time for him to move on from the marriage that ended a decade earlier, when his wife died.

While he considers life with a new person, in the Leadbetter household tragedy strikes for a second time. Will Stacey Leadbetter lose the only man she has ever loved?

POWER MOORE INVESTIGATION TALES
Crime solving

~The books of the Power Moore Investigation Tales series are standalone stories and can be read in any order

RESOLUTION OF HAPPINESS

Fiona Thompson - better known as Flo to everyone who knew her - took a plunge and stepped out of her comfort zone and into the world of online dating.

With persistence she found her prince. He ticked all the boxes. He was handsome. He was financially secure. He loved her. He married her.

She was warned by friends and family that there was something off about him. She didn't listen. Then she woke up cold, inside the darkness of a wooden box.

HOME BY THE SEA

A decade ago, homeless people began disappearing from four neighboring towns. A young woman, eager to find out where her grandfather disappeared to, began trying to find him. When four police departments dismissed her, telling her that her grandfather would no doubt turn up when he wanted to, she was too young to realize she should pursue the matter further. Now, ten years on, she's stepped up and pushed harder for something to be done to find not only her grandfather but also the countless other people who seemed to have disappeared around the same time.

Called in to investigate the disappearances, Special Agents Ashley Power and Tim Moore find themselves searching for - and finding - so much more than they thought they would

DJ OF INCAPACITY

High numbers of shootings in one small town after another begin to put people across the country into a panic, wondering what could have inspired such horrific occurrences to happen. Called in to work as part of a large taskforce to try and figure out not only why the shootings are happening, but also how, are Special Agents Ashley Power and Tim Moore. Neither have before seen death on such a large scale in their law enforcement careers, and what they have to see during their lengthy investigation isn't for the faint-hearted.

~ Author's Note: DJ of Incapacity is not a whodunnit. You'll figure out, rather early on in this book, who is doing what, so be prepared to be taken into the darkness of the suspect's mind…

CATCH A CATFISH KILLER

After a suspicious gas explosion wakes a usually peaceful community, what is left of the home reveals the charred remains of Bob Masters, a hospital orderly who has a solid reputation as someone good-hearted and caring. When fire scene investigators confirm their findings that the explosion was intended, so begins a murder investigation. The one question that's on everyone's mind is why? Why would anyone intentionally try to hurt such a kind and hard working man?

Called in to work out what could have gone wrong in what appears to be a simple, quiet life, and who could be behind such a horrific act, Special Agents Ashley Power and Tim Moore start to realize how much more to someone's life there can be other than what people see on the outside.

Embark on a murder mystery involving crime solving of the digital kind. Initially, through studying online actions and conversations, it becomes evident that catfishing - an unfortunate and sad aspect of modern day dating - seems to be at the root of what begins to be a pattern. Even knowing this, the journey of discovery the agents are subjected to still surprises them.

Catfishing: a deceptive activity in which a person creates a fictional persona or fake identity on a social networking service, usually targeting a specific victim.

With it being such an easy way to take advantage of people in the modern age, it may take quite some detective work to solve the mystery of who is ever behind any screen, at any time.